KV-014-072

THE LONG ENCHANTMENT

Elizabeth Byrd was born in St Louis, Missouri, but now lives in a fifteenth-century cottage outside Edinburgh. Her previous novels, *Immortal Queen*, *The Flowers of the Forest*, and *The Famished Land* were all highly successful. Her most recent book is a novel about the nineteenth-century Edinburgh murderers Burke and Hare.

By the same author in Pan Books

IMMORTAL QUEEN
THE FLOWERS OF THE FOREST
THE FAMISHED LAND

THE LONG ENCHANTMENT

A Novel of Queen Victoria and John Brown

Elizabeth Byrd

PAN BOOKS LTD
LONDON AND SYDNEY

First published 1973 by Macmillan London Ltd
This edition published 1975 by Pan Books Ltd,
Cavaye Place, London SW10 9PG

ISBN 0 330 24273 3

© Elizabeth Byrd 1973

Printed in Great Britain by
Richard Clay (The Chaucer Press) Ltd, Bungay, Suffolk

CONDITIONS OF SALE

This book shall not, by way of trade or otherwise, be lent, re-sold, hired out
or otherwise circulated without the publisher's prior consent in any form of
binding or cover other than that in which it is published and without a similar
condition including this condition being imposed on the subsequent purchaser.
The book is published at a net price, and is supplied subject to the Publishers
Association Standard Conditions of Sale registered under the Restrictive Trade
Practices Act, 1956

For Elizabeth Gladych

Prologue

Hampered by her long skirt and the picnic basket, she found the climb difficult; briars scratched her bare ankles. But at last she was on the grouse moor and there was the flat rock they used as a table.

Had she brought enough food this time? Johnny Brown was a great one for the eating, and she wondered where it all went to for his stomach was flat as this rock and his waist scarcely wider than her own, for all of his big-boned height. Playmates all their lives, she had taken his fine looks for granted. Until lately, when she began to notice how the village girls preened themselves to get his attention. It was more than his great height that set him apart. His father had once been a schoolmaster, so Johnny was educated beyond most – and far beyond her. Now he was stableman at Balmoral Castle, working for Sir Robert Gordon and meeting fancy maids who wore shoes and stockings all summer, even on week days. What chance would she have against all those?

For one thing, she thought as she unpacked the basket, there's few can make bannocks as well as I. And she had invented something from sausage and oatmeal that even her sister Jean – often so dour these days – grudgingly admitted was good. If Johnny didn't like it, the bannocks, apples and cheese would fill him.

Below her the Dee was a shimmer of silver winding between firs and larches. Above her crouched the heathered hills, violet-colored, dwarfed by Lochnagar. You could tell what the weather would be by the look of that mountain. Haze meant heat, mist rain. From late autumn until April or May it was crested with snow.

The winters were brutal here but they could be cosy too if

you were wise. When the heather scorched dark, when the leaves turned, then you took in your wood from the pile and gathered heaps of twigs to feed the fires. You salted down mutton in vats, dug up the last of the carrots and potatoes and turnips to store in the shed. Then there was the ill-smelling chore of candle-making, the reek of sheep-grease. Folk didn't move much in the winter, only to take a dram or a pot of tea with a neighbor.

Below she could see the rowan trees, their berries like tied red bows on a Christmas tree she'd once caught sight of through the castle window, Johnny lifting her up. Rowan was supposed to bring good luck (and it also made good jelly) so tomorrow she'd gather some, bringing Jean if she felt well enough. But it wasn't Jean she worried about now − it was Johnny. Perhaps he wasn't coming. Perhaps he'd forgotten, though he'd said last night ...

Perhaps he knows me too well, she thought miserably. He's seen me grimed from the peats, he's pulled me out of streams, my hair like wet weed. I have no mystery for him − he even saw the stain on my dress when my bleeding started. Of late he had kissed her twice, but only lightly, as a brother might, and in comfort of her worry over Jean.

'Linty?' She heard his deep voice before she saw him. Then he was up the rough trail, his curly red hair catching the sun, always somehow larger than she remembered him from last night or the day before.

He came up and slid down beside her, his brown shirt open at the neck. 'Have you been here long?'

'Only minutes,' she lied. He mustn't think she had waited; God knows he was vain enough, not of his looks, but of his strength and skills.

He brought a bottle from his pocket. 'Will you take a dram?'

She hated the taste of whisky but accepted it because it pleased her to share whatever pleased him. In turn he drank from the bottle and took from another pocket a brace of grouse wrapped in newspaper.

'And who roasted those?' she asked. The cook at the castle was very pretty.

8

'They were forlorn in the kitchen so I took pity on them. Sir Robert doesn't need all he bags.' He took a knife from his belt and slit the birds.

'Are you not eating?'

The trouble was that in the past few months she had been unable to eat in his presence. It was partly fear that he would find her manners lacking after seeing those fancy maids eat in the servants' hall. But mostly because love had driven off appetite.

She nibbled at a wing, watching him demolish the sausage loaf and the rest of the grouse. Perhaps all that food went to the massive shoulders? Perhaps men in love didn't lose their appetites. At seventeen, she had so few of the answers.

'And how is Jean today?' Johnny asked.

'Still the headache,' she said. 'They change her, you know?'

'I know,' he said, mouth full of apple.

'But shouldn't those headaches ease, after a year?'

'A kick on the head from a pony takes time . . .'

'Aye, but Dr. Robertson said the bruise is long gone. Will she heal, Johnny?'

'Oh, likely, in time.' But she saw a shift of the gray-blue eyes, heard a falseness in his voice.

'I could take the truth,' she said.

He reached for another apple, flinging the core of the first down the ravine. 'I'm no physician, Linty.'

'But you've the second sight.'

'Away, woman!' He raised a huge hand as though to slap her.

'But you have. It was yourself warned that Jean shouldn't ride that pony—'

'Because Andy hadn't gentled it.'

'But have you forgotten that – for no reason – you left the stables and found your way to the path as though you knew you'd find her there?'

He shrugged. 'I'd a fair idea she'd take that path, easy as it is. And I have a fair idea her headaches would ease if Andy came back from Glasgow.'

'He's not like to come back to a farm after service in a city.'

'He should.' How strange, that new look in his eyes, like candles softly lighted. Bright, bright as candles but the blue-gray almost black. 'He should come back.'

'But what's there for him here? The good jobs at the castle are taken.'

He didn't seem to hear her, looking off across the hills. 'Great changes, Linda.' He used her full name only in deep seriousness. 'Something – I dinna ken what – is coming. Coming in purple and gold and silver. Carriages, I see ... and look to those peaks. Cairns will grow there from piled stones and the castle pulled to the ground.'

'Balmoral?' she asked, incredulous.

'Aye, Balmoral. But stone by stone and tower by tower it will rise again. I see a great quarry – and building.'

'Is it fire will destroy the castle?' she asked fearfully.

Again he didn't seem to hear her. 'Torn to the ground, but spires rising. Gardens planted. Someone – a woman. Och, what a woman!'

A woman he would love? She reached across and clasped his arm. 'Who? Who is she?'

'What?' His eyes were no longer strange, though he shook his head as though to clear it. 'What's wrong? You look as if you've seen a spookie.'

'No,' she said, frightened. 'You did. This woman you spoke of.'

'What woman? Now, why do you stare like that?'

'Do you mind what you said?'

'If I didna say it, then I should have. That loaf of meat was gey fine.'

So he hadn't remembered. It was as if he had been talking in his sleep. 'You said Balmoral would be pulled to the ground!'

'Likely it should be.' He stood up and stretched, gathered the grouse bones into the paper and flung them down the ravine. 'The drains stink. It's too small for Sir Robert's family, crowded and mean. And it's mean he'll be if I'm not back within the hour. Come, I'll reach over with you to the house.'

He helped her down the rocky path until they were on level ground. Whistling, he mocked a blackbird. Crows rose above

10

the pleated green fields, then settled darkly. Past Little Mill, with its great, groaning wheel, they came to her cottage clothed in its worn heather-thatch and dead honeysuckle.

'I'll be over tonight,' said Johnny.

Why? Linty wondered. He could put his long legs to any hearth-light, warm himself at any fire. And there must be a great warmth blazing from the kitchen at Balmoral, and all manner of girls anxious to cheer him. It was said, too, that whisky flowed free and the food left from dinner (dinner meant supper in a castle) could be chicken or turkey, not just game.

Was Johnny playing some game with her? No, he wasn't sly, nor had she anything but love to offer. But she'd not offer it easily. He must not be so sure of his welcome, so sure of her. Perhaps he was only in pity of her, orphaned, with a strange, sick sister.

So she must say, No. I've a lad calling tonight.

'I've a—'

But if she said, 'A lad coming,' he'd know it a lie; there could be no secrets in Crathie Parish, small and gossipy as it was.

'I've a bit of work to do,' she said. 'I'll see you another night.'

It was hard to say. Looking up at him, at the red-gold of his hair, the long sideburns, the full mouth, she almost went back on her words.

'If you're making bramble jam,' he said, 'you'd not deny me a taste? Or have you gathered the rowan?'

'No,' she said, 'It's the rowan I'll gather tomorrow. But tonight, as I said, I've some work.'

'Tonight,' said Johnny Brown, 'I'll be by to help you.' And he was off up the path, whistling again.

Arrogant. Conceited. All the big words she'd ever heard, and all from him, who was so educated, who could read and write and spell, who knew more about life outside the glen than anyone, even the minister.

And he knew, God help her, that she'd be waiting tonight.

Chapter One

Jean's headaches were bad that month. Unable to help with the chores, she lay near the hearth in the main room, hands pressed to her eyes. Only twenty-two, thought Linty, but she looks thirty now. Her fair hair was all tangled, for she said it hurt to brush it. She screamed when Linty put a shawl over it against the cold.

For it was cold early this autumn. Linty stuffed cracks with sheepswool and fires burned from dawn until bedtime. The girls were usually abed by nine unless Johnny Brown came, or some other neighbor. Jean shrank from company, preferring a brick-warmed pallet in the next room.

The little house had seemed crowded in their parents' time; now they used the tiny room on the upper floor for storing such few things as they had. A brown chest of scarred pine contained her mother's wedding veil, her bride's bouquet of withered white heather, and scraps of old dresses for quilt-making; then there were boots and fishing tackle, an old gun, a skinning-knife. This was all that was left of Margaret and Ian Clarke, both dead of the coughing sickness.

Downstairs, past the main room, was the bedroom, with its two pallets, a stool and clothes chest, a cracked looking glass. Beyond was the kitchen, with its fireplace and iron pots that swung from long hooks, a griddle for baking. Each room was limewashed except the tiny rock-walled one where cheese and butter were made and the indoor shed where chickens roosted on bitter nights.

They still kept chickens, but only two cows were left now. Milk and eggs were sold to Balmoral, which housed so many guests, and servants. Those shillings were their livelihood, except in spring when they made a few pennies with rhubarb jam or, in summer, raspberry or blackcurrant. It was a slim existence, though Johnny helped with a bit of mutton or game from the castle. Linty hadn't believed Johnny's fantastic tales of cooking up at the castle until he had brought her a haunch of lamb, a sauce of cherries on it, glazed red. But what she was most grateful for was raw meat for salting down. Johnny provided almost like a husband, ever careful of their larder; but then he was a man who valued food.

More and more often now, as the trees tartaned in gold and crimson, she worried that he didn't share her love. So many small adventures from childhood, but the great one of marriage seemed not to enter his mind. He was twenty-one, earning a good wage, and his family's farm prospering. Bush Farm supplied much of Balmoral's garden fare, its cream and crowdie and butter. Aye, Johnny could afford a wife.

On this mid-October night Jean, shivering into bed, said, 'Will he be coming?'

'I never know for sure.'

Linty bent to secure the candle in its holder. 'It's after eight.'

Jean eased her head carefully onto the pillow and pulled up the rough blankets. 'I think you should ask him outright what he plans.'

'What!'

'There are other lads, if only you'd notice them. Johnny is wasting your youth.'

'You speak like an old wifie. And I'm only seventeen—'

'Our mother was only fifteen when she married. But it's not that worries me, Linty – so much that he's like a' – she turned toward the candle placed near the bed on a stool – 'like that. All shine, but apt to go out and leave you in the dark.'

But it would be a strong wind to bend Johnny. 'I'm the one should fret,' Linty said, 'not you. It will only make your head hurt.'

Jean said, 'I'm not saying he may not love you. But what man would want to take on the burden of me?'

'Of all the spindly talk! His farm's big enough for us both, and well you know it, and his brother's leaving for the town, he says, someday. Educated men are not content here long—'

'And will Johnny be?'

There was a rap on the door of the main room, the sound of big boots, and Jean said, 'He's here!' and blew out the candle.

Linty closed the bedroom door, then at sight of Johnny she said, 'What is it?'

She knew his moods so well. Anger, contrition (rarely), triumph, and once, at twelve, the close-to-tears when he saw his dog's head raw on the road, the body smashed by a drover's cart. 'What is it?' she repeated, alarmed.

'Sir Robert's dead. Suddenly, just like—' He snapped his fingers, then sat down on a stool. 'A good man, a fair master. Only Sunday he was there in the stable, watching me bring out the foal.'

'Oh Johnny.' She went to him, stroked the wiry red curls. 'What shall happen to you, then?'

He sighed. 'What's to happen will. All I've heard is second-gossip. I suppose it will all be settled by the Earl.'

By the Earl of Aberdeen, the dead man's brother.

'You'll not leave here, then, for a city?'

'I'll be where I'm needed,' he said. 'That's all I know.'

That was so simply the way he was. If the need – whatever it might be – were there, Johnny would remain. Or if he found helplessness. One night at a barn frolic, between the flaunting of the pipes, he had heard the scream of a rabbit, went out into the snow and found it trapped. Not a soft man, you'd think, but he nursed that paw back to health. He hated traps; game should be shot swiftly, cleanly. Then there was that oafish guest of Sir Robert's who had left a wounded doe, not caring as it was thin and small – Linty's cottage had rocked with Johnny's rage and next day at Balmoral, speaking his mind, he had all but been sacked from his job.

'Then you'll not be leaving here?'

Again, the odd brilliance of his eyes, sharp and gleaming as needles. 'I'll wait for what's to come.'

'That woman?' She hadn't meant to blurt the jealous question.

'What woman?' He stared at her. 'Have you been at Jean's medicine?'

He meant the laudanum Dr. Robertson brought to ease the

14

headaches but which sometimes made Jean strange. 'I have not! It was you yourself spoke of that woman and the changes that would come here. On the moor, it was . . .'

He chuckled. 'Then I was fou. If ever a change comes to Crathie I don't see it a woman's doing. More likely some English bastard, and the worse for us.'

The wounds of the past were still sore in the Highlands: the banning of the kilt and the plaid a hundred years ago, the order against carrying arms, the clans broken. But it wasn't all English cruelty and craft – later there had been the treachery of their own lairds, absentee landlords who left Scotland to wine and dice and wench in London, and grew fat on the profits of the sturdy new Cheviot sheep. Aye, sheep driven north in hundreds of thousands to displace the people from their crofts; people burned out like rats. The Clearances of twenty years ago were as vivid as last night's nightmare.

'I'd sooner go back to farming,' Johnny said, 'than kiss the boot of some son of a bitch. One thing I'll be is free.'

Perhaps of me, too, she thought. Did he think of marriage as a shackle, was he like an animal which would not be fenced, however gently?

Gently, she said, 'It will all come right, Johnny. Now when did you eat?'

'I supped,' he said.

So grief was really on him. 'I could make brose,' she said, 'if you've the heart for it.'

Ah, well, he could do with a bite. He followed her to the kitchen and stirred up the fire while she mixed oatmeal, butter and salt in a pan and heated water in the iron kettle. Then she combined the mixture and set the pot on the hearth to swell the oats.

Johnny peered into the rock cupboard. 'Good, there's plover left,' and he brought it out on its plate.

She smiled; he was himself again.

Linty could not remember so hard a winter. Lochnagar, snowed-over, was invisible against an ice-white sky. When she leaned toward the looking glass she could scarcely see her face for the steam of her breath on it.

A small, serious face dominated by brown eyes that tilted up at the corners. Her hair was fair, like Jean's, tumbling loose and thick to her waist, a tiny waist. A body delicately boned but strong enough for the chores, for the endless bringing in of wood and sea coal and turf, of water from the well. Jean was unable to help with the animals, but on her good days she boiled the kale or the turnips or sat in the inglenook piecing a quilt. She was patient with her pain, but more and more dependent on the medicine. It brought oblivion, but it didn't cure, and sometimes it thickened her tongue as though she had taken spirits. But when Dr. Robertson came by from Ballater in February he said she would surely heal by spring.

If ever spring came . . .

The Gordons remained at Balmoral except for two of the ladies who took refuge from the cold in Aberdeen, lodging with the earl. Johnny continued his tasks. It was all the same, Linty thought — the same visits to neighbors, the same talk of plantings-to-come, of crops, the same gossip. Her world was small and its extent bounded by journeys with Johnny on his pony. To nearby Little Mill, where Gordons — no relation to the Balmoral family — ground barley. Across the Dee to the Mill of Inver, where Ian Davidson ground oats, and warmed drinks of sowans in his cottage down the road. A visit to Torquil Briggs, the tinker, who sheltered in a barn near Loch Muick, a barn long deserted but still firm to the winds. Rarely, a frolic at the Inver Inn, the stop for the Braemar–Ballater coach where Linty listened to the talk of strangers and marveled. Edinburgh, Glasgow, London seemed fairy cities built on dreams, some houses towering higher than Balmoral's tallest spire.

In March the snow-capped towers of Balmoral thawed, like peaked hats dripping. Sun sent mountain snow to spate the streams to roaring. There were the first snowdrops, like foam on the land. And in April, Johnny helping with the birth of lambs at Balmoral and Bush Farm, and finally, shyly, on tiptoe, as if embarrassed by being so late, the first fat buds of spring.

Johnny was free of duties on Sundays and on the first warm day, after kirk, they mounted his pony and took picnic fare past Inver Mill up to the hills. Here were the ruins of tumbled houses and the old kirk with its gutted windows, dead hens in straw where once there had been pews. A stench, a despair here, and even outside on the slow-flowering slopes was a desolation of rubble that had once been a cottage, a manse. Here stood fireplaces without fires, huts without walls or roof, and far down the glen, in the valley, a phantom mansion, a wraith of a peel tower. Places which had once known and welcomed the hopeful, swaggering soldiers of Bonnie Prince Charlie — proud clansmen, fierce, merry, hard-drinking, elegant, exquisite, ragged or velvety, but all of the Stuart cause, who called themselves Jacobites and dedicated themselves to a dream now lost.

The evictions came later — the typhus, the cholera, the famine.

'Och,' Johnny said, looking down, 'this is no place to eat,' and they rode a mile further on, where there was only the sweep of wild daffodils and the cry of the curlew, no lament but the mourn of wood pigeons among the silver birches.

Unschooled as she was, Linty knew the pibroch of her people, handed down from grandparents to parents. Again she wondered why Johnny stayed on. He could make twice his wage in a city. He was no sloup of a farmer only, he could even be factor to someone, good as he was at sums. Why, then, did he stay on here, unless . . .?

But he could take her with him if he cared to. If he cared beyond friendship.

After the crumbs of the crowdie-cheese, washed down by a dram from his bottle, sitting close on the grass, she said, frightened by the question but needing to ask it, 'Why do you stay on here, when even men like Andy go?'

'I'd be prisoned in a city,' he said. 'I've not forgotten the time Sir Robert sent me to Aberdeen, to the horse fair. Aye, a fancy lodging at Campbell's and my boots put out for shining — but it was as if my throat closed and I couldn't breathe in foul air. Three days and you mind I came back like an old man to his hearth, with a cold on me that wasn't cold at all — but disgust.'

She remembered that he had seemed glad to return, but

hadn't probed the reason. 'Disgust at what?'

'The fancy ways. The cheating. The belief that, being a countryman, I couldn't tell a good horse from a false one or ken the spiels or the lies. Or even know the value of a shilling from a ha'penny or the difference of cod from haddock. Being laughed at.'

'*Laughed* at?' Who on earth would dare?

'Some pretended not to understand me – the horse dealers from London. They scorned my clothes, as though the kilt were still "a crime." But a lad who called me "Redshanks" will bear a broken jaw to the rest of his days. And Mrs. Campbell, of the tavern, charging two shillings a bottle for whisky because she thought I'd not know about prices. A Scots thief is no better than an English, Linty. It's a rumply world outside.'

She had never been further than Ballater, seven miles across the hills, and then with her parents as protection, astonished that there were five shops and windows displaying ribbons and lace and bonnets with flowers. She could still remember the smells – the scent in a chemist's from a glass pot of rose leaves; oil lamps, like warm scorched earth; wheels of strange yellow cheese in the greengrocers, brine from pickle vats, brown beans of coffee; and of course the familiar smells of the cattlemarket, which were like home but with everybody wearing shoes and their Sunday clothes.

'I'd not give a gipsy's oath for the world outside,' Johnny said.

And so he would remain, and so she was happy – or if not happy, content. Jean would heal, as Dr. Robertson said. Summer would come, and the harvest plump and the dances to celebrate. And who knew if on some night of moon and stars Johnny might not kiss her – a kiss of love, not friendship – and ask her to marry? And then, oh, then, what would matter the world outside or cold or even hunger?

She was aware of the hunger for him stirring her body, but there was no shame to that, only the need that he wouldn't suspect. Two years ago she would have sat closer to him for the chill of the damp primrosed grass and the wind from the hills. But now she must be aloof.

'To thine own self be true,' the minister had said this morning. But that was kirk talk. If she were to speak truly, she could lose Johnny to that thing that was eagle-free in him, and her pride as well as her caution forbade it. In her mother's youth a girl was an old maid if not married by seventeen, but times had changed. One might worry at twenty, but not now, not yet.

'Don't be fretting,' Johnny said.

She turned to him. So he knew, as he always did.

'Fretting?' she asked. 'About what?'

'The future,' he said, and tangled a weed around his thumb, then looked up, smiling.

June was a burst of blossom, and in July wild strawberries and gorse gold as the sun. Haymaking, and then the frolics to remember in the wet mists of another autumn. Torquil Briggs, the tinker, deserted his barn for his hedgerow, where Linty, seeking raspberries, found him one warm afternoon.

'You've been away,' she said. 'Did you do well?'

'Aye,' he said, and showed her a basket of coins. 'All the way to Huntly I walked – and everyone believed.'

She giggled. 'And you wore your white robe?'

'The brown for bogs, the white I washed before I entered villages.'

'Johnny Brown says you're a rogue.'

'And who is he to judge?'

'Only in fun,' Linty said. 'So don't be frowning.'

'I never frown,' Torquil said, kneeling to make a stick fire, filling a pot for tea, 'except at Mary Magdalenes, and there's not many round here. Besides, I'd forgive them – afterwards.'

'After what?'

'After, that's all.' He brushed grass from his trousers and eased his thin body next to the fire, keeping an eye on it, feeding it peat. She was afraid his long beard might catch as he leaned forward, but he pulled back quickly. Forty, was he, or more? No one in Crathie seemed to know or to remember. It seemed as if he had always lived here, in his winter barn or summer hedgerow, sharpening scissors or scythes or axes for a living, mending pots, traveling to parts where he was unknown to work his miracles – or so he called them.

She had never been sure whether he believed in his miracles

or played on the credulous. Johnny said perhaps Torquil didn't know himself, after so long at it. But most surely he looked like a prophet, with that gaunt frame and gray-gold beard, and once, seeing him in his white robes beside the loch at sunrise, she had sensed a great power in him – that tall, silent figure standing in the light of a pink sky, the arms out-stretched as though to bless. Though when she'd told Johnny he'd said more likely he was stretching himself after a night on the hard ground.

The minister had tried to oust him but it couldn't be proven that he did harm, nor did he call himself Jesus or Moses or anything but his own name. And the name, he said, had come about very simply. His mother, Janet Briggs, finding herself with child by a man who ran away, took service with Sir Torquil and Lady Sutherland up beyond Braemar. So what could be more natural than naming the child after a fine, good master – though Lady Sutherland had not been appreciative of the honor, and Janet was forced to seek work elsewhere. Otherwise, Torquil was vague about his early life. His mother, he said, had gone to heaven in his youth after some alterca-tion at the Stag and Hound – which is why he drank nothing but water from the stream, or tea.

Accepting a mug of tea she said, 'Torquil, could you heal my sister Jean?'

He hesitated. 'She has her own doctor, hasn't she?'

'Aye, but she gets no better.'

'I can't meddle with one who has a doctor,' he said. 'I'd be stoned out of town. That's what happened in Tillyfriskie last year. I went to heal a poor man who had bad lungs. Three nights I spent with him, and he was easing, and then a neigh-bor told another and it reached the doctor's ear and some old wifie said I was up to witchcraft. At the same time there came a disease to the cows ... I escaped with my life barely.' He rolled up a rag of his trousers. 'That's a rock cut will scar me always.'

She was surprised by the youth of his skin, the even white-ness of his teeth. Without the beard he might be younger than she'd thought. 'It's a bad scar, but you're strong of limb. How old are you, Torquil?'

'How should I know?' he asked. 'My beard is graying. Perhaps I'm forty. But I don't know. I'm not tired as old men are.'

'Have you never had a wife?' It was a bold question and she instantly regretted it, for he frowned.

'Ministers have wives,' she added hastily.

'I've little to offer a wife,' he said. 'No woman wants a life of wandering. There's this thing in me that must make me leave a place and seek another, not just for the shillings of tinkering, but for the need in me.'

'Yet you always return here in summer.'

'To commune with beauty. To look to the hills whence cometh my help. And then, the castles along the Dee and Don are full of profit. Yesterday at Balmoral alone I made three shillings, and a fine meal into the bargain.'

'I hear the cook is pretty?'

'I saw only her hands, which put out a basket of beef and haggis. Mending harnesses I was, in the barn . . .'

'You could mend Jean,' she said. 'At least, you could try—'

'Try? I *do*, when I please to. There is no "trying" about it.'

'Then please to mend her. We'll not tell a soul. No neighbor will know. You could visit after dark—'

'I don't force my healing. I may come; I may not. If there are impurities on me, then my powers are poor.'

'What sort of impurities?' she asked. 'You never even take a dram.'

'My personal impurities,' Torquil said with dignity, 'are not for the ears of lassies. Would you admit to yours, Linty?'

'Aye,' she said in a rush of confession. 'I am jealous of that castle cook and all the maids. I could kill each one who flaunts to Johnny Brown.'

'So it's come to that,' he said, pouring more tea. 'Has he spoken for you?'

'No!' She was suddenly angry at the waste of it. 'Almost every night he comes to me, or we picnic. But it's like—' She searched for a way to explain. '— being so hungry and having just a bite to eat and then the food snatched away until hours later when there's another wee bite. But no full supper.'

21

He nodded, frowning again. His brows were thick, still fair in contrast to the gray in the beard, tufty brows that nearly met above calm blue eyes. 'I see. But Johnny may have to sow his wild oats.'

'What do you mean?'

'That he's not ready to settle. Perhaps he'll want a slice of the world first. Once he spoke of going to sea.'

'But he was only a lad then; it was years ago. I can't understand what holds him here.' She put her mug of tea down on the grass. 'Torquil, you're wise. What shall I do? Jean says to ask him straight out, but I'd be ashamed.'

'Of course,' he said. 'You must not ask. A man but wants the pleasure of the chase.' He smiled. 'Just bide your time, Linty. What's to happen will happen.'

'You sound like him, sometimes.'

'But I am not like him – at all. I live in my mind, he in his body. We are only alike in needing freedom, space to move in, but I think his need is from youth. He might settle down for reasons I cannot.'

She was about to speak when Sheena Davidson, with her berry basket, came through the bushes. She looked at Linty's basket and said, 'So that's why I canna find any – you have them all.'

'There are plenty over there,' Linty said, pointing. 'Go and pick over there.'

But Sheena sat down and demanded tea of Torquil. 'I like you,' she said. Then, turning to Linty, 'I hate you, Linty Clarke.'

And that was true, Linty thought, and wondered why. As Torquil brought out another cracked mug and poured tea from the iron kettle, she felt impaled on Sheena's cold-eyed hatred. Her eyes were so pale a gray that they were almost white; her hair was the color of sun on snow.

For sure this was a queer child. 'Spawn of the devil,' Johnny had said, but laughing, not meaning it. Her father, Ian Davidson, the miller, was as kind a man as one could meet, and his wife Katherine lovely and gentle. Both had brown hair and brown eyes. Yet this only child was so different in look, in mood, in thought. Last autumn just, Johnny had caught

Sheena laughing at a hare caught in a trap. 'It's funny when it cries,' she'd said. 'I've been here an hour listening.'

Johnny had slapped her and removed the dead hare. 'It's the way some children are,' he said, 'but they grow up.'

But would Sheena, at twelve, ever grow out of that need to hate, to enjoy torture? Linty could remember herself at six, fascinated by the cat's way with a mouse. It was Johnny who had helped teach her about animals, their ways, their needs, their helplessness. To kill was for food, not otherwise. To enjoy torture was mad.

And Sheena was still mad, for she was always hanging about the traps set for foxes or hares, and God knew what she did to the dogs and the cat when her parents weren't looking.

'Why do you hate Linty?' Torquil asked mildly, giving her the mug of tea.

'Because,' Sheena said, tossing back her long white hair. A strange, narrow little face, with a mouth like a bright string. To Linty, that mouth was the worst of her, like that of a cat bloodied by its catch.

'Because what?' Linty asked.

Sheena ignored the question and turned to Torquil. 'Do you have any cakes?'

'I do not. And if I did, I'm not sure I'd give you one. You're not being nice to Linty.'

'I don't like Linty.'

'Why?' Torquil asked.

Sheena wriggled her thin shoulders. 'Just because.'

But Linty had heard all this before. 'Never mind,' she said to Torquil, rising and picking up her basket. 'Thank you for the tea, and I'll go along.'

Because I'm frightened of this child? Surely not. But some sort of evil is in her and the day is dirtied.

It's only by chance, she thought, that the sun has gone and the air chilled; that's mountain weather, ever changeable. Yet as she walked home she thought of the old stories of witches, in whom some folk still believed. It took no imagination to think of Sheena as a young witch. Even at twelve her face was old in malice. What, then, would she be at fifty or sixty? Seeping into herself the foul and filth of the world?

23

You're daft, she told herself. She's simply a bad child, spoiled by Ian and Katherine because she's their only one. It is only that and nothing more. She doesn't like me because I don't like her; it is simple as that.

In late August Jean was better, able to help with the milking though Linty would not let her do the heavier chores. She was well enough to build the fires to cook, to make the broth and the bannocks. The ache was still in her head, she said, but not the piercing pain. She was even able to speak of Andy lightly, as someone might a song or a scent once beloved. He had moved into her past, and that, Linty thought, was as well. For no man who left these mountains ever returned – except the gentry who came for the seasons of fishing and shooting. It was as if cities got into their blood like drink. Of all the men she knew, only Johnny had wanted to come back.

Nothing had changed with them; only her love for him had grown firmer and strengthened through these twelve months. If he had another girl, she didn't know it or sense it. Almost every day or night she saw him, welcomed him, thanked him for the food he brought, cooked it or preserved it. Together they visited neighbors, danced at harvest frolics held in barns festooned with strings of shallots and heather and beetroot, with torches of pine fastened to the eaves. Courting couples after a dram or two climbed to the straw of the haylofts, but Johnny never asked her there. She comforted herself that he was too discreet.

'The loft,' Jean had said with a chuckle, 'is where many a bairn is made.'

'If he'd marry me I'd not care how or where.'

On 7 September Jean felt well enough to venture with Linty to the store in Crathie where they needed to buy salt and thread. To their astonishment a crowd was gathered outside and a flag was being raised on the pole of a slender birch.

'What is it?' Linty asked Ian Davidson. 'What's happening?'

'The Queen comes tomorrow.'

'*Here?*'

'Aye, though I didn't believe it until the minister said so himself.'

'She's to visit Balmoral,' said Katherine Davidson, holding Sheena's hand. 'The men are putting up a flowered arch at Lodge Gate.'

It couldn't be true. The Queen would never come here, of all places.

'She's to visit the Gordons,' said the postman, 'and all her family, too. The Prince and the bairns. She's to be here at half past two in the afternoon.'

'I don't believe it,' Jean said.

'It's myself that delivered a letter, all fancy it was, to Balmoral, though—' He paused. 'I'd nae idea what was in it. It was three weeks ago. But it was kept secret, y'ken.'

The crowd mingled to exchange gossip, speculation, rumor. If the minister said so, then it couldn't be a lie. And Mr. MacLeod, the postie, said he'd delivered a fancy letter. Still, it was like a dream, for Balmoral was a wee, wee place and the Gordons not so grand that they merited such visitors.

Listening, Linty felt betrayed. There must have been wild preparations going on at the castle, cleaning and airing and cooking and all. But Johnny had not said a word. She remembered he had mentioned a special cleaning of the stables, but she'd thought nothing of that, with winter coming on.

'The Queen,' said Sheena, letting loose her mother's hand and mocking a curtsy. She looked at Linty. 'She might throw you a penny, if you're close.'

'Sheena!' Her mother caught her hand again. 'You mind your manners.' Then, to Linty, 'I'm sorry, her tongue has a nasty twist.'

Mrs. Anderson, the minister's wife, came forward. 'If any of you have flowers in your garden, we'd be grateful for them to make the arch. And my husband thought some little girls might present a bouquet.'

'I will,' Sheena said.

'Several little girls,' Mrs. Anderson said. 'And no one may talk, only curtsy.' She looked about at the hopping, excited children and sighed. 'Linda, would you be willing to find the flowers for the bouquet and bring them to me at the manse? Nothing thorny, mind.'

'I'll do my best,' Linty said, flattered yet still unbelieving.

25

'They must be ready at noon tomorrow.'

Linty and Jean bought their provisions and returned home in a daze. They agreed that Linty's search for flowers could not begin until morning so that the blooms would be fresh, but now the problem was what to wear. They had their Sunday dresses but both were shabby.

'I think it time we went to Mother's trunk,' Jean said. 'She'd want us to if the Queen is coming.'

'If . . .'

By dusk they each had a lace collar sewed on old gowns, and Jean took her mother's red shawl. They would not have used them, out of respect, had it not been essential. There was the Sunday black and the sprigged merino, but no time to alter them. The best they could do was to refurbish two old bonnets with bits of ribbon from her bridal hat.

Linty sighed, standing at the looking-glass. 'I'm glad I do not have to present the flowers. She'd laugh at me.'

'Nonsense. You're pretty. No, perk the bonnet to one side, so.' She adjusted the tilt. 'Now, we'd best wash our stockings and hang them to dry. Are yours mended, or shall I—'

A knock, and Johnny came in. 'What's this?' he asked.

'We're getting ready for tomorrow.' Linty turned accusingly. 'Why didn't you tell us?'

'I was sworn to secrecy,' he said. 'Lady Gordon said if one of us told we'd all be dismissed after the Queen left. They don't want journalists here nosing about during their holiday.'

'Then it's *really* true. How long shall she stay, Johnny?'

'I'm not sure. There are all sorts of tales – that she was ill and is coming here to rest; that she's weary of city life; that the Prince wants to shoot.' He sat down on a stool. 'I hear you're to gather flowers, Linty. We have a few blooms the gardener said he can spare from the house. And there are wild chrysanthemums at Bush. I'll lend you a pony.'

'Weeds, for a Queen?' Jean asked.

'What can she expect? And what more does she deserve? Bloody English coming here to clear us out is my guess, with her German puff along to make a thorough job of it.'

True, the Clearances were continuing in far places, but

surely not here. As the girls stared, appalled, he said, 'What have the English ever brought us but misery? Did she do anything to prevent the Clearances? Don't tell me she doesn't *know*. She has a finger in every pie. This Irishman works at Abergeldie, he was telling me about the terrible famine in his country – a million starving, he says, and does she lift a finger? Or is it so heavy with diamonds she can't?'

He swung off the stool, brought out a bottle and drank. 'I'll not be there to welcome her. I'll keep to the stables and find it cleaner air. Will you take a dram?'

The girls shook their heads. Seeing that he had frightened them, he said, 'Och, I may be wrong. Maybe they only come to flaunt and flatter the Gordons out of good shooting. There's none better, though I don't see that German puff with a gun – him and his top hat. But whatever's their reason for coming, I don't like it. It's not natural. They're up to no good.'

'Is it that the Earl is so important that she decided to come?' Linty asked.

'What's an earl when she's with kings and princes and dukes all the time? Och, she sees earls as no more than anybody else. And damned if I like what they're putting up on the gate "Welcome to the Queen of Scots."'

'But she is,' Jean said.

'By law, not in the heart. There was never a Queen of Scots but Mary Stuart nor ever will be – and she looks a pudding to boot.'

But the girls had thought her pictures beautiful. It was just that Johnny hated all things English, with that long memory of his. That's what book-reading did; it soured you and made you suspicious. Besides, Linty suspected he'd had more than a few drams.

'What will you eat?' she asked. 'We have—'

'Nothing,' he said, and went to the door. Never had she seen him in such a black mood. She followed him outside and put her hand on his shoulder.

'Johnny, there's such a darkness on you. You're spoiling it all, the one thing that's ever happened here.'

His eyes softened, and his voice. 'Forget it, woman. I'll bring a pony round at eight, and the castle flowers.'

'Mind there are no thorns.'

He laughed, 'To prick the royal hands? I doubt she runs blood, Linty. But we'll not take a chance.'

No chances were taken next morning. Whether there were letters or not, MacLeod the postie was told to rouse everyone on his rounds, though the farmers had been up since five as usual and nobody but the gentry slept until nine. Mr. Anderson added 'And England and Ireland' to the poster on the lodge gate, then smudged it with his sleeve and inky fingers and hurriedly lettered a new one: *Welcome to Our Queen and The Royal Family.*

'I've not enough paper to add Wales and all,' he told his wife. 'Besides, they should have sent a proper banner.'

But when Linty came with the flowers she thought the gate looked wonderful. The blacksmith had built a wire arch and women had festooned heather and pine and rowan to cling to it, watching men teeter on ladders and handing up asters to tuck in the foliage. Mrs. Anderson took Linty's flowers into the manse to fashion a bouquet, grieved by the lack of roses. Still, she said, it was a gesture and surely there would be plenty of roses in the royal apartments.

At home, Linty tethered Johnny's pony at the fence, wondering if he really meant what he'd said, that he'd not join in the welcome. So golden a day, the sky cloudless, and he sulking in the stables ... As she washed herself in the shed, she called to Jean, 'Whatever he thinks, it's a day we'll never forget.'

'Aye.' Jean came to the open door, fastening her bodice. The little silk buttons were frayed, but the lace collar was delicate against her throat. 'I could almost be happy today. If—'

'If?' Linty turned, drying herself with the homespun cloth.

'If the headache doesn't come back. And if there were a lad.'

'Perhaps someone will come from Ballater or Braemar. If we see a handsome boy we'll go up and speak to him. You can't afford to be shy when there are so few chances to meet new folk.'

'It's not just handsome I'd care for,' Jean said. 'I don't want another Andy, but someone steady to be here always.'

'Just smile, and he will be,' Linty said. She felt suddenly young and giggly. 'Smile at a lord or a duke. There are sure to be some.'

'All married or after rich brides.'

She couldn't tease Jean as she used to, or make her join in the daydreams they'd played as young girls. The headaches had sobered her, though today she looked younger, her hair tidy under her bonnet. If only she were not so pale, with her skin so candle-white and something like fear in her eyes.

'I've small needs,' Jean said as she followed Linty into the bedroom and watched her put on the cotton petticoat and Sunday stockings. 'Just to be safe, that's all. And to know you are safe.'

'I'd rather not be safe,' Linty said, climbing into the long brown skirt, fastening its hooks. 'Safe is never to know anything; safe is to be in your coffin.' She put on the tiny-waisted jacket and buttoned it, frothing the frill of the collar. 'We're not *old* enough to want that.'

'You're not. But you might be, someday.'

Safe in Johnny's arms is the only way I want to be. And why should it not happen? Was he lending her the pony so that he would be here tonight for sure to take it back to the farm? There was no need to worry when he was here so often.

They walked to the village, for Jean was afraid of riding the pony, through the fallen leaves and the tall, spiky broom. It wasn't yet noon but the crowd was dense – nearly two hundred, and more coming from outlying farms. Pipers practiced near the lodge gate, walking gravely back and forth, to and fro. And there was Torquil Briggs, decked out in a black suit Linty had never seen before.

'Where did you get it?' she asked, admiring the wide lapels and tight waist.

'I bought it off the widow Donaldson and had it taken in.'

'Aye, he was a fat one, was the big Donaldson.' Linty motioned toward Jean. 'You've not seen my sister in some time.'

She hoped that he would look beyond the grace of bonnet

and lace collar and see Jean's odd expression, but he simply made a little bow and said, 'A fine day isn't it, Miss Clarke?' and went off to look at the men who were placing new flowers into the arch.

Accustomed to noon-day dinner, the crowd had brought their own — oatcakes and cheese, cold meat and bread and ale. Och, but on such a day Linty wondered how they could even think of eating. In the warm sun she and Jean settled under the shade of an oak and watched as more and more people came, on foot or on horseback. At least they had a place close to the gate through which the Queen must pass.

'She'll never be here on time,' Jean said. 'Folk like that want folk like us to wait.'

'But the minister said half after two.'

Some little boys tried to raise a flag on a pole. Sheena Davidson fought with two other girls for the privilege of hand-ing the Queen the bouquet, and the minister's wife came to instruct them: 'After the minister's speech of welcome, you, Sheena, are to toss these petals. You, Janet, are to come for-ward and throw the white heather. You, Fiona, are to curtsy and present the bouquet to Her Majesty. And not one of you is to speak, only to smile.'

Then she turned to the crowd. 'There must not be a bottle seen nor a crumb of your dinners. You are to cheer, aye, and loudly. Then the pipers will play Her Majesty through the gate to the castle.'

'Isn't the Earl to be here?' asked Mrs. Davidson.

'He'll be with them, and his ladies waiting.' Mrs. Anderson looked droopy as a flower off its stalk, Linty thought, usually a pert and pretty woman but now aged a good ten years by the weight of the occasion. 'Once the Queen is through that gate, we need not fret. But—' She turned again and faced the crowd, and Linty had never heard her voice so flinty. '—there will be no unseemly behaviour. You women will watch your bairns, and you men your manners.'

'I think,' Jean whispered to Linty, 'that she's about to cry. It's Mr. Anderson should be doing this.'

'Likely he's thinking over his speech. It's him has to face them.'

'The Earl should do the welcome,' Torquil said, coming back. 'Even if he is with them he should do it. It's for the nobility to do the welcome.'

'But at the lodge gate?' Linty asked. 'They'll be in the castle.'

He didn't reply, and she saw that he was looking past her at Jean, who sat with her back to the oak, one hand pressed to her forehead. So the headache was back. But Jean turned, and smiled reassuringly. Perhaps that gesture of hand to forehead was habit now. 'It's warm,' she said. 'We should have brought ale.'

'Likely Johnny Brown will have more than that with him when he comes,' Torquil said.

'But he's not coming,' Linty said.

Torquil raised a shaggy eyebrow. 'I hear they're all told to come, except the butler and some of the maids, to make a great showing. The ghillies, the beaters, everyone's been told to come.'

'It's past the days when his head could be cut off if he doesn't,' Linty said.

'But the Gordons could sack him, and he's no fool to lose a good job.' He glanced again at Jean. 'If it's a cold drink you'd like, Miss Clarke, I'll be off for it.' They watched him push his way through the people toward the well.

'He's nicely mannered,' Jean said, 'for a – a – what's it Johnny called him?'

'A tinker. A gypsy, almost. And you know, he has the power to heal. So if your headache comes back, I thought—'

'Och, no!' Jean laughed. 'I'm not one for some witches' brew. Look, there's Johnny!'

And angry by the look of him, Linty thought as he came toward them. 'I've just one hour to spare,' he said, sitting down beside them. 'If they're late it's too bloody bad. I'll be off.'

Too proud to say he'd been ordered here, Linty thought. And in good order, too. He wore the kilt and his bonnet, and from the deerskin sporran he took his father's turnip watch. 'Fifteen minutes,' he said, 'they should be in Ballater. But likely they'll linger.'

'For what?' Jean asked, accepting the cup of water Torquil brought, smiling her thanks.

'For welcome speeches and all. And don't forget,' he said, deep in sarcasm, 'Ballater is a "fashionable watering place." Good enough to water their horses.'

'You've too long a memory,' Torquil said. 'The past is done with. We're part of England now, and that's it.'

'The better part,' said Johnny.

'What have the English ever done to you, you should be so blustery?' Torquil asked.

'Not to myself. To us. They're a race apart. By God now, do you know what our whisky would cost a bottle without the greed of their duty on it? One and nine. They make fivepence on every bottle.'

'Then why don't you give it up?' Torquil asked.

'Give up the water of life for a pack of scoundrels?' He motioned toward the cup of water Jean was drinking. 'Would you give that up, Torquil Briggs, for the sake of the English or anybody? Oh, I'm not saying we Scots are all so bloody perfect; there's lairds that have sold out – and their sons soft as butter. There's a laird up the Braes O' Mar – I'm not mentioning names – who disgraced himself just last winter. He and his clan were out hunting and dusk came on, and a mist, then snow. What did he do, that soft degenerate, but make a *pillow* of the snow to lie down on!'

'I've done the same myself,' Torquil said.

'But he'd an *example* to set. You're free to do as you like, but it's a father to his clan he was until they saw that. Now he's in London pillowed on his rents or on some—' He glanced at Linty and Jean. 'Never mind. Who'd like a dram?'

Jean and Torquil shook their heads but Linty accepted one. Anything to please Johnny, to share. Putting it back in the pocket of his jacket, he said, 'I was glad to leave the castle. All the fuss going on about food and flowers, one of the ladies needing the smelling salts for her nerves, the cook in a fit because there's no mint for the sauce – you'd think it was the second coming of Christ or Mary Stuart herself . . .'

The minister came out and the crowd hushed. After appraising the flower gate, he nodded approval and said, clearing his throat, 'Now, I must ask you all to be quiet the moment the carriages come in sight. Then you rise and cheer. The little girls know what to do, after I have spoken my welcome. Then you cheer again. Remember, this is an historic occasion for us all, and a blessed one. You must not forget that Her Majesty is head of the Church, as a lay – laywoman.'

Someone snickered and was glared at.

'As lay-leader of the Church, as well as being our Queen, she is due all of your respect. I have asked my wife to tell you that there must be no bottles – absolutely none – apparent, and no litter of food. So those of you who are eating, please make haste to finish and dispose of the remains. And now, may God bless you and place you all in proper reverence . . . Is there any question?'

The widow Donaldson stood up on her cane. 'How long will the Queen be here, sir?'

'We don't know. Perhaps a day or two, perhaps more.' He was obviously nervous, and took a handkerchief to his sweating forehead. 'It might be that she even comes to kirk on Sunday. If so, you are to leave the front pews vacant for her retinue, and of course the gallery will be in readiness for her and the royal family.'

He went back toward the manse and Linty said, 'I still don't believe she'll come *here*. There's no purpose, is there?'

'I'd guess it's the puff's need to shoot,' Johnny said. 'They say she agrees to every wish of his.'

'In love,' Jean said softly.

'Love?' Johnny laughed. 'Not likely. These royal folk marry for political reasons, and she's some sort of need for Germany, it being part of her heritage. Along with the madness of George the Third.'

'Stop your bitterness,' said Torquil. 'I may not read the journals as much as you, but I can read. And I read it was a love match from the start. It's said that she never had a room to herself, poor lass, always with her mother until the very dawn she was come to and declared Queen. At eighteen, mind you—'

'And married the first man she could, to rid herself of Mama,' said Johnny. 'Well, anyway, she's foaled five, more than I'd believe the puff could do. Or was it Melbourne?'

'Johnny,' said Torquil, 'you watch your tongue or I take these young ladies away, else demand you go.'

'Who's Melbourne?' Linty asked.

'A *prime* minister,' Johnny said. 'And now she has Sir Robert Peel? Anyway, she married the puff eight years ago and we'll all have the immense pleasure of seeing the bairns, if the cook heard right, she making jellies and porridge and all, and ginger-pudding men.'

That pretty cook again, Linty thought.

There was a sudden skirl of pipes, then a hush. The minister came out of his manse, and Linty, seeing a cloud of dust, helped Jean up and stared, dazzled.

First came an escort of horsemen, wearing uniforms and tall hats – 'Police officers,' Torquil said. These were followed by more men on horseback in the Gordon tartan, with pipers marching ahead. And finally the first carriage, open, shiny black, drawn by black, white-plumed horses – and a cheer went up for the Queen.

Linty had imagined her as tall, but sitting beside her husband, her bonnet scarcely came to his black velvet collar. She wore a gown of fawn-colored silk, a frilled brown bonnet trimmed with tiny plumes caught under the chin with ribbons. Under the bonnet gold-brown hair was looped in coils over her ears, and something bright – surely diamonds? – sparkled there. But what dominated the small, round face were enormous dark blue eyes, and Linty thought, almost with a shiver, *they see everything*. Even me, right down to my patched stockings.

Victoria waved a small, fawn-gloved hand and smiled and then, turning, waved and smiled again, the sun catching the sparkles of a bracelet.

'Och!' Jean whispered, 'how handsome he is!'

In dark gray, the Prince was, all in velvet from what they could see, the top hat off now, showing his high forehead, the long, dark sideburns. His mouth curved red under the brown moustache, almost as red as a woman's. But not a patch on Johnny, Linty thought, for all of his elegance, and the wide shoulders. He looked like the tailor's dummy she had seen in the shop window in Ballater – not quite real.

'She's plain,' Torquil said, through the cheering. 'In time she'll be fat.'

But those *eyes*. God help me, Linty thought, if she looked straight in my face she'd know every secret.

Behind the Queen's carriage was another with a gentleman, two ladies (governesses?) and three young children. These must be Prince Edward, Prince Alfred, and Princess Victoria, the eldest, a poised eight-year-old in a great flat-topped hat tied with pink flowerets. But the royal children held little interest – and weren't there three more back in England? Anyone could have children and dress them up fancy; it was the Queen who interested Linty, and the carriages that followed with the most elegant ladies in satins and velvets and wearing bonnets and jewels you'd not believe existed . . .

The Queen's carriage paused, her escort rode aside, and Mr. Anderson, trembling, came forward and made his speech of welcome. It seemed longer to Linty than most of his sermons, and the Queen lifted a fawn-coloured sunshade and put a gloved hand to her lips. Smothering a yawn?

'. . . so greatly honoured are we of Crathie . . .'

Aye, Linty thought, small as she is she looks as a Queen should. Perhaps she wears one of those things in a corset that keep the spine up, so erect she is. How old, now? Thirty or so, but not a wrinkle. The chin was a trifle short, the mouth small, petulant now as Mr. Anderson droned on. But she kept her glance steadily upon him, politely, and finally when he had finished she spoke:

'We thank you for so warm a welcome, sir . . .'

Her voice was like the tinkle of bells, exquisite, soft but clear. Then came the cascade of petals and heather, the presented bouquet, the skirl of the local pipers, and the carriages moved forward through the lodge gate and out of sight.

'Well,' Johnny said, taking out his bottle – nearly half left – 'so *that's* over.'

'Ah,' Jean said, 'I wish it had gone on forever! Linty, did you notice her earrings? Diamonds, for sure, and her bracelet, and her hands in those gloves, small as a bairn's but so – so—'

'Graceful?' asked Johnny with a growl. 'If you were the Queen you'd have had lessons all your life about what to do with your hands: fan *this* way, fan *that* way, wave to the peasants *that* way, and under cover of that coach-rug, tug on the puff's hand to keep him quiet, for he can't speak decent English, much less Scots.'

'I thought he was handsome!' Linty said. Then, seeing Johnny's frown, 'I mean, he suits her. He looks like a prince should. Tall and all – and can he help it he's a foreigner?'

'And aren't we foreigners to them?' Johnny capped his bottle. 'I'll be by for the pony tonight, and with beef. Could you make collops for supper, Linty?'

It was the first time he had ever actually invited himself to supper. Aye, he brought food but was casual about the times for it. She forgot the Queen, the Prince, the merrily gossiping crowd. She forgot that this was history just made. She even forgot to hesitate and pretend to think before she said, 'Aye, Johnny, but mind they take an hour to simmer.'

Thank heavens she had gathered the nuts and brined them last week. Now, at six, she split them and fried an onion and waited for him, for the bits of beef must be fried too, and then the beef put in the pot, and when it was done, the dumplings added. Stirring flour and suet, she thought, suddenly, almost with certainty, that he would speak of marriage tonight.

Jean must have sensed her thought for she said, 'I'll just have an egg with my tea, and go to bed early.'

'Tired?'

'Not very. But I think you should be alone with him.'

Bless her ...

'Only Linty—' She placed an egg to boil in the small pan. '– You must be sure, if he asks you.'

'I've been sure these three years. But you don't like him?'

'I never said that. He's a grand man. So good to us, God knows. But I wonder where he wears his heart, not to have spoken sooner?'

That cook? Ah well, she'd a feeling that she'd know tonight for sure.

Jean ate and then retired. The wind rose, billowing smoke into the little room. The hands of the clock moved toward six, but he didn't come and she worried about the pony tethered outside and wished she had hay for it. She went out with apples and carrots. Nothing moved on the road beyond. A golden scar lay across Lochnagar — the last of the sun — and above it, a fragile crescent of moon, forming shyly.

She could smell autumn — leaf mould, the death of moss, the death of another summer. Going back inside she wondered where she and Jean would be this winter. At Bush Farm? Or would Johnny prefer to live here, with them? They could take a room for themselves upstairs . . .

A knock on the door. It wasn't Johnny, but the lad who helped him in the stables, holding forth a paper package. 'It's beef, Johnny said. He can't come. I'm to take the pony.'

'Can't *come*? Why?'

'I don't know.' But he didn't meet her eyes.

'Angus, is he sick?'

'Och, no, I wouldna think so.' He started edging out the door but she caught at his ragged sleeve and pulled him back.

'Then what is it? I want the truth. Is he having supper with — maybe the cook?'

He shook his head. 'He just said to say he couldn't come. And to give you this meat.'

She took it, feeling chilled and miserable. Of course the cook would be busy now, fixing what they called 'dinner' for the Queen and the rest of them. But afterwards, with fine food left over, and wine maybe, the two of them alone, and then maybe Johnny up to her room . . .

'Angus.' She spoke so sharply that he jumped. 'Tell me or I'll beat it out of you.'

Poor little lad, only thirteen, and scared. Softly, he said, 'He's fou, that's all.'

The relief was immense and she patted Angus's shoulder. 'Why didn't you say so?'

'Like tattling.'

She laughed. 'Tell him when he sobers up I'll give him a bit of my mind — and collops. He's abed?'

'Aye.'

'Tell him tomorrow night, then.'

She watched him unhitch the pony and ride off into the gathering darkness. Disappointed, aye, but so long as he wasn't with that cook she need not fret.

If she started tonight and worked all day tomorrow she could take in her mother's sprigged merino and, with Jean's help, look pretty for his proposal. Perhaps she could even buy tuppence worth of pink ribbon at the store, if Jean agreed (for they always conferred on expenditures) and tie up her hair with a fall of curls and *then* see if Johnny Brown didn't show his heart.

The door closed, the one beyond it opened, and Jean, in her nightdress, said, 'He's gone already?'

'It was just Angus,' Linty said. 'Johnny can't come.' And then she lied to protect him. 'With the Queen there, and all the fuss, he can't get away.'

Jean agreed to the pink ribbon and by five Linty was dressed in the sprigged gown, pleased with the ruffled hem, by the smell of the collops, by Jean's insistence that she and Johnny must be alone at supper. During the day Linty had justified Johnny's behavior to herself; hating the English as he did, resenting the visit, it was quite natural that he should have got drunk. Better that than if he had lost his temper with some earl or duke.

'You look beautiful,' Jean said again, preparing to retire. 'If he doesn't speak tonight he's no more brains than a vole.'

Alone in the kitchen, an apron over her dress, Linty dropped the dumplings into the pot. And then, with a knock and a push of the door, Johnny was in the room.

Kilted again, handsome as never before, but – strange. She didn't think the drink was on him, but some mood she had never seen before. He said, 'I'm sorry about last night,' but he didn't look penitent (had he ever?) and he didn't even notice her dress. He sat on a stool and glowered, watching the fire.

'Now look,' she said, 'I'd thought to have a happy evening and you're dour.'

'No,' he said, still not looking at her, 'but something's happened.'

'What?' She took the pan off the fire lest she should forget the dumplings while they were talking.

'She looked at me last night, straight through me as if I was a lace curtain. I was passing and she in the garden—'

'Who?'

'That woman. The Queen. I didn't think much of it except then before supper Lady Gordon said I was to be in the stables at nine this morning, as Her Majesty wanted to ride. Y'ken I'm up at seven, but to be *commanded*, well, I've taken it from the Gordons, our own people, but that woman? So, I got fou. I thought of leaving Balmoral and rose up in bed and nearly did. But I couldn't walk to Bush, and then I thought, don't be a fool, she's here only a day or two. So I slept and I was in the stables at eight.

'And it was before nine that she came in, all alone, in a plain green kind of skirt and jacket. She looked at the horses in their stalls and at the ponies, and I stood back wondering which she'd choose. I hoped it would be Tammy, who'd thrown more than a few – you remember Tammy. Then she said, "Is anyone here, please?"

'I came forward. She was not much taller than Sheena Davidson, and she said, "I want a pony for climbing."

'Not *may* I have, but "I want." Well, the stables are my charge, and it was on the tip of my tongue to ask whether the Gordons had given her permission, but I held on and kept silent.

'Then she said, "My husband and I want to climb Craig Gowan. I want ponies for us and four others."

'She looked up at me, those blue steel eyes, and then she said, "Well?"

'I said, "*Cha n'eil Beurla agam.*"'

'Oh, God!' Linty said. 'You didn't! So you're sacked!'

'Wait. She moved back a step or two and said, "I hope to learn the Gaelic. Shall I ask someone to come and translate? Or perhaps you have enough English, Mister Brown?"'

'She called you *Mister . . .*?'

'Aye, and then, by God, she laughed and laughed, and so did I. Her laughter was like bells, but it was from her belly, too. And then she said. "Mr. Brown, I love these mountains: and I love this land and I want ponies that know the trails."

'Well, I was so surprised and maybe still a little unsettled from all the drink, but not a fool, for I said there's a cold wind and rain coming. Then she said, "I have never allowed weather to stop me," and looked up at me again and damned if I thought any weather would stand a chance against her, those eyes, and the set of her mouth.

'So I chose the ponies, and not Tammy, and she watched me from stall to stall, following and learning their names. And then she said, "What was it you said to me in Gaelic, Mr. Brown?"

'Any other woman I'd have lied to, but I'd a feeling she'd remember those words and find out, so I told the truth: "I have no English." She laughed again and said sometimes she didn't understand the English herself. Then she chose a saddle, and it wasn't the fanciest, either, but just right for her little bott – I mean, for her size. She said her own groom would be in later to lead the ponies out, and then—'

'Aye?' Linty asked.

'She asked me how long I'd worked for the Gordons, and where I was born – so I told her. Then, lifting up her gown at one corner, she walked through the bits of hay and turned back at the doorway. Damn me if the sun wasn't shining. I'd never expected sun, and I said, "Look, Your Majesty."

'She smiled and said, "Queen's weather, Mr. Brown; it rarely fails me," and then she was gone with a wave of her hand.'

And you, Linty thought, who hated her and her breed, were won over because she called you Mister.

'Then she paused, and came back and said, "Oh, a moment, Mr. Brown. How shall you say goodbye in Gaelic?"

'So, well, I said it: "*Beatha fhada leis gach beannachd.*" And I meant it. "Long life and every blessing."

'She repeated it after me, stumbling, then getting it right, for a new language is slippery, you know. She got it fine on the third try. Och, what a woman!'

'You said that last year,' Linty told him quietly. 'You said it before you met her.' But who could be jealous of a Queen, up so high he could never follow, a star to remember but never to wish on. Perhaps never again to see.

'When does she leave, Johnny?'

May it be soon! For such a daze was on him he still hadn't noticed her dress or the smell of the collops. Drink would be better than this, she thought.

'No one knows; at least we aren't told. Or why she's here. It's not sickness, I'm sure, for they climbed Craig Gowan. The puff wants to hunt. The beaters are gathering, and the ghillies, for tomorrow. Deer, pheasant. She doesn't hunt but she's interested, they say ...'

'Johnny.' She stemmed the tide of talk. 'Are you hungry? Shall I serve the collops and dumplings?'

'If you like,' he said, as if he didn't care, and he ate as if he was only filling himself, not with his usual appetite. Very odd. Johnny was not one to be impressed by rank or money. She tried to put herself in his place. To be so honored by 'Mister,' to have a queen talk to you, and with the drink still upon him.

After supper she took off her apron. 'Do you like the dress?'

'Aye. I remember your mother wore it to the frolic in Braemar. Pretty, she was.'

And am I not, too? But his glance was beyond her; he sat in the inglenook and stared into the fire.

They had often been silent together – waiting for a fish to bite, listening to the rare song of a nightingale, or bemused by a setting sun. Silent he had been after both her parents' funerals, not talking that stale talk of 'time will heal,' simply holding her hand, letting her weep. But this was a different, secretive silence, as though he was thinking of things she could not share.

It grew oppressive. 'Tell me,' she said finally, 'why was it so comical that the Queen laughed when you said you didn't understand English?'

'It just was,' he said. 'I'm thinking she knew what had been in my mind and it amused her.'

Perhaps I'm stupid, Linty thought, but I see no humor about it. Johnny was rude, he lied, yet she had laughed.

'Perhaps,' he said, still staring into the fire, 'you might call it a sort of private joke.'

Another week, and the Queen was still at Balmoral. If Johnny was taken in by her assumed interest in all things Highland, Linty was not. She and Jean agreed that she was playing some sort of game, like politics. What middle-aged woman — twenty-nine she was — really enjoyed treks through the wet mists of Lochnagar? For 'Queen's weather' hadn't held and gossip had it that she had picnicked in the rain more than once, her bonnet a squashy pulp, so that she'd borrowed a shawl for her hair. And her insistence on eating native food, like haggis, disdaining the fancy foods the cook offered; and — most incredible of all — shedding her silks and velvets and having a dress made of tartan. Ah well, wool was warm, but folk like Johnny could be taken in by such trickery!

'But why would she bother?' Jean asked, after the week had passed. 'There is nothing political here.'

Linty quoted Ian Davidson, the miller — a wise man. 'He thinks she and the Prince are buttering up the Gordons for free hunting rights so they can bring their friends here without cost. Whatever the reason, there's something queer about it. She doesn't shoot or fish, and that climbing is fair daft.'

'Unless it's to please the Prince,' Jean said. 'It's said she's daft in love with him, and no wonder.'

This Linty grudged. He *was* handsome, in his thin, dark way. Johnny had stopped calling him a puff; there was respect now for his skill with a gun, and the ghillies and beaters who went with him on shoots were speaking of his fairness at the sport. But they agreed that he was on the dour side, rarely smiling, and very strict with the children.

'All we get is second-hand talk,' Linty said. 'Folk like that put on masks all the time.'

And Johnny too, usually so forthright, had put on a mask in a way. When she questioned him about the Queen, he half-answered, or evaded. She comforted herself with the knowledge that he wouldn't admit to ignorance, but on the other hand there seemed actual reluctance to speak except, 'No, she didn't ride today,' or, 'Aye, she likes walking more than most women.'

'Perhaps to keep herself from being a pudding, she—'

'For the love of Christ,' he said, and his voice reeled her silent, 'she *likes* it.'

Always before, she had spoken her thoughts, her doubts, her fears to him. Now she felt constrained. But what had caused such a change in him? Surely by now he had recovered from the pleasure of being called 'Mister'? He hadn't mentioned it since, nor had he bragged in company. In fact he seemed more subdued than she'd ever known him, as though there was a great weight on his mind.

One thing was sure: Johnny Brown could not have fallen in love. He wasn't the sort to live a fairy tale, and to love a queen would be just that. Besides, without jealousy (she told herself), what could a fine young man see in a plumpish woman eight years older than himself? A married woman with six children? It was nonsense to imagine that he had more than mere respect for her. And in any case, she would surely be leaving Balmoral soon.

But another two weeks went by. Why did she linger in these mists, these wild winds, these tumbling leaves – unless, of course, it was Prince Albert's wish? Then Linty learned the truth.

It came from Mrs. Anderson, the minister's wife, told to Katherine Davidson, who told the postie, who told everyone: Victoria had leased Balmoral from the Gordons as a holiday retreat. The Prince, enjoying the sport, was reminded of his native mountains here. The Queen had 'fallen in love' with the Highlands, so different from Windsor and London, which she called 'stifling.' But there was yet another reason. Sir James Clark, their physician, had advised the climate as being beneficial, and of course there were the children to consider. Royal children must have healthy mountain air, a place to learn swimming and fishing, riding and hunting. And in case of a typhus or typhoid epidemic, what better place to take them to?

'Did that doctor,' Linty said to Jean, 'say that the coughing sickness goes everywhere? Consumption, they call it.' Consumption was the new name for what had killed their parents.

'Never mind,' Jean said, 'they'll only holiday here, and with all the servants they have, they won't be needing Johnny.'

That was relief, but a worry, too. Where else would he work but here at Balmoral? Unless, of course, he emigrated. For there was nothing at Braemar or Ballater. Aberdeen?

Linty thought, I suppose I should be glad for him. A man as well educated shouldn't stay in stables all of his youth. It had to come to this, and loving him I should be glad for him wherever he goes. *Love is selfless*, Mr. Anderson had said in the kirk. So easy to say, but suppose his own wife was to have a better chance elsewhere. Would he still be selfless?

'Perhaps he'll join his brothers in farming Bush,' Jean said.

But that would split the profits, and besides, Johnny would rather be free of his family, that she knew. More often than using his room there he slept in the loft at the castle barn. Perhaps the reason he had not asked her to marry him was that he was waiting to get his own croft house.

Och, her thoughts were spinning in circles, getting nowhere. She was not what Johnny called a 'fatalist'; she could not be content to wait for the flow of chance to sweep her. Planning was the only wisdom, building towards a future step by step, thinking ahead, as one did now, against the winter. In the last sunny days of that September she and Jean washed clothes and blankets and hung them between the birches, praying the weather would hold, for nothing stank like wet wool steaming by the fire. They were prudent as squirrels with nuts, having Johnny fasten down the flapping window-shutter and look to the roof for holes. And of course, like everyone else, bringing in and storing the root vegetables from the garden. If Johnny left for a town there would be little but brose and meatless soup until one could fish again in the spring.

They weren't at the lodge gate to see the Queen leave – after three weeks – but they went to the kirk the Sabbath following and heard Mr. Anderson's astonishing statement:

'Her Majesty told me we must consider her and her family as parishioners now, and she gave forty pounds to the Poor Fund. More than that, she hopes to help improve the village when she returns next autumn.' He paused. 'We will now join in prayer for her . . .'

On the way home from the kirk, Linty asked Johnny, 'Shall you stay on until her return?' and tried hard not to sound jealous or malicious.

'As long as the Gordons stay. No one has asked me to leave. Why do you push so, Linty?'

'Push?' She walked ahead with him, as Jean chattered to Mrs. Davidson on the path. 'I am only asking! I'm thinking of your future, that's all.'

'It will care for itself. Her coming here will make more work for us all,' he said. 'Likely, when the news gets round it will bring the visitors. And she wants improvements made to the castle, so it will mean work for joiners and roof-men and all. You've no idea, Linty, what a queen's whim may mean to a community. There are people now reading about her visit here who never even heard of Scotland, much less these wild parts.'

'But I don't understand why she wants to come back.'

'You dinna ken how it must be, Linty, chained in those palaces and all that strict fancy stuff. Here she can breathe, and be herself. It's what you haven't got that you want. It's all new to her here.'

Then likely she'd tire of it in time. Balmoral would be a doll's house to be exchanged for another – and another. But what was important, Johnny would remain here, at least until the Gordons dismissed him. They wouldn't be moving out to leave the Queen a cold, empty house, but one that was cared for from turrets to stables.

She turned to look up at Johnny. What a strange man, knowing so much, well educated, well spoken, content to be a stableman, with not a thought for the years ahead. Or if he had plans, she didn't know them. Perhaps he was right in running with the tide of life, but if her life was linked with his she wanted to know what to expect. Didn't he want children? At eighteen and twenty-two, they were at the right age to start a family. But you don't start one with a kiss on the cheek, she thought wryly, or a 'thank you' for a meal.

He went off to the castle, but the next morning Linty and Jean met him in the road.

'I'll be by tonight,' he said.

She hesitated a moment, then mounting resentment got the better of her. 'I'll not be home.'

'Where, then? The Davidsons? Little Mill?'

'No,' she said, rebellious, lying to him for the first time, 'I've met some folk up – up at—' Och, he knew everyone within miles; she could never invent a name, much less a man to fit one. 'Never mind, you don't know him.'

'Him,' said Johnny. 'Well, then, with nothing to do myself I'll drop in and play some whist with Jean. It will keep her company.'

Was there a twinkle in his eyes? Would she have to hide in the bedroom, pretending to be out? Undoubtedly she would sneeze or something and give herself away. If only they lived in a larger village, she might invent something to make him jealous; but here it was hopeless. People knew every move you made.

She summoned her wits and called back to Jean, who had stayed a discreet distance behind, 'I was just telling Johnny we'll not be home tonight, since we've a frolic to go to.'

One could trust that sisterly wink, surely? That feminine bent toward conspiracy? Jean caught the idea. Quick as a cat, she said, 'Aye, another night, Johnny?'

Later, they wondered if he believed them. To make sure, their curtains were drawn at half-past six, the fires doused.

Damn that Johnny Brown, they said, speaking softly in bed. Not that he'd spy, but he might just ride past on his way somewhere.

'Still,' Jean said later, wakeful in the darkness, 'you did right. He can't just think he can come any time at all. He must learn a lesson. If he's courting, that's different. But when we see him again, what do we say?'

'I don't know.'

Jean giggled. 'You got us into this; now get us out.'

As Linty thought, Jean added, 'You said "a frolic." That makes it harder, for everyone knows about a frolic around here.'

'Aye, and he'd be the first to be asked to it.' Linty snuggled into the pillow, eyes open to the darkness. 'Could it be that two young men we met the day the Queen came – from Ballater – asked us there?'

'And their names?'

'Och, of course he'd know, or find out. Even Ballater is too small. *If* he's interested, he'll find out.'

Jean sat up in bed. 'I'm hungry, rushing that broth as we did. And how do we get food in the dark?'

'I think I could find my way to the kitchen,' Linty said, and got out of bed, grasping a blanket around her. 'Nothing hot, of course, but we've gammon and bannocks if I can get to the larder and back.'

It was five minutes before she could grope her way past the bedroom door. Then, in the kitchen, she knew what it was to be blind, oversetting a stool, mistaking a cupboard for the larder. If only she had left a bit of the peat fire, as would have been natural; but no, they had smoored it. Now, the larder at last, with it's smell of boiled gammon, which she kept on its plate. Carefully touching, she found bannocks, which she put on top, and the two boiled eggs and some cheese.

Warily she made her way back, saying, 'Jean?' to get her bearings.

'Are you sure those eggs are boiled?' Jean asked. 'I'll not forgive you this night if they're not.'

'Dinna worry.'

The only worry, as they ate in the darkness, was what to tell Johnny. They put the plate aside and conferred. 'Ah well,' Jean said sleepily, 'we've all of tomorrow to decide.'

They slept, and at dawn they rose and made tea and straightened the rooms. 'Have you any idea yet?' Jean asked.

'He may not even ask where we were. But I think I'll say some new folk came to Braemar, just visiting—'

A knock on the door and there was Johnny, holding a necklace of sausages.

'A fine day,' he said.

Linty rattled down her tea cup. He never came so early, for he had his chores and knew she had hers with the cows and hens.

'Aye, fine.' Please, may my brain stir to some story . . .

'Tired, are you, being out so late?'

'Oh, we're fair enough,' Jean said. 'Only our feet hurt from all the dancing.'

Linty changed the subject quickly. 'Sausages! Now that's grand; you've not brought them for a month or more. Shall I cook some for you, Johnny?'

'If you've the time.' He sat down. 'But why didn't you bring them in last night? Some animal could have got them. I hung them on your doorlatch on my way to the inn, about eight.'

The girls stared at one another.

'It was so dark when we got home,' Linty said.

'That we didn't see them,' Jean added.

'Now, that's odd,' Johnny said. 'All round your door latch they were. I'd have thought you could have felt them. But no matter, I'll have three, please, if you've time for the cooking?'

Linty thought, I should have known I could never fool him. Whether it's the second sight or just that he knows me so well, I'll never chance a lie again, nor place Jean into one. We're made out fools.

A final sip of tea and he rose. 'I might be by tonight.'

'And welcome,' Linty said humbly. How kind of him not to trick them with questions, not to embarrass them further.

'There's a frolic at the inn, pipers coming. But then, you may be too tired of dancing?'

Was he mocking? Was he serious? As Linty hesitated, Jean said, 'My feet hurt and I don't trust my head not to bother me. But if Linty wants to go—'

'I'll go,' Linty said.

Stupid, childish, she thought later, as she fed the hens. She needn't have been so swift to agree. She could have pleaded weariness like Jean. But then, she was certain he knew. Those damn sausages.

The Inver Inn lay across a curve of the Dee on the road that travelers took and it did a lively business until the weather worsened. Paneled in local pine, its fireplace blazed between the two small public rooms. Above were quarters for overnight guests or for such folk who, being fou, couldn't manage the journey home. These were given a mattress on the floor and a bit of porridge in the morning for sixpence. No sheets, mind you, only a rough blanket or two, but many a local man

48

took advantage of that hospitality, glad for lodging and a pine-stuffed pillow under his head.

Sandy Scott, host of the inn, gave them special welcome with a dram on the house before they made their way into the room where the dancing was. Johnny was the best of them, light on his feet for all of his bigness, whirling, spinning, fast as a top, but never treading on toes, always catching her hand when others came between them. Out of breath finally, he took her aside into the other room where the drinking was and brought her a cool ale, buying a dram from Sandy for himself.

'A song?' Sandy asked. He, too, was a big man, with yellow curly hair and red cheeks. 'Sing to us, Johnny.'

A fiddler came forward, ready to accompany, and folk gathered round, drinks in hand.

A love song, Linty hoped, directed toward her. Johnny had only a puckle of a voice, but when he sang, somehow it meant more than just the words or the music. It was the way of him . . .

Johnny whispered something to Rob, the fiddler. And then he looked toward the hearthfire and sang:

> 'But I had dreamed a dreary dream
> Beyond the Isle of Skye
> I saw a dead man win a fight
> And I think that man was I . . . .'

The sadness of it, the way he made it seem true, quieted the drinkers. At its end, Sandy said, 'Well . . .' and then, 'What's the dirge for?'

'Aye,' Rob said, 'my fiddle's like to die. What about a nice rollicksome song, like—'

'You sing, then,' Johnny said. 'You've a better voice; no need to play, just sing.'

But Rob had quieted like the rest. Strange about Johnny, how he could put a mood on people. Sandy said, to the silence, 'That Irish fella from Abergeldie, he was telling about wakes and all the drinking goes on. You had that in mind, Johnny, to help my trade?'

'Aye,' Johnny said, smiling now, 'that was my very intention. Linty, shall we dance again?'

They rejoined the dancers for a while, then went back into the bar, where folk were watching Sandy and Rob at darts. The Davidsons had come and sat on a bench with Sheena. Sandy won and was paid tuppence.

'Now,' Sheena said, jumping up, '*I'll* play.'

'Hush,' said Katherine Davidson. 'It's a game for men.'

But Sheena picked up a dart, faced the board, aimed, then turned. Linty felt something whizz just under her eye.

Sheena!' said her mother, running to the child and bringing her back to the bench. 'It's the board you're after, not people.'

It could just have entered my eye, Linty thought. It was not by chance. For a moment she clung to Johnny's outstretched hand, then fury took over. She rose and went over to Sheena and said, 'You meant that, didn't you, you little gowk!'

'Och, no,' Sheena said, cuddling against her mother. 'It was just that you were in the way of the board.'

'You turned,' Johnny said. 'We all saw it. You threw it at Linty.'

'I was nowhere near the board,' Linty said, 'and you know it.'

Sheena burrowed closer against her mother. Voice muffled, she said, 'It just flew out of my hand.'

If I had her alone, Linty thought, I'd give her a slap she'd not soon forget. But out of deference to Katherine and Ian, and not to make a fuss in public, she returned to sit with Johnny.

'That was no accident,' he said softly, 'I think the lass is somehow daft. If I didn't know Ian and Kate, I'd say she was spawned of some other family and adopted by them.'

Ian came over. 'I'm sorry, Linty. I'd guess she sneaked a little drink.' He lowered his voice. 'And her time is on her – you know – the change from a child. I am asking your pardon.'

'Och,' she said, 'it's forgotten.'

Though it wouldn't be. Johnny bought Ian a dram and then the pipers paraded in. Old tunes, old friends, old dances, and the night ended in a whirl of stomping and laughing and then

Sandy turned them out into the starlight and Linty was lifted onto Johnny's pony.

His arms around her as they jogged homeward lay like an ache on her heart. As she had told Torquil, being so close was terribly frustrating. The moon rode high above Lochnagar; there was a soft stillness. If she turned her head and lifted her face toward his . . .?

But pride as always forbade that. If he wanted to kiss her, he would. She had lost all sense of what was right according to Mr. Anderson and kirk talk. A heather bed would suffice. Any bed. Any place. Anywhere.

There was a scream as they approached her cottage and she tried to shut her ears to it. Nothing so terrible as the cry of a hare eaten by a hawk, eaten alive and savored, a lingering thing. 'Oh, God,' she said, 'I'll never be used to that, not ever.'

Johnny said nothing, spurring the pony on. 'It's hawks I'd shoot,' she said, 'and no mercy—'

'Linty.' His voice was grave, slow, even. 'It's no animal hurt.' The scream soared higher, nearer. 'It's Jean.'

They found her half off the bed in tumbled blankets. By guttering candlelight they saw splintered glass on the floor – the laudanum bottle.

Still she screamed until finally, head cradled against Linty's shoulder, she whimpered that it was easing. In reaching for the medicine she had overturned it.

Johnny said, 'I'll get a fast horse and ride to the doctor. Linty, you've whisky? Then give her a dram, and make it big.'

Aye, the whisky might ease the pain. Jean sipped in small, sobbing gulps. Then, head against the pillows, she said, 'I'm sorry.'

'For what? You couldn't help it.'

'I could help living,' Jean said softly.

'That's heathen talk! The pain has turned your mind.'

'That's what I'm afraid of – that it will. I haven't said – I haven't told you. But sometimes my memory goes. Tonight, before the pain came on, I started to piece the quilt and . . .

51

ah, Linty, it was minutes before I saw there was no thread in my needle.'

'And no wonder, in light like this,' Linty said, slashed by pity but pretending crossness. 'We're not starving of candles. And who is not forgetful?' She hurried to a lie. 'This morning I left the water jug in the shed and brought in the milk pail – almost washed our dishes in milk, I did. So there's no need to fret about *your* mind, for I'm the goose.'

Jean's smile was tremulous. She watched Linty fasten another candle onto the dying one and then she said, 'I want your promise on something. If you ever find me witless—'

'*Hush.*'

'–if you ever do, send me off to the—'

But she couldn't say the word.

'Och, you won't need hospital,' Linty said quickly. 'Now, lie back and close your eyes or else—' She managed a giggle, 'I'll dram you again and Dr. Robertson will find a drunk on his hands.'

For a while she sat near Jean. Then, hearing her even breathing, she tiptoed into the main room to make sure it was tidy. It would be two hours before Johnny brought the doctor back, perhaps more. She stirred up the fire and sat waiting.

Is my life to be all waiting? she wondered. Waiting, in panic, for another of Jean's headaches, helpless to prevent them. Waiting for Johnny to speak of marriage. And if he left here, waiting to die. But these were dark night-thoughts and she tried to shake them off, went to the kitchen and put the kettle on to boil.

When Johnny came with the doctor, she gave them tea in the main room before she asked, 'Could there be some new medicine for my sister, sir?'

He shook his narrow, balding head. 'Laudanum is best, but she may have a stronger dosage. I think she's probably used to it now and needs more.'

'But she *will* heal, in time?'

'One can only hope so.' He spoke tiredly; he looked tired, poor man, roused after scant sleep.

'That laudanum,' Johnny said, 'does it cure or just ease pain?'

Dr. Robertson said, 'I hope time will be the cure, John.'

He left them, with his brown bag, to go into the bedroom, and Johnny said, 'There are other doctors. If she's no better I've a mind to get the one from Aboyne.'

As a husband would speak, as if Jean were part of his own family. 'Just because he's closest doesn't mean he's the best. Or she might go to hospital.'

'Johnny—' Linty spoke over a lump in her throat. 'She is afraid of her mind going. She tried to make me promise, if it does, to send her to a madhouse.'

'My God!' He came to her and put his arms around her, but as one snuggles a child. 'I'll not have that. Nor will it come to that.' He bent and kissed her wet eyes. Then, abruptly he moved away as though ashamed of his tenderness. 'I hope he'll not be long. I've got to get that horse back to the stables before it's missed.'

'It wasn't from Bush?' she asked, aghast.

'Of course not; I chose the best. By damn, and he liked the exercise too. It's like folk in castles, going to fat if they're not—'

He paused as the doctor came in. 'She'll sleep again,' he said. He gave Linty two bottles. 'Three drops now instead of two, you know the amount of water. Cold compresses – never heat, mind. That will be two shillings, Linda.'

There were only seven in the old cracked cup where they kept their money. Johnny said, 'Here,' and took coins from his sporran.

And after they had gone, Linty thought: Just as a husband would. Aye, it was surely love – of a sort.

The bonfires of Hallowe'en died, snow came and melted, the wise cuckoo spoke of spring in early May and the woods burst into green. A rampage of daffodils, and purple lilac spilling over stone stiles. Sandy Scott polished the sign that hung above the Inver Inn, and his wife Mariad scoured and prepared rooms for travelers. Mr. Anderson preached about rebirth, a sermon left over from Easter, and the Davidsons rethatched the roof of their mill. Lambs chased one another in the fields, stopped with no reason at some invisible barrier, and chased back again. Torquil Briggs deserted his barn for the hedgerow, washed his clothes and hung them to dry between two larches. The widow Donaldson took up with MacLeod, the postie, as she did every spring as if some sap rose in her. It was all as it had been last year, Linty thought, except that Jean kept more and more to her bed in a strange drowsy way; but it was better the medicine than the pain. Better a thickened tongue than no words at all.

Johnny rode to Aboyne to bring back a new doctor but was told he was too busy with consumption and typhoid to travel all that way – and aye, laudanum was all he could suggest himself. 'The good clear air will heal your friend,' he'd said. 'Put her out in the sun as often as it shines.'

So Jean sat in the little garden, sometimes dozing, often awakening with a muffled scream, and then Linty ran for the medicine. Her mind didn't wander often, only at times when the pain took over and she called Linty 'Mother' and didn't recognize Johnny. Two to three weeks might pass and she would be herself, helping with the lighter chores. One could mark her recovery by new patches on the quilt, by her wish to brush her hair and wash it. In August she said, with a smile, 'I have kept my reason.'

More than I have, Linty thought. Any reasonable lass would have given up on Johnny Brown long since. I should go to the Inn and meet the travelers . . .

'So many lonely young gentlemen,' Mariad Scott said, 'some even rich, all asking for company. Not bad company, mind – I'd not suggest that for you – but those pausing on the way to business in Aberdeen with nothing to do, and sometimes the rainstorms keeping them.'

'Aye?' Linty asked softly, mindful that Johnny might come in from the bar any moment. 'But what have I to offer?'

'Company, I said. Someone to talk to, dance with. You're bonny. And you're wasting yourself. There's a world beyond that Johnny. It's like there's some enchantment on you.'

'I know.'

'Och, he's a fine lad, but the ones that come here are fine too! I'm not saying they are all so handsome, but they have money and a future. Now you come on Friday – I'll send Sandy for you – and you can help me with the food and washing up. Then you'll be free to meet some Navy men on the way to their ship; they're staying over until Sunday.'

'I've Jean to think of.'

'Bring her then. If she's well, she will enjoy it too.'

'I don't know—'

'I'll pay you a shilling, too.'

That settled it. They went to the Inn that Friday, Jean and Linty on Sandy's old horse, he walking. At the gate Sandy helped them down and Mariad came out, wiping floury hands on her apron. Shrewd eyes appraised Jean, then she smiled. 'You're looking fine. Come, have a bit of tea and we'll talk.'

In the kitchen, hot mugs in their hands, Mariad said, 'I'll not test your strength, Jean. If you feel well enough, there's tablecloths to mend and pewter to polish. You can do it sitting down. If you feel like it you can join the sailors when they come; but if you've the headache stay in the room as if it was home.'

Jean said, 'I'm well enough to help.'

Linty said. 'You're so good.'

'It's for your good, lass. Does Johnny take it well?'

'Aye.' Linty sugared her tea. 'Too well. He calls it a paid holiday. And when I told him the sailors would be here he said to cover our ears for the swearing, and laughed. He's not caring as a jealous man would.'

'But you're to forget him,' Mariad said, 'and should he come by, pay your attention to others.' She took a deep breath and the plump bosom seemed to burst its bodice. 'How I hate waste! Waste of two pretty girls just ripe for marriage. I'm not a matchmaker, y'ken, but I like to put folk in the way of folk and I like a good time.'

She has had a good time with Sandy, Linty thought – both happy, though there were no bairns, nor like to be any now that they were in their forties. It was Mariad who had cheered her mother's last days, coming by with treacle biscuits, sitting down for a gossip. Now she was trying to help the daughters.

'Jean,' she said, clearing away the tea mugs, 'here's tatties to peel. Linty, gut those trout and roll them in meal.'

It was cheerful in the kitchen, and there were good smells.

Rabbit stewed with onions. Soup of mutton and barley, cabbage and dried peas. When the lads came, fourteen in all, there would be plenty to eat. 'And not that terrible fare they have at sea, so they'll pay well.'

At five they could hear a great to-do in the inn yard; Sandy was welcoming them, and Mariad sent the girls upstairs to get ready. 'I'll do the serving,' she said, 'and later Linty can help me wash up. But for now, you're to enjoy yourselves.'

They wore their best dresses, their hair smoothed back and tied with bows. As they entered the grog-room there was sudden silence from the sailors. Behind them, Sandy said, very dignified, 'Gentlemen, Miss Jean and Miss Linda Clarke.'

As if they were guests! The young men sprang up, caps off. They made a place for them on a bench. A big bearded one, older, perhaps a petty officer, asked 'What will the young ladies drink?'

Linty started to say 'Ale,' but Sandy said, 'Clary,' and wine glasses were brought. Och, this was fun, lads bending over them, asking where they came from.

'Just across the river,' Linty said. No reason to play like fine ladies just because they were treated as such. 'My sister and I are helping out until Sunday.'

There was no surprise, no lessening of respect. They said they were bound for Aberdeen, then probably Stonehaven. And where had they been? All around the world, and the gloss of the world was on them in their tidiness, the way they talked, with strange foreign names slipping off their tongues easy as you please. The prettiest port? Some said Genoa, others Gibraltar. But the mightiest was New York, with so many ships you couldn't believe it and houses so high you feared they'd topple in the big winds.

After supper, Linty helped Mariad wash up and returned to find Jean a-sparkle, surrounded, gay as she'd not been in months. Then Rob came with his fiddle, and other local folk, and dancing began in the next room. A good-looking blond boy paid special attention to Linty, asking if she was spoken for, or engaged.

'No,' she said.

'It's not true,' he said bluntly, 'that we've a sweetheart in

56

every port. When we meet someone who – I mean, I might write you?'

She shook her head. 'I can't read. Besides, I—'

'What?'

Why lie? 'I'm not spoken for, but I hope to be. And he's all I can think of.'

'Then where is he?'

'Likely he'll be along.' She smiled up at him. 'I'm sorry. May we dance?'

They danced, she and Jean and Mariad teaching the sailors the Highland way and Mrs. Donaldson (where *was* the postie?) dancing the Hoolichan alone, not a thing for a woman to do, nor even a man not skilled in it from his early years. Outside the pipers marched, playing until Sandy came out and gave them their drams and brought them in from the rising mist.

Jean left the room to go to the out-shed and Linty followed her. 'You're enjoying yourself?'

'Aye. But I'm for my bed soon.'

'So am I, when I've helped Mariad wash the mugs and glasses.'

'And leave that nice young lad with the gold hair?'

Linty said, 'It's no use. It's Johnny – but he hasn't even come by, and y'ken he always does on Friday nights.'

'Too proud. Or scared.'

'*Scared?*'

'To be put aside. He knows the men are here.'

But not one here could compare to him. 'He just doesn't care. I must face it.'

Lying sleepless in the bed with Jean she summoned all of her will to face it. So be it, then; but not another man, not ever. If he didn't want her then she would get along without him. At least, she thought wryly, I know where I am going – nowhere.

She was up early and no one was about but the hungry birds that swooped down hoping for food. Standing outside, she thought: It is nearly autumn despite the green of the trees – the death of another year. She scattered stale bannocks to the birds. Then she went inside to brew a pot of tea and was setting out a cup to take to Jean when MacLeod, the postie, came.

'You here?' he asked, surprised, 'I stopped by and wondered at no one home.'

There was never a letter for them, so she knew he had news. 'What's happened, Jock?'

'The Gordons – they moved yesterday. For the Queen.'

So she was really coming again. There would be just what the housekeeper called 'a skeleton staff,' Jock said, to keep the place warmed. New servants coming in, dozens likely. Already there was said to be freight on the way, luggage and boxes of food marked *Balmoral*.

'And Johnny?' she asked. 'Does he stay on?'

Jock said, 'She wants the stables clean and neat, so I think he stays – until some fancy Englishman takes them over, anyway. But don't be taking this as gospel, Linty, it's only what I've heard.'

These things didn't happen overnight. Johnny must have known. Johnny had known about the great cleaning and scouring last year, but he'd said nothing. Strange and secretive was not his way – or was it, now? He was keeping things to himself that surely needed no hiding.

'When does she come?' Linty asked.

'In a month, I think.' He looked up at the shuttered windows. 'No one about but yourself?'

Poor man, he wanted to repeat his great news to Sandy and Mariad, but there'd be no one stirring yet. Gently, she said, 'I'll not tell a soul except my sister, if you like.'

He smiled, showing broken teeth. 'You're a good wee lassie.' He paused. 'And you'll not be saying I was by.'

'So you've told no one else?'

'Well—' He lowered his voice. 'There just happened to be Mrs. Donaldson feeding her hens before she went to bed.' He chuckled. 'A fou night out, was it? And there was Torquil Briggs I met at the well. There was Miss Farquharson who had a letter from her brother in Perth. Aside from them, no one knows.'

And Johnny, she thought as he rode off on his pony. It took a while for her anger to heat. What was she, an outsider not

58

to be told? Or trusted? Did he think he was part of the royal household that he could not drop a word? 'Sworn to secrecy?' as he'd been by the Gordons? Getting above himself, that's what he was. Oh, she'd show him a thing or two if ever she cared to see him again, high and mighty.

'Aye,' Jean said when Linty brought up the tea and was told, 'I've been saying that Johnny needs a lesson. But what will you do?'

'I don't know – yet.'

It was a bright blue day and the sailors went climbing, with picnic lunches. MacLeod came by again, telling his great news to the Scotts. The latest rumor was that Prince Albert was ailing and the doctor had suggested an autumn holiday here. But better, they all agreed, if the Gordons had remained, for their servants brought trade to the inn all the year round. There had been work for both millers, also. If the Queen and her staff spent only weeks here once a year, Crathie would be honored – but impoverished.

The girls worked in the kitchen that afternoon, preparing the herring to flake with tatties, boiling woodcock with onions. Sandy brought in the inevitable salmon, which Mariad said she was embarrassed to serve, it being so common, but the men would be hungry enough to eat anything after a day in the hills. Then Jean retired to their room and said she'd take a nap.

'The headache?' Mariad asked Linty, worried.

'No, she's been well. But she's saving her strength. She does enjoy the dancing.'

'It's her eyes I don't like the look of,' Mariad said, scrubbing a pot. 'They're somehow too bright.'

'But that's a sign of health!'

'Not that kind of shine. My grandmother—'

She paused and Linty stared at her, an apple half-peeled.

'My grandmother always said – och, never mind. It's a tale for the old wifies.'

'What? What did she say?'

Mariad contrived a laugh. 'In those days they knew nothing. You know fine, it was all superstition. Why, they even thought that the fairies stole away new-born babes unless you put a bit of bread under the pillow as a bribe, or barley in the cradle. She thought bright eyes meant ill-health, that's all – stupid talk, meaning no disrespect to her.'

Linty relaxed, relieved. Dr. Robertson would have said something of Jean's eyes if there were reason to. She finished peeling the apples and folded them into a crust. Jean's eyes were bright with interest, with excitement, with the fun of last night and more to come.

But I, Linty thought, I would rather be home, for I must know what is happening with Johnny. Perhaps he'll be by to-night, and if he is, I shall pay special attention to everyone but himself.

After supper, the golden-haired lad named Cullen was attentive again, and perhaps a bit fou, for he seemed to have forgotten that she loved someone ... but she kept him close on the chance that Johnny might come by and see them sitting on a bench outside in the garden, sharing a cup of whisky. But the whisky could not lift her spirits.

He reached for her and she moved away. 'What do you do aboard ship, Mr. Cullen?'

He was not too fou to realize he'd be a fool to persist. 'I'm aid to the medical officer.'

'Oh! A doctor?'

'Not me, unless I stay ashore and study, which I might.' He drank from the cup. 'In Aberdeen, if I thought you'd care.'

'You should care,' she said, 'if you want to be a doctor. It's nothing to do with me.'

He *was* fou. He began to hum a tune to himself. And he took her hand and held it tightly, looking up at the far, faint stars.

Something troubled her – not his hand – not even Johnny's absence. She said, 'Mr. Cullen, did you ever hear bright eyes were a sign of bad health?'

He thought that over. 'Consumption,' he said, 'and flush. The cheeks flushed.'

But Jean's face was pale. 'Could not bright eyes be youth and happiness?'

'Of course,' he said. 'Or else—'

She leaned toward him. 'Or else?'

He began to hum again and then to sing:

> *'There's nothing like the sadness*
> *Of the strange bright eyes of madness ...'*

She snatched her hand from his and jumped up and ran inside, hearing him call, not heeding, bumping into Sandy as he came through the hallway.

'What's wrong?' he asked. 'Did that lad—'

'No,' she said on a sob. Through the open door she could see Jean smiling, laughing, sharing a meat pie with a man, then bending to give a titbit to the collie.

'No, Mr. Cullen is a perfect gentleman,' she said. 'It's just that he sang a sad old song, and me a little fou.'

Johnny didn't come by. Jealous, sulking? Not likely. Perhaps he wanted her to meet a new man, hoped for release. Yet she had never tried to cage him. Still, if he thought of her as a sister, he'd not want to spoil her chances.

Of course, the harvest was late this year. He might be busy at the family farm ...

Stop fooling yourself, she said sternly, lying awake as Jean slept. If he'd have cared to come here, he would have. He's with that pretty cook, unless she's left with the Gordons. Or with someone else.

Slipping into a dream, she saw him building a throne with Kenny, the joiner, hammering in golden nails.

He came by that night, casually as ever, with not a word about what had happened at the inn nor an explanation of what he'd been doing the past two nights. 'The postie,' she said finally,' said the Queen is coming but that you're staying.'

'That Jock! It's a wonder he can deliver a letter straight. I've been paid ahead for a week, then a Master of the Stables comes from London.' He chuckled. 'I can just see him, frock coat and all, trousers rolled up to keep the hay from them and a scented handkerchief to his nose. All the grooms lined up in frills and shiny boots. A mare starts to foal, they'd call a vet — unless they've all fainted first.'

Her pity for him thrust deep, for behind the chuckle she sensed his bitterness. He wouldn't be needed. Perhaps he would think her pushing, but she had to ask, 'Then you'll farm?'

He nodded. 'There's work enough for us all at Bush. And with no gardens laid out at Balmoral – only flowers – we'll be supplying food as we did to the Gordons, only more. The cook, she said the mother of her friend worked at Windsor and the Queen is a great one for food—'

'The cook's left?'

'Aye, the Queen's own servants are coming...'

So there was *one* woman less to fret over.

'... and four meals a day served. Breakfast, and what they call lunch, tea in the afternoon and dinner at nine.'

'Nine!' Why, most folk were abed by then unless there was a frolic.

'The Queen's dinner at nine. With her own family and guests. And then four separate meals there are – for the guests who aren't invited to eat with the Queen, for the upper servants and for the lower ones. My brother Hugh said we should lay out more in the way of vegetables, get more hens and cows. Maybe you'd help at Bush, Linty?'

What a proposal, she thought wryly. Yet just to be near him – and the extra money.

'I'll help,' she said. In gardens or dairy or wherever he said. For it could be worse by far. He could have decided to leave.

The folk of Crathie couldn't believe that the carriages that streamed in were only of servants, for these people looked like ladies and gentlemen, even to high white collars and ribboned bonnets and gloves. Then came wagons loaded with crates, dozens of them. In early September more carriages swirled the dust, and these carried more servants, only so grand you couldn't imagine them talking to anyone but the Queen herself. And finally, on a breezy day, her pink veil flying, her cheeks round and rosy as apples, came Victoria, drawn by four beautiful grays, her husband beside her.

She looked happy, Linty thought, younger than before, looking back and waving to her children in the carriage behind, pointing to mark a flight of crows that swept down to the fields. Then, as last year, the pause while Mr. Anderson delivered his welcoming speech and Crathie's oldest resident, aged 89, hobbled over to present a bouquet, trying to curtsy, nearly tripping over her long skirt.

Her Majesty's smile was gracious. She said something to old Mrs. Barber and leaned to pat the skinny wrist. Then, to the shrill of pipes, the cavalcade moved on through the flowery gate.

Next day at noon Johnny came to Linty. 'It's hard to believe,' he said, 'but the Queen remembered me and sent for me early this morning. I shouldn't be telling you but – do you swear to keep this secret?'

'Aye,' she said, but feeling queer, uneasy.

'She and the Prince told Grant and me to take them up to Craig Lowrigan. There was mist thicker than my body, but she never minds dirty weather. Just me and Grant with them and our ponies, and not a thing to see, but she seemed to like it, the climb and the air. Then when we got to the top she said for Grant to go back to the castle and fetch up things to make tea. I knew it was a way of getting rid of him. And then Prince Albert said, "We want to know about all seasons here, the shooting and the fishing."

'It wasn't too easy to understand him, the way he gluts in his throat like Germans do, but she made it clear. Then she wanted to know if I thought it true that the climate was healthy and good for the lungs, and I said, "Aye, except nobody was ever sure about typhoid." But she said she had noticed a lot of old folk about and healthy children with pink cheeks. "We love this place," she said, and the Prince said something in German and she laughed like a young girl and said, "Both of us, Mr. Brown. It just might be that we will buy Balmoral." '

'To *live* here?' Linty asked.

Johnny shrugged. 'I don't know for sure. But, I'd guess, to be here often, for she asked about the weather and the hunting in all seasons. And then she said, "Of course it's too small, but if we buy we'll tear it down and build another castle on the site, right there on the Dee – his Royal Highness has plans." '

'Oh, my God!'

'But think what it will mean to us all, Linty. Workmen, masons, joiners, the quarrymen – what's wrong?'

'You told me all that *before*,' she said. 'You told me before you knew! On that picnic – my God, it seems years ago – you said you saw a great quarry busy, ... and the castle pulled to the ground, and building and spires going up.'

'Are you daft, lass? I only just heard of it this morning. And mind, this is a secret. I should not be telling you, for she said, "We're not yet sure, Mr. Brown, and there must be no talk of it. We do not wish to raise hopes only to lower them." So, Linty, not a word, even to Jean.'

'I promise,' she said.

He left her then, hurrying off because the Queen wanted to ride again this afternoon, rain or not. And alone, bemused, she remembered something else he had said last year on that picnic, in that strange way he had of visioning: 'Gardens planted. Someone – a woman. Och, what a woman!'

Chapter Two

The folk of Crathie marked the passage of years by the visits of the Queen and her family – eight children now. Linty, too, was prone to say, 'It was the year she and the bairns took lessons in Highland dancing,' or 'It was the first year Johnny cooked her trout up at Loch Muick...'

Och, he'd bragged about that, all right, but he'd seen Linty cook it a hundred times, rolled in oatmeal and fried. The splendid thing to Johnny was the intimacy of it all – just him and the Prince, the Queen and Lady Jane Churchill, with Grant the ghillie looking on. But it was that very intimacy that worried Linty, for the Queen had done a daft thing. Though she complained about the cramped little castle where the billiard room had to serve as dining-room and sitting-room, for her own use she chose an even smaller retreat five miles away in the wilderness above Loch Muick. Here were two little shielings – mere huts – suitable only for shooting parties or as ghillies' homes. But the Queen had had them joined together by a covered passage, and Alt-na-Guithasach became her favorite place now that it was refurbished inside. Just four rooms in the Queen's hut (was not *that* cramped?), and the other hut for Johnny, Grant and Duncan.

Jealous of a queen? Yes, and why not, with Johnny away up there on moonlit nights in the big rowing-boat, so close to the Queen he could touch her skirt ... the tall pines about, and the fragrance of them, and the piper playing softly from shore. Was it the fishing that enchanted the Queen, or the look of the moon and the red-gold shine of Johnny's hair? Oh, it was *said* she was mad in love with Albert, but then why did she always want Johnny dancing attendance on her. Miserably, Linty thought: Just because I love him I can't believe she doesn't, and for sure what she wants she takes. Torquil said her ancestors did, and not so long ago, and that hot blood is in her and that means passion.

Didn't the Queen know or care that Loch Muick, for all its wild beauty, meant 'Darkness' or 'Sorrow'? But according to Johnny she had banished the ghosts, and no one would believe she could laugh so much, or smile even at the simplest thing, like a leaf fallen on Albert's shoulder, or giggle at the sudden patter of rain, lifting her face to take it like a greedy child. 'Poor Lady Churchill hasnā much fun, I can tell you. A storm comes up and the Queen orders me to row ashore *slowly* and looks up at the sky all excited, while Albert pulls up his muffler and Lady Churchill huddles in her shawl, holding her feet off the wet planks.

'And then, inside, it's "Brown, make up a fire," and I do, of birch logs, and Albert and the lady sit there drying and talking of chills, while the Queen opens a window and takes the blast of the storm without a care of herself. It's myself takes and dries her shawl and suggests maybe hot tea. "I never liked tea," says she, but the others clamor for it so I put on the kettle. Then I nip in *her* tea some whisky from my flask and take her a mug there at the window. I think she took it just to be polite. But after she's finished the mug she says, "Brown, that was the best tea ever I had." So I told her what was in it.'

'It's a wonder you're still in service,' Linty said.

'But the tea was a wonder to her, so she said. "Brown, always have a bottle handy wherever we go, that's a command." '

'One you're not likely to forget,' Linty said.

It was hard to hide her resentment as, autumn after autumn, and sometimes in spring, the Queen took over Johnny's life, and thus her own. Working at Bush, with Jean doing simple tasks for fear of the headaches, treated as members of the family by the Browns, her mind was not on the churning, the fowl-plucking, the helping in with the hay. For Johnny was off up some mountain with the Queen, commissioned now to lead her pony. And if Albert wanted to deer-stalk, often he went alone with Grant and Duncan. Such a strange man he was to Linty — whoever heard of a man that paused on a deer-stalk, waiting, opening a Gaelic dictionary so as not to waste a mite of time? Making the ghillies talk the language to him, eager to command it as he commanded everything else at Balmoral but the Queen herself.

It was Albert who seemed to have a hand in every pie, Johnny said, for he served as the Queen's secretary and advised her what to do. It was he who superintended the children's lessons – too strict by far, Johnny thought, even choosing a tutor named Birch for the Prince of Wales, though perhaps the lad needed a hard hand. The trouble was that Bertie, as the family called him, was a strange blend of mischief, sullenness, impudence, rage and love – and fear. 'Just nine, but y'ken his father pushes him too fast and too far – and never a smile for him.'

'Not even for the Queen?' Linty asked.

'Not often. He's not the smiling sort. But by God, a good hard worker. And nothing too small for his attention, be it a loose button, or a lazy footman, or a war.'

But surely these big things outside would finally drive the family from Crathie, so far from the world? Linty clung to the hope that the Highlands were only the Queen's whim, until Johnny told her, one night, the most incredible and awful thing:

'They have bought Balmoral, Abergeldie Castle, Birkhall and all of Ballochbuie Forest . . .'

No whim, then.

'They will pull down Balmoral and raise a larger castle, and use Abergeldie and Birkhall for guests. Now what in hell's the matter, Linty? It will be the making of us all. She wants the servants here all Highland.'

She said nothing.

'Stop looking like that.' He put out a big hand. 'It's fine, great news for all of us.'

'Don't you remember,' she reminded him, 'that you foretold all this?'

'One dram,' he said, 'just one, and it turns you fey as a March hare. How could I know what I never knew?'

The new castle rose through the years of the Crimean War.

From the quarries of Glen Gelder came great blocks of granite, so pale a gray as to seem white by moonlight. Slowly, slowly rose dunce-cap turrets embellished with iron thistles. It was planned by Prince Albert with architect William Smith. 'The Queen,' Johnny said, 'can never seem to remember Smith's part in it.' And it was Albert who created the new gardens. He ordered thousands of conifers to be planted to insure a hedge of privacy. Finally the new Balmoral stood shining, with the Dee to ribbon it and the mountains to frame it – and the Queen to call it 'This dear paradise . . . my dearest Albert's own creation, own work, own building, own laying out . . .'

Crathie celebrated with the Queen on her arrival that September, and bonfires burned on the hills to celebrate the fall of a place far off, called Sebastopol. Linty stood with Jean and Torquil in the torchlight of the gardens, where free whisky was passed by footmen in fancy velvet and silk knee-breeches. Johnny was tending those fires on the hills but soon he would be down to join in the dancing, which Her Majesty had ordered must be reels.

Why can't I be happy for him – each year growing more in favor, trusted as no other outdoor servant was. But that selfless love isn't in me and likely never will be.

Jean said, 'It's so hot.'

'It's just the look of the fires,' Torquil said.

She had taken off her linen cap to fan her face and he looked down at her. 'Aye, it's bloody hot,' he said. 'I'll walk you over to the fields for a breath of air.'

Linty watched them go, wondering when Johnny would join her. There must be a dozen fire-makers; surely he wasn't needed for so long.

She felt a hand on her shoulder and spun around to see Sheena Davidson.

Avoidance of the devil, she thought, can't last forever. Always at the sight of Sheena she had moved away – prideless, in panic. At the Inn, at the sheep trysts and fairs, she had had Johnny to protect her, but even then she had moved. Now she was caught in this crowd.

'Are you alone?' Sheena's voice sidled through the torchlight and the shadows and the colors of coats and dresses made golden by the glow from here and the hills. 'Where is your Johnny?'

The face was no longer a child's – but had it ever been? The wild white hair was primly braided over the ears, as everyone wore it in imitation of the Queen, smoothed and parted in the middle. Her white waist was neat, buttoned tightly over full breasts, and her skirt spun out in red and black stripes. Some of the lads at Bush were attracted, as Linty felt, like dogs to a bitch. But Sheena had made no choice nor, indeed, any gossip.

'Johnny's up at the fires,' Linty said, and started towards Sandy Scott.

But Sheena moved at the same time and barred her way. The slash of her mouth was smiling but the gray-white eyes were cold and intent. Linty looked into them and felt a wash of memory. Years ago she had seen a rabbit held fast by a stoat ... with just such a glance.

She felt a nerve jump in her cheek and shaped the words, 'Let me by,' but she heard no sound as she spoke except the crowd's hum and laughter, the clink of mugs and crackle of a cook-fire. She swallowed. Again she tried to speak, but if her lips moved, no words came.

'You're afraid,' Sheena said softly, still smiling.

And then, thank God, Torquil was back with Jean and the spell – if it was that – was broken. Sheena pushed past them as pipers blared the Queen's entrance.

'I'm taking Jean home,' Torquil said. 'Oh, I'll have her to rights; it's the excitement and standing so long. Stay here till Johnny comes, Linty.'

'I'll be fine,' Jean said, 'if you don't upset me by leaving.'

She knew now that Torquil had the healing power for Jean, had used it, was using it. And in the past few years his summer wanderings were shorter, or he broke them to return for a week. The laudanum bottle had long since been empty; it wasn't needed – if Torquil were there.

Perhaps they did want to be alone, needed to be alone for the healing, and so she watched them go and stood safely by Sandy and Mariad lest Sheena return.

'Look!' said Mariad, 'she's coming among us!'

69

Incredible, but true — and Prince Albert behind her. But the torchlight seemed only for her, making a glory of the smooth hair, sparkling the jewels on her wrists. She was plumper now, which made her seem shorter. Her white satin gown was crossed with a great tartan ribbon — the Balmoral tartan of black, red and lavender on gray designed by her husband, who wore the dress kilt. She stopped to greet the mothers of Grant and Duncan, to give her hand to Dr. Robertson, now factor of the estate, and to smile on everyone and laugh as her collie swept past her toward the cooking fire.

No one dared to move toward her; she moved to them, a princess in a fairytale. She bent to ask the name of a child, touched a babe in Mrs. Stewart's arms, paused to inquire of old Mrs. MacRae's health, even remembering to ask of her son in America. Linty was close enough to overhear that crystal voice saying, 'It is such a wonderful, wonderful night!' and to see those little velvet bows set in back of her hair, and the way a strand had fallen down her plump, bare shoulder. Linty moved; she edged back and found herself standing next to a man, a stranger. He was taking a mug from the tray a footman held, and seeing Linty without one, took one for her and said, 'A good evening, isn't it?'

If only Johnny would return. 'Yes, sir.' She accepted the mug and sipped. Guns were going off, and fireworks spinning up. Above the blaze of the hills blue and gold and crimson rockets tore the sky.

He was tall, thin, perhaps thirty, but one never looked at a man closely for fear of being bold. She thought of him as a refuge in case Sheena returned. But why was it safer to stand beside him than near the Queen?

The good whisky calmed her, so that when he asked her name and gave her his, she said, 'Ian Wyness — you'd not be a journalist, would you?'

He laughed. 'No, Miss Clarke. But why?'

'We are not supposed to get into talk with journalists.'

'I know. No one should nose about the Queen's private home. But I'm a footman, seeking work here tomorrow.'

She turned to look at him then, a craggy face, but merry, full-lipped, with fine black eyes. The dark hair was turning sparse, like Prince Albert's. Would it be a fashion, she wondered, and was relieved to find a chuckle in her.

'You'll be from Aberdeen?' she asked, for the accent was broad, but somehow nice.

'Born there, but in service to the Gordons of Huntly. I heard the Queen was looking for Highland help and so I asked for a letter—' He patted his pocket. '– and they've given me a good reference. If I fail to get the work, they say I may come back – a fine family.'

It was then that the pipers and fiddlers began in a burst to the left of the lawn, and word went around: 'Dance, the Queen says to dance.' But first off she was dancing with the Prince, as if she'd known the Highland way all of her life, though her ladies and gentlemen were not that graceful at all.

Dance! came the roar, and couples moved forward. And where on earth was Johnny Brown? Still with those long-lit fires on the hills?

Suddenly she saw him. The dirt of the hills, the briars, were off him and he wore the dress tartan, his own, the curly white frills at his throat, the cairngorm clasp – and he was dancing with the Queen.

'Will you dance, Miss Clarke?' Wyness asked.

Now the Queen was swung to another partner, Duncan, and other couples obstructed her view. The music shrilled and shrieked.

She shook her head. Johnny had kept her waiting here over two hours; now her feet felt sore and dull and cheated.

'You don't like to dance?' he asked.

'If I'm in the mood. But I'll take another dram.'

One should never drink in anger. As she drank she thought that Johnny could have sent her a message by someone. What was she, his dog to wait and wait? Now she could see Sheena among the dancers, but good riddance. She'd not be back here as long as Johnny was there in that whirling mass of skirts and flung bonnets; it was long love of Johnny that made her so terrible, though he of course would laugh at the idea.

People were going across to the cookfires, where servants stood waiting to serve them at trestle tables.

'Will you let me get you some food, Miss Clarke?'

Och, he was a nice man, but surely not fetched to a woman who didna want dance nor food nor fun. The smell of roasted ox and deer sickened her. Once Johnny stopped dancing, his first thought would be of food, of course, but a dozen flasks would delay him – or the drink-trays of the footmen – before he remembered to seek her.

'No, Mr. Wyness,' she said, 'I think I'll take my way home.'

She didn't need his company, but he insisted. They walked through the littering leaves into the cool of the starlight and along the fields, some still stooked with the harvest. Owls called; a hare fled their path in the light of her lantern. She hoped Ian Wyness would not touch her, more than to help her over a stile. He didn't. He just talked quietly about indifferent things.

A great darkness was upon her. The years had sped so fast. Could she be twenty-five, a spinster, but just the same girl – woman – who had made that picnic for Johnny across the cut of the forest and heard him predict the future? *Och, what a woman.* Well, tonight he had danced with that woman, touching her hand, looking into her eyes.

The cottage was lit with more candles than usual and she said, 'My sister wasna feeling well; I hope—'

But Torquil had seen them and came bounding out like a boy and said, 'Linty, Johnny, come in—'

'It's not Johnny,' she said, relieved that Torquil was smiling. 'Mr. Ian Wyness has brought me home.'

Home to Jean, who was making spice bannocks as if it were Christmas, and the candles were the wax ones they saved for special occasions. Jean tucked back her hair and curtsied to Mr. Wyness and seated him on a stool and brought whisky. Torquil said, 'We've been waiting for company.'

Usually grave, he had a gaiety on him, and then Jean said, 'Mr. Wyness, it's a family celebration. We're to be married.'

While he rose and drank to them and congratulated Torquil, Linty, hugging Jean, thought: This is the way such things happen – long friendship, then that burst of knowledge that knows it's more. It could happen with Johnny too; it must happen.

'No more wandering,' Torquil said, turning to Wyness. 'I was a tinker; now I'm tamed.'

'More than that,' Jean said, passing the bannocks, 'he's shaving off that beard and seeking work at the castle – in the gardens.'

Mr. Wyness was now Ian, one of them. He too was sure to find work, when he presented his fine letter. He kept saying that he mustn't impose on their hospitality, really must go to the Inver and sleep; but though Torquil drank only water he saw no reason to thrust it on anyone else, and the mugs were refilled. Jean took Linty aside and said they would furbish their parents' room upstairs so Linty could have privacy, too. It would be all the cosier down here when Johnny wanted to stay late.

'Johnny,' Linty said, 'didna even bother to seek me out tonight. He was dancing with the Queen . . .'

'When he comes by, then, he'll find Ian. Now you make the most of it; he's a fine-looking man and a good chance to brew jealousy.'

'But Johnny won't be by, not now.'

It was just after two when Johnny came in, a bottle in his hand and his bonnet askew. But his legs were steady, and his speech, and his nod to Ian was polite.

'I looked all about for you, Linty,' he said.

'Oh, Ian and I – we left early,' she said, deliberately vague, and saw Jean's nod of approval. 'We were celebrating a marriage . . .'

Johnny clapped Torquil's shoulder in a way that nearly floored him, picked up Jean and danced her around. Then he sat by Ian and told him just how to apply for work. Sir Thomas Biddulph, Master of the Household, wasn't a bad old stick – a wee bit stiff maybe, but underneath fairly human. It was Prince Albert did the final approving though, and there you had to watch out. He'd see the tiniest mote of dust on your jacket and read that reference letter between the lines.

Johnny jealous? My God, he was *advising* Ian, and helping him, and telling Torquil how to go about getting work in the gardens. There was MacFee to see first. So dour was MacFee

73

he'd have found fault with Eden itself, never mind the behavior of the people in it.

Finally Johnny and Ian left together. In her bed, Linty thought: All I've done this night is wait for Johnny and make him a new friend. But when she heard Jean and Torquil's footsteps upstairs she was glad. Why should they wait? The banns would be posted today, and her sister was safe in the healing that was love.

That night, the banns posted at Crathie Kirk, Torquil said, 'I was not in the mind to bother with this MacFee. He'd have rubbed the juice out of me. So I went straight to the Prince, like you do to God without the mess of the saints in between.'

'But how?' Jean asked.

'I saw him out ordering the gardens, top hat and all, with papers in his hand. There was a wind, and I saw one of the papers blow away, so I went up and warned him. He thanked me, and before he could turn away I said, "May I have a word, your Highness?" and drew him off away from the gardeners and told him why some new-planted trees would die, and how to save the old ones. He listened carefully. He asked about my experience and I said, because the truth is best to a man like that, "I have lived among trees all my life. I understand them, sir. I have seen them hurt and torn, and believe me, they can cry out like any living thing. I have comforted and prayed and seen new life."

'He said something in German, but softly, and he didn't go away.

' "You will see proof, sir, if you let me tend the trees. Because for trees, I am the resurrection and the life." '

As you are with Jean, Linty thought, but she said nothing. 'The Prince thought for a long while and then he said, "I see no harm, Mr. Briggs. Will you — what is the word? — stake out six old trees, and mark them? To prove what you can do?"

' "Gladly, if you'll send someone for paint. I'd not mark a tree on its bark." '

'So it was the red paint he sent for, and he watched me among the old trees, and said meanwhile he would tell MacFee to use me in the gardens as ordinary labor.'

74

Torquil looked so much younger without the beard, his hair more yellow than gray, yet still there was something about him that could impress even a prince. It might have to do with his hands, Linty thought, big and sun-browned but slender-fingered and graceful as a woman's. Or just in the quiet way he spoke and the soft shine of his eyes.

Johnny urged her to work at Balmoral too. 'The Queen is ridding herself of the English staff, all but a few Uppers. Now's the time to see Sir Thomas, while the Prince is here to approve.'

Or disapprove. Still, she knew her way around a kitchen or dairy. And she'd be closer to Johnny, for the lower servants ate together, he said, and there were fifteen minutes free in the afternoon for tea or a walk, as you pleased. And when the royalty left there'd be a great relaxing, like a family when the guests had gone.

'Somehow I'm afraid, Johnny.'

But of course she would do as he suggested, especially as he said he'd go with her and leave her outside Sir Thomas Biddulph's office. There were many windey corridors, as if meant for people to get lost, but he'd see her safely in.

It was nine o'clock when they were passed by a policeman and allowed up a flight of stairs; but there was nothing elegant here, just whitewashed walls. He took her cold hand and said, 'Scared? Of what?' Though she tried to speak, her teeth chattered. He laughed and brought a flask from his pocket – a new one, she thought, cased in red leather. 'Drink,' he said, 'I'll keep watch.'

'Oh, I couldna!' The porridge lay heavy enough on her stomach.

'Do as I say.'

A command obeyed since childhood. She drank hastily, and Johnny pocketed the flask, 'I'll smell of it,' she said.

But Johnny carried the remedy, a little vial of coffee dregs, and she chewed the bits he poured in her hand, but worriedly. 'I'm sure he'll smell it.'

'I'll just see,' he said, and pulled her into his arms and kissed her.

Not a gentle kiss, but a deep one, the sort she had longed

for. She held it, not caring who might see them, pressing close against his rough jacket, feeling a leaf in his hair as she put up her hand in caress.

Gently he drew back. 'Dinna fash yourself, your breath is fine.'

So the kiss was only a test of her breath, a friendly way of finding out if she stank. Nothing to build on, nothing to treasure, just a test.

He led her around a bend in the corridor to a dark pine door with thistles carved on it and knocked. A voice called 'Come in,' and Johnny, opening the door, said, 'It's Miss Linda Clarke seeking work,' and left her.

She closed the door and stood helplessly, then remembered to curtsy. The man at the desk was small, and tidy as its pigeonholes. He sat so straight it seemed he might have a lady-busk up him or worn a corset. His brown beard was luxuriant, his brown eyes sharp. She was too intent on him to notice much about the room except blue velvet draperies at the windows.

'What sort of work?' he asked abruptly.

'Dairy, sir, or kitchen.'

'Experience?'

'Bush Farm, sir.'

Her legs wobbled with nervousness. Why, she could pick trenches of potatoes and never tire, but this standing still and straight, and looking into his eyes, which seemed never to flicker . . .

'We are very particular here, as you must know.'

And then he asked a dozen questions – age and religion and all that, whether married and with children, who would vouch for her honesty. She said The Browns of Bush, and Mr. Anderson, the minister.

'Come back at four this afternoon,' he said, and turned to some papers.

He wasn't even polite enough to say 'Goodbye.' Well, it was a known fact that the English gentry had no manners, but leaving in the chill of his silence she wanted to cry. One comfort, folk of her own kind would be working with her – if she was accepted.

Out in the corridor she saw a man in gray shirt and tartan trews, very smart, and as she stood aside to let him pass she recognized Ian Wyness.

'Linty!' Like an old friend greeting her. 'Are you working here?'

She told him maybe. 'And you had no trouble — but of course you had that letter to show.'

'Still, I'm only a "pupil footman." And on the rush with messages from tip to toe of this place, but I've fifteen minutes free. I'll see you outside.'

They walked into the pale gold sunlight, passing women with egg baskets, Kenny the joiner carrying a chair; but Johnny was nowhere about. He hadn't said he'd wait for her, but still he might have found a way, just out of concern. Then, through the courtyard that led to the stables she saw him helping a bunchy-skirted woman onto a black pony. Her voice came softly but clearly across the grass and separating cobbles: 'You won't forget the "tea," Brown?' and a giggle like a girl's.

Linty turned in the other direction and Ian said, following toward the gardens, 'How does Johnny find her?'

'It's hard to say. He admires her, I think — and God knows he's not afraid of her like everybody else. And he's the favorite outdoor servant, that's for certain. But he doesna talk about her much. He talks about himself and what he does for her, finding the trails that please her, showing her the country.'

Ian laughed. 'I'd say that she and the Prince have a conspiracy to show the footmen every room of the castle in the shortest possible time. She writes messages the moment she's awake, or how else could I have delivered fourteen this morning? And two, if you please, to her husband, and two back in reply — and they had only to open a door between them.'

'Is she pleasant to you?'

'She nods without smiling, but I doubt that she really sees me. The notes are sealed, of course, but one she forgot to. I sneaked a look. It was to Lady Churchill: "*None* of our ladies and gentlemen to leave the house until I am back after tea-time." My God, on a fair day like this, to have to stay in and read or embroider or play billiards. It's a fair shame.'

'Why shouldn't they come to the gardens, at least?'

'She's afraid of some kind of scandal. She sees a mating in everything. My laird told me that himself. He said, "Her grandfather's court was dissolute, and her ancestors', and she's turned a new leaf." But it's bloody hard on the ladies-in-waiting, the maids of honor, the upper gentlemen, the gentlemen visitors. And if the Prince doesn't ask the gentlemen shooting they sulk around like children and smoke too much.'

'Smoke – here? I'd heard she was fierce against it.'

'She is.' He chuckled. 'They have to lie down on the hearthrugs of their fireplaces and blow smoke up the chimney.'

He turned and faced her. 'I must get back. When shall you know? – four, did you say? I'll be in the corridor at a quarter past, if I can. I'll want to hear all about it.'

As he left her, she thought: Already he cares for me as much as Johnny – perhaps more.

Torquil saw her as she rounded the path of new conifers, put down his spade, and waved. One must thank God for him, and Jean's happiness, and the friendliness of Ian. For health and perhaps some beauty. That was the right way of thinking.

But she picked up a pinecone and crushed it until blood oozed from her palm.

She had not really believed that Prince Albert would want to approve a dairy or kitchen maid, but within minutes of her arrival in Sir Thomas's office a footman announced him; she backed against the wall and curtsied as Sir Thomas rose. And he kept Sir Thomas standing, a lovely thing to see.

The Prince was too pale, she thought, his skin like tallow against the black and silver of his sideburns and moustache. His lips were red as a woman's, and his hands as cared for, though he wore a rough kilt, as men wore for stalking. He held a pair of deerskin gauntlets embroidered in gold, and a great gold ring sheathed his marriage finger.

Tall he was, nearly as tall as Johnny, and somehow more like a marble monument than a man, with a stillness about him. His eyes were sad and circled; she felt they missed nothing, but expected nothing either. The high forehead was furrowed, but then he was thirty-six, like the Queen, only with no glow on him as she had.

He looked Linty up and down, not boldly, but as farmers eyed stock before purchase. Then he said, in a rasping kind of accent that was German, 'You are on trial for two weeks. If you satisfy, you remain. I have seen Sir Thomas's report lacking one question.'

Sir Thomas looked embarrassed.

'That question is, Miss Clarke, it is known your sister suffers from migraine. Dr. Robertson says you might be needed at home for emergencies. If this is so, you cannot divide loyalties.'

Did she dare speak? Was it a question? Evidently, for he waited. 'Your Highness, my sister is to be married in October. She is healed.' And not by that blabbing doctor. Dare she mention Torquil, whom he knew? Safer not.

'Very good,' he said. 'You may start work tomorrow, as Sir Thomas will direct. You are as a student, here to learn, perhaps to rise in position.'

He left to her curtsy and Sir Thomas's bow at the door. Sir Thomas sat down and said, 'You will start at six in the morning as scullery and general kitchen help. Mrs. Newlands is housekeeper there. I hope I shall not have to see you again.' The rudeness of him! 'For I am the one who engages – and dismisses.'

Pompous ass, as she told Ian when she joined him at the end of the corridor. She hadn't even dared to ask her wage, but the housekeeper could tell her that, and whatever it was, she'd be sure of meals. But wasn't it queer to keep servants here all year round?

'A staff must be kept in great, cold houses, Linty – besides, we're being trained while the family are away. It was expensive bringing servants to and from London, Windsor, Osborne – och, the Prince has it all figured to the ha'penny what each household should cost. But you'll find they're generous here with the food. We don't eat leftovers from the Upper tables.'

'Why on earth not?'

'Because we eat first, you goose. The gentry don't breakfast at six and lunch at noon and dine at six.... May I come by tonight, Linty? I owe you all a bottle, you know.'

But she said she wanted to be asleep early. Tonight, of all nights, Johnny would be by to ask what had happened, and to crow about another day with the Queen in the high hills, among the scarlet leaves.

When Torquil came in to supper he said, 'I knew you'd be hired – Ian told me. And he asked me if you were promised to anyone.'

'Johnny wouldn't give out such an idea,' she said bitterly.

Jean slipped off his working boots, patted a stockinged foot. 'What did you tell him, then?'

'That I wasn't sure.'

'One thing I'm sure of,' Linty said. 'If Johnny doesna come here tonight he just doesna care at all. For tonight, it's like the beginning of a new part of my life, and he's shared everything else.'

Jean went to the griddle and laid on smokey haddocks. 'I'll cook some extra for him. He likes them cold with vinegar.'

'Don't,' Torquil said. 'I'm sorry to tell you, but just after tea-time – about five, it was – they set off in the carriage, with Johnny on the box and the ghillies ahead, for Loch Muick.'

Of course. Most of the day with him wasn't enough. And tonight was full moon.

'Now,' said Mrs. Newlands, sitting down in a pantry corner, 'let us get it all straight at once. And *stand* straight, Linda, you're in royal service – if you suit. The pay is one shilling and sixpence a day and food. The hours are from six in the morning until seven at night. Sundays off when the family are not in residence ...'

Black beady eyes in a long pink face and surely six eyes in the back of her head beneath the white cap. A beaky nose gave her the look of a parrot, and her way of tilting her head. Not English, thank God, but Edinburgh-born, brought from the palace of Holyrood, she said, 'to train you all to Her Majesty's pleasing.'

What pleased her, and the Prince? The invisibility of all servants except those in personal waiting, such as ghillies in attendance, footmen, those serving at the royal table. It was most unlikely that a royal personage would descend to the kitchen, but if it happened, the help were to scutter for the nearest cover. 'You are ghosts, never to be seen or heard. You will never venture up the stairs, nor into the corridors. The kitchen, pantries, game porches and dairy are your boundaries, and the kitchen gardens for your fifteen minutes free at different times – yours, Linda, shall be at three o'clock.

'The punishment for being late is to go without breakfast – but a third such offence means dismissal. Theft, be it a crumb of cake, means instant dismissal.'

Prince Albert had been disgusted by the behavior of servants in England. The old skulduggery between cooks and butchers, with money passing hands, was impossible now. No longer might a kitchen maid sell dripping back to the butcher or a scullery maid expect deer or rabbit skins.

'You will start today scrubbing, a brown apron and cap provided. In training for kitchen chores, there will be a white cap and apron.' She rose in a crisp of blue skirts. 'Breakfast.'

This was served in a big room off the kitchen for the humblest servants – indoor and outdoor – on a plain deal table without cloth or furbish. The fare was just what one might eat at home – porridge and bannocks and tea – and except for Mrs. Newlands' long prayer, which seemed more to Prince Albert than to God, it was cosy, for here were familiar Crathie folk, men and girls she had known all her life. Johnny gave her a smile, a wink and a wave, but he was far at the end, with the men.

'I always reiterate, for new help, that we are a helpful family here,' Mrs. Newlands said, passing down the tea pot. 'Bickering and strife – never.'

Johnny laughed aloud at this, but in that beguiling way he had. 'The cooks, Ma'am?' and wagged a finger at her.

'Och, that!' But she was smiling. 'They are creative geniuses, Mr. Brown, and so above us.'

'I dinna notice any genius about this porridge,' said Elspeth McFarland. 'There were a lump in mine the size of an acorn.'

'I shall speak to Mr. Duff.'

What a queer way the breakfasts were – chefs Duff and

81

Macose, Scottish and French, eating in separate pantries; then the deal table cleared and covered with linen and flowers brought in a pot, and nicer plates arranged. Linty had only a glimpse of the people going in half an hour later, but, as she said to Jenny Strang, who scrubbed near her, they were surely gentry, all starched and laced and handsome? No, these were the personal servants of visitors, and Lord, what a fuss if they weren't seated properly, a thing Sir Thomas saw to. The maid of a Duchess took what they called 'precedence,' or the valet of an Earl, or whoever ranked highest in his master's service. It was terrible, Jenny said, when some Indian Maharaja's personal attendant was placed below the Prime Minister's valet because the Queen-Mother's lady's maid was there – och, a muddle. *Their* breakfast was different, of course – eggs and bacon or fish, rolls and toast and jams, tea or coffee.

The third breakfast was sent upstairs for Upper servants of the household like parlormaids and footmen, and at the same time orders were taken for trays for the Queen's Ladies and the Prince's Gentlemen and guests. 'You will see such trays, all silver, and what's on them you wouldn't believe, like a roasted grouse on toast at *nine o'clock*, with eggs poached in port or whatever.' And then the Queen's own breakfast, which she might or might not eat in her dining room with her family – plain Scottish fare: eggs and gammon, black puddings, finnan haddie, mealie jims. But at luncheon – that strange new word for mid-day meal – Monsieur Macose shared the cooking with Mr. Duff, so there were French things along with the usual salmon and cold beef and lamb. And it was Macose who cooked for the castle at night with his two sulky assistants, who hated Scotland worse than a fallen soufflé.

The big kitchen was divided so that each chef had separate reign – his own wood and coal stoves, pots, pans, worktables, stools, cabinets and cutlery. There was a huge expanse of floor to scrub, and difficult, because it was white cobbled stone with chinks for food to fall in and no time to do more than soap and rinse the surface before space was needed for the chefs. And then the dairy, after the maids had churned and patted the butter into beautiful shapes of horns and butterflies and hearts. But those were only for everyday – for special occasions the butter was formed into the initials V.R., with coronets above; HRH or flowerets to please the young princesses; a butter gun for Bertie. But the dairy was an awful place to scrub if butter bits had fallen, or eggs; and you could sicken on the game porches, with the animal guts to take up in buckets.

Nothing was wasted. Offal and scraps went to the gun dogs, and the pigs, which were styed well away up the glen. Stale bread was saved by Macose — on purpose, imagine — to fry in tiny cubes and float in soup, or to sprinkle on dishes of vegetables before baking. If she'd had the time that first day she'd have watched Macose at his stove because of the wonderful smells.

'Will we get any of that?' she asked Jenny as they shed their aprons at noon and washed their hands at the maids' basin.

'The soup——'

A footman, fancy-dressed, had appeared. On the blackboard above Duff's chopping block he wrote

READY
One-twenty, P.M. Queen's picnic, for Six Persons . . .

and then spoke the command aloud. 'Ready . . .'

And I know who one person will be, sharing

Sandwiches, Gammon, chicken, salmon mayonnaise.
Scotch eggs.
Mince Pies.
Cherry cakes. Gateaux.
Implements for Tea.

'It's raining,' Jenny said, 'they'll never go. The food will just sit here and get stale.'

Another footman appeared carrying a large silver-scrolled box, and gave it to Mrs. Newlands.

'The Prince's own picnic box,' Jenny whispered, 'a gift of the Queen. Only of course they'll never go.'

After luncheon Johnny came to her and said, 'I'm sorry

I've had no chance to see you. Are you getting on fine?'

'My back,' she said. 'I could do with a new one.'

'And I can do with sleep. We were at Muick until she rose with the bird chorus. Fresh as a warm egg she was, with Grant and me the worse for a bit of the bottle and the Prince and Lady Churchill blue with the cold. They wanted their tea but she said no, we'd breakfast here at Balmoral and drive through the sunrise. All the way she kept exclaiming about the colors and wasn't it too beautiful and poor Lady Churchill sneezing and saying it was. And now, by God, an order to go out again.'

But the rain was steady, the kind that could go on for a day or two.

'Never mind,' Linty said, pleased that he seemed to be complaining at last, 'the rain's hard.'

'Has it ever stopped her?'

At a quarter to two the picnic party left Balmoral in a light drizzle, and shortly after the sun came out.

'Queen's weather,' said Mrs. Newlands, looking out of the window toward the stables. 'Nine years I've been in her service and noticed how nothing stops her. Uncanny it is how she gets what she wants — always.'

During the next week Linty was trained two hours a day in other chores than scrubbing. How to polish a pot just so. How to strip a fowl with those new clipper things. The way Duff liked suet chopped; the way Macose required carrots and leeks to be cleaned. She watched Elspeth's clever fingers, marveling at the pretty things to garnish the food.

'Now you do it, Linty — so. Scrub the radishes. Gently remove the tips — so. Plunge into cold water. And after ten minutes you may rosette.'

'Must I? I'd break the little things sure.'

'You must learn in case of emergency,' Mrs. Newlands said. 'No Upper food *ever* goes undressed — a shame to the kitchen, it would be. Last week...'

Two footmen bound for the Queen's dinner had collided with trays of hors d'oeuvre just outside the dining room. 'Smoked fish, pâté, caviar — all that we could replace down here within minutes. But not the frivolités, as Monsieur Mac-ose calls them – the flowered tomatoes and radishes. Elspeth was off; there was only myself to do them, for none of the late maids knew. That's why we must master one another's work. Time being so short, I had to slice on tomatoes just plain, and fill in with parsley. And the Queen noticed.'

'She was angry?'

'I received a note by a footman next morning "The veget-ables *must* look pretty and I was *most* embarrassed at sight of them." '

'Because they was undressed,' Elspeth said, with a snicker.

'It's not for joking. The point is, the Kitchen must never be shamed. We are a team to help one another. Linty, start on the radishes.'

Gradually she progressed to flowering the tomatoes, to flut-ing a cucumber, to making a cup of an orange which might be filled with its own segments or a salad. Told to decorate a plate of cold luncheon for Sir Thomas, she found her hands steady. He could find no fault, surely, when Mrs Newlands couldn't.

But back came the tray with a note: *The orange must be precisely leveled so as not to tip. There were two seeds. A sense of color must be developed so that pink radishes do not rest near pink ham.*

Though the chefs might bicker, the girls did not. Elspeth hid Jenny's blunder with a trout ('a fillet is never *torn*'), saying a cat must have crept on the porch. Janet scoured a pot Beth had forgotten. Maggie took the wrath of a burst salt bag from Cathy. Cathy covered Morag's clumsiness with the lie that *she* had upset the barley sack. All were like sisters, overworked, protective, linked in fear of Up There.

Up There, it was said, voices were never raised; servants tiptoed and whispered and suffered the terrible agony that they might be seen by the Royal Family despite all the pre-cautions taken. In each corridor there were warning bells rung by Upper Housekeeper or Linen Mistress, Wardrobe Mistress or any passing footman – yet still one could be caught in a passage with nowhere to run to and the Queen herself bearing down, when it was advised to stand flat against the wall and close one's eyes. So who would want to rise from here, the cheery Below, even for more pay?

Johnny was lucky, Linty thought, to have work that suited him, even if he did grumble about that painter fellow Landseer always being underfoot when the deer were brought in, wanting the torches just so to throw the proper light and shadow for getting them onto canvas, when the ghillies wanted only a feed and a dram and bed. But the Queen liked Landseer, allowed him to paint her on a horse, though Johnny said the horse was always a better likeness. She seemed to appreciate his help with her own sketches, and the two of them would sit side by side on a brae, with Lady Churchill sitting apart as chaperone, and the ghillies stalking with the Prince.

'This Mr. Landseer—'

'Sir Edwin. Aye?'

'Is he handsome?'

'Well – well set up, yes.' He was frowning.

Johnny jealous? The Queen a flirt? Could a queen behave foolishly so as to cause talk? Yet there was talk in the kitchens about the new footmen, all good-looking, the older ones banished to England. It was said Sir Thomas knew she liked handsome people around her, and hired for Upper accordingly.

She heard so much as she peeled and chopped, scrubbed or washed or fashioned the frivolités: that Bertie – Edward, the young Prince of Wales – had terrible tantrums as a result of long-enforced studying; that he trembled in his mother's presence but was rude to servants. Johnny, teaching him to shoot on the grouse moors, said he was bright and full of fun one minute, angry the next, 'when he stamps his feet and screams at the loss of a bird. I told him no sportsman behaved that way and I think he wanted to kill me too. But he knows I'll take no insolence.'

'He sounds horrid.'

'He needs playmates his own age.' He paused. 'I think he could make a fine king; but at fourteen, y'ken I was no angel myself, only nothing was expected of me, I wasn't pushed – he's made to work too hard, and this a holiday. What's more, I heard the Queen ask to inspect his diary.'

Och, she could hate the Queen for that, nosing into young privacy, which was none of anyone's business.

'It's a mercy she canna see yours,' Linty said, teasing.

'I've a lock on it,' he said, and was serious. Who on earth would suspect Johnny Brown of keeping a diary?

'Since I entered permanent service,' he said, 'I started a kind of record. It's history of a sort, isn't it?'

'Aye.' She wondered if the smallest line mentioned her. But there was little time for thought during the last days of the royal holiday, when guests crammed the Castle and overflowed into Abergeldie, from where a lady-in-waiting complained that her luncheon was brought in a wheelbarrow and the soup and cutlets stone cold. But it was the best that could be done until the kitchens of Abergeldie and Birkhall were made modern, and more staff hired.

Mrs. Newlands never seemed flurried, except on that October day when Linty asked release to attend Jean's wedding next day at noon. It was granted, through Sir Thomas, but with loud complaint that the request came at the very worst time. The Queen had refused to relinquish Johnny. Weddings, she said, could have been arranged for after her departure.

It was a small, pretty wedding at Crathie Kirk, with a frolic later at Inver Inn which Johnny joined at midnight, bringing the gift of a fine oak clock that had been his sister's. Och, there were plenty of gifts – a barrel of oatmeal, delivered at the cottage with iron cooking pots, a painted jug, wax candles, a sewing box, a hanging vase for ivy. Ian Wyness, who lodged at the Inn but would soon be quartered in Balmoral, came with the gift of music. No one had known he had a guitar and could play it so well.

'You should be playing in great halls,' Johnny told him, 'not wasting your time in service. Where did you learn?'

On a ship out of Glasgow when he was a boy, from a Spanish mate. He'd seen a bit of the world before he'd returned to Aberdeenshire. And now would Linty dance?

If only Johnny would frown and be jealous. Not he. He was off having a drink with the Davidsons. Sheena was not there, for a wonder. . .

'. . . so beautiful,' Ian said, as they danced.

Talking of her hair that she wore long tonight, not strict in a cap. She hoped it was only the drink in him, not serious, the way he clung to her hand afterwards and looked at it and said, 'All it needs is a ring.'

Jean and Torquil would honeymoon at the Inn for a night; the Scotts' wedding gift was their fanciest room. At home in her cottage with Johnny, she said, 'What use to go to bed with work two hours away?'

'Spoken like a man,' he said, and poured a dram for them.

'Not for me!' she said, 'I've had far too much. And I'm not wanting to work all day with the shakes.'

'Who does?' he asked as she put on the kettle, brushing up the fire. He slid down to the hearth rug, piled on logs, then stretched out with the mug in his hand, looking up at the bare boards of the ceiling. 'You can always come to the stables for a dram if you need to. My bottle's behind the old saddles marked *Duncan's*.'

She laughed. 'And the coffee beans – are they there, too?'

'Fresh every day in a blue bowl . . . God, it's a comical thing to see her toss off her dram now, neat as it was born, and prudent too, on the cold trails or up at Muick.'

She took the kettle off its hook with a rattle as she set it down, filling the tea pot before she spoke. 'And does she smell of it?'

'Och, she smells of pine and spruce and all the outdoors. And some kind of scent like fern is on all her mantles and shawls.'

So in love that he held a shawl to him after she'd tossed it off, treasured it to his face? Nothing can come of it, of course, but then nothing can come of us either, as long as he's in this thrall. She filled her tea mug and sat down beside him, stirring in sugar, depressed beyond words.

He looked up at her and smiled. 'Fair tired out, are you? You should rest on your bed. I'll waken you and we'll walk the road together.'

Afraid she would lie down with him, on the cushion of his shoulder? She rose and said, 'Aye,' and took the tea into her own room, shutting the door carefully lest she slam it in fury.

Johnny roused her with a push. 'Quick, I overslept ... Hurry.'

Time only to throw cold water on her face, to cap her snarled hair and stumble out after him into the lifting darkness. The walk seemed interminable, and now rain began in a cutting stream. Johnny gave her his bonnet to keep her hair dry, but her best dress, worn for the wedding, would be a wet ruin. Luckily she'd be wearing an apron over it.

As they reached the gardens the castle clock struck six and she said, 'It's no use to rush now – and I don't mind missing breakfast.'

'I'll tell Mrs. Newlands it was my fault—'

'And have her suspect you stayed overnight? Just say nothing, and walk in before me.' He was not kitchen help; he would be fed. And of course the weather would clear to give the Queen her daily outing.

In the shelter of the courtyard he said, 'Wait. You're not running in there breathless and scared.' He took his bonnet from her and patted rain from her face. Then he took her in his arms and kissed her, and she knew it was not for a test – it was for love, or what he had to give.

But when he left her to walk in ahead she felt more shaken than before. It was, of course, the dregs of drink in her and no food since six last night. It was bewilderment that he had kissed her deeply, and at such a time when she felt low as a water-rat, and blowsy and all. She put out her hands to see if they were steady, but they were not. She was all un-steadied, and she had the awful feeling that she would begin to tremble all over if anyone looked at her.

She'd never been much for praying except in kirk. But now she whispered, 'God, help me,' and walked into the kitchen.

No one was there but Mr. Duff's boy, tending the cook-fires, and she put on her white apron and stood hesitant at the dining room door, which was open. There was clatter and talk.

I must report to Mrs. Newlands *now*. Late as I am she mustn't think me even later ...

With a deep breath she entered the dining room and stood near the door, and the talk died as the housekeeper turned and looked at her, as they all did.

'I'll wait outside,' she said humbly. 'I'm sorry, Ma'am.'

It was hard to speak from a frightened throat.

'You should be, and particularly today. What an example to set a new girl!'

It was then that she saw Sheena sitting by Jenny, perky and clear-eyed and smug from righteous sleep. So that's why she hadn't come to the frolic last night – resting up for her first day's work.

'I am sorry, Ma'am. It won't happen again.'

'Twice more and you're sacked.'

'Aye, Ma'am.'

'You're not begging breakfast?'

Och, the insult of that. She tried to form words to say that she was only reporting in but no words came, and she felt daggered on Sheena's bland smile.

Johnny said, 'With all respect, Ma'am, none of us are beggars. We are *Highland* help.'

The worst thing to say if Mrs. Newlands took it as slur to her native Edinburgh. She was frowning and about to speak when her glance clashed with Johnny's and she said, almost mildly, 'I am only reminding Linda of her duties here, Mr. Brown. She goes without breakfast.'

'I *know*,' Linty said, bolder in Johnny's presence. 'I came to ask what work you'll put me to this morning?'

'Scrubbing,' said Mrs. Newlands. 'The game porches.'

Does she know the reek will sicken me? 'Yes, Ma'am.'

'Go, then.'

At the far end of the kitchen she changed the white apron to a brown one and faltered out onto the porch. The castle butcher had left beef and deer entrails on the wide board tables, the red slime slipping down to the floor, and the terrible yellow hash of a dog-mangled partridge. She brought the bucket and held her breath and rubbed with a bloody cloth until the tables were free. Then she began to clean the floor, going to the well for water, trying not to look at what she did, smell it.

Mrs. Newlands' voice above her: 'Linda, you haven't scoured the tables.'

How to talk without retching? How to explain that first you

took the stuff off onto the floor with the rest, and this bucketed, you came back with fresh rags and water, and then the soap and more water? And didn't Mrs. Newlands *know* that was the sensible way, so that you didn't work in filth under your feet?

If she didn't have to speak she might swallow down the nausea.

'Well? Another fine example for our new girl.'

Linty looked up and saw Sheena, also brown-aproned, standing beside the housekeeper. The white brows were raised in little arcs, the eyes widely open as if shocked at the state of the tables when she damn well knew this was the way the job should be done – all countrywomen knew.

'Well, Linda? Why aren't the tables clean?'

'I – was – going – to.' Another word risked and she'd be sick sure.

'What's the matter with you, girl?'

She dared not answer.

'Och,' Sheena said, with a kind of coo in her voice, 'Linty's all right. The wedding yesterday and all the drink – I'll help her put things to rights, Ma'am.'

'*Drunk!*' said Mrs. Newlands.

'No,' Linty said, anxious to get up but afraid of slipping, 'it's not . . .' and scrabbled up and out into the rain, reaching the privy just in time.

Under a cool dripping still she took deep breaths and righted her stomach, then washed her face. The job which had seemed so cosy was as ruined as her character. Working day after day with Sheena would be nearly unbearable. But for pride's sake she must finish out the day somehow. She would not run. When Mrs. Newlands reported her to Sir Thomas she would stroll out knowing she had been nothing but foolishly late.

If only she could talk to Johnny. He'd be in the stables, with the rain so sheety, but she didn't dare linger. She walked back to the game porch, received Mrs. Newlands' stiff nod, and was told to learn from Sheena how the tables should be properly scrubbed, '*If* you are sobering enough to fix your mind to it.'

Alone with Sheena, she said, bending to wash the table legs, 'You knew I wasn't drunk; it was the stench.'

'Oh? What do they call it here – "a delicate condition?"'

She ignored the taunt because she hadn't the wit or the strength left to fight.

'Well?' Sheena asked, a soap cloth in her hand.

Linty didn't reply.

'He'd have to marry you then,' Sheena said in that soft relentless voice.

'I'm not, and you mind your tongue!'

'Or else ...?'

'Oh, be *quiet!*'

It was fortunate that Jenny came then to say the kitchen was ready for scrubbing and Sheena was to do it. Jenny helped Linty finish that porch, and on the next one – not so bad, with the small birds' entrails – did the worst of the job, leaving Linty to the feathers. That had been the way in the kitchen, the girls knowing how one another felt without words; and Jenny, who had been at the frolic herself, just whispered, 'You'll be fine after luncheon. Sit by me. I don't like that Sheena.'

'Does anyone? Did she do anything?'

'She's sly. You know Elspeth's practicing on the butter shells? Well, Sheena held hers up and said, so Mrs. Newlands could hear, "My, someone must have dropped this one," and snickered. Poor Elspeth went red like beet-root. It's like we had the kitchen all sunny but this morning fog came in. But we'll stick together.'

Linty smiled at the round, indignant brown eyes, and leaned to pat a feather from her cheek. Jenny was married with two bairns but there was something so young and trusting about her, as if evil surprised her. 'We'll stick together.'

After that it was other evil-smelling chores, like cleaning the lamps and then the privy the girls used – Mrs. Newlands' way of punishing the sick stomach. So that when she sat down by Jenny at luncheon she took only a few spoonfuls of the soup, a wisp of bread and cold mutton. Johnny, from his end of the table with the men, seemed not even to see her, deep in argument with Grant about the prospects of Milly foaling before sundown.

Mrs. Newlands rapped on the teapot for attention. 'You know I've no objection about conversation among yourselves *if* it is suitable to the table, but Mr. Brown, Mr. Grant, how do you think Her Majesty would feel if she heard . . .?'

'Beg pardon, Ma'am,' Johnny said, 'but Her Majesty would be very interested in *this* foal as Milly is her pet, in a way. She'll be wanting to see it herself and bringing Bert – I mean, Prince Edward. Perhaps tonight.'

'Aye,' Grant said, gulping ale, 'the foal is sure to be "darling." Or "*so* cunning."'

'Do I detect mockery there, Mr. Grant?'

'Oh, no, Ma'am. It's like women – ladies – talk.'

Linty stared uneasily at her plate. Mrs. Newlands and the outdoor servants had always had a sort of truce, it being understood that the Master of Horse, and he alone, was their superior – and he, of course, had luncheon Upstairs with those of equal rank in the household. But some demon was in Mrs. Newlands today, because she said, 'Mr. Grant, the Queen is not "a woman" or even "a lady."'

Linty had avoided looking at Sheena but now, in her nervousness, she did. *She's enjoying this.* She had stopped gorging her mutton and roasted potatoes to put down her fork and smile.

Johnny, who had fought with Grant about everything from fishing rights to who owned the stones of a discarded fence, said, with a terrible kind of quiet on him, 'Ma'am, are you saying to Grant that the Queen is not even a lady?'

'Why, I never—'

'Then I am glad we misunderstood you, Ma'am. I was sure I hadn't heard right.'

It was strange to see someone like Mrs. Newlands silenced by a ghillie. It came to Linty then, for the first time, that Johnny was able to put down people in higher positions than himself, and maybe had even done it before. She was almost sorry that Mrs. Newlands had made the blunder because, aside from today, she'd been fair enough to everyone.

Luncheon went on, served by Martha, who was waitress of the day. She forgot to wait for the bell but received only a timid reprimand from Mrs. Newlands, and no correction when the gooseberry pie was passed first to the men. But as the day progressed Mrs. Newlands found her old self back – only worse, because she found fault with everything.

'It's the rain,' Elspeth whispered as she and Linty washed up after the last luncheons. 'Maybe bad humor's catching. They say the Queen's like a caged thing when she has to stay indoors. They say she writes in her journal and hears the childrens' lessons and—'

'Attend to your work,' Mrs. Newlands said, angry as if they'd dropped china instead of just gossip. 'Sheena, come here and dry the cutlery, and make sure it's clean.'

She left them to scold potato-peelers at a nearby table.

'Linty,' Sheena said, clear and distinct, 'look at the soap on this knife. It'd poison someone.'

'Bitch,' said Elspeth, but softly. 'We don't tattle on one another here.'

'A bitch!' Sheena said, so that the word carried. 'To call her that when she's *mistress* here!'

Mrs. Newlands came over to them. 'So I was called a bitch, eh? And by whom, may I ask?'

'Och, Linty didn't mean it, Ma'am,' Sheena said.

'She never said it, either,' Elspeth said. 'It was what I called Sheena for being a trouble-maker.'

Perhaps she believed them, or wanted to for the sake of peace. For she said, 'Next time that word is used in this kitchen the person is dismissed,' and ordered Sheena to the carrots and turnips in the far corner. It was then that Ian Wyness came in with a note, and the usual scared look jumped into Mrs. Newlands' eyes as she took it and read it, everyone watching. Sometimes she told them what was in those notes – the Queen's commands through Sir Thomas, or else his own, generally critical. Duff and Macose stood at their opposite stoves and waited like soldiers stiff at attention.

'Thank you, Mr. Wyness,' she said, in that respectful kind of dismissal required for Upper footmen, even those in training. He looked at Linty as he went out and she thought he was smiling, so it couldna be too bad.

'Monsieur Macose, you are notified to prepare to leave tomorrow morning at nine o'clock sharp with Her Majesty's Household for London.'

So finally they were going – to return in the spring, of course, but leaving the castle free of fear, and Sir Thomas would certainly go with them. This left only Upper and Lower housekeepers in power, with someone called Security and a policeman . . .

'Get on with your work, all of you. Morag, go to the Dairy and tell Janet to await my orders on eggs, butter and cream . . .'

Oh, it would be different tomorrow – if it weren't for Sheena and her tricks. But surely in time Mrs. Newlands, who was no fool, would catch her out in mischief and lies.

We should all be happy that they're going, Linty thought, but no one looked it. The queer thing was that no one spoke unless she was spoken to, as if there was a funeral for the afternoon. Only Sheena raised her voice in some question to Mrs. Newlands, pattering after her from pantry to pantry, learning where each set of dishes was. But later she hooded her hair for a dash to the Dairy.

'Well,' said Mr. Duff, as the door closed behind her, 'tomorrow night they can call it dinner if they like, but it's High Tea until Macose is back.'

'Provincial,' said Monsieur Macose, but in the old teasing kind of way as if they were friends underneath. Gossip had it that they really didn't fight at all but played at it, and that at night in their quarters they played chess and drank claret. 'You will miss me, friend. Who but I taught you the croissants you call "butteries"? How to marry a potato with a turnip? How to start a soup from a sauté?'

'Now, gentlemen,' Mrs. Newlands said, but smiling. 'If either of you can boil water, it's time for tea.'

Or, for Linty, a free fifteen minutes. Johnny would be in the stables, so she said, 'Ma'am, may I go out?'

'In this rain?'

'Please.'

A shrug that meant 'Go, then,' and she went to the hook and grabbed her shawl.

It wasn't far through the inner courtyard and around. She found Johnny in the harness room and he came forward, away from the other men, wiping his hands on the leather of his pockets.

'I had to see you,' she whispered. 'It's been an awful day ... that Sheena ...'

'Och, she'll settle in. Dinna fash yourself.'

'But I can't go through another day if she—'

'It's been a foul day all round. The Queen in a mood because of the weather, coming out like a spoilt bairn with nothing to do but hang around and ask about Milly, as if she could hurry the birth. Then she decides to leave for London with no notice to her packers but these few hours. Now she says she wants a Ghillies' Ball tonight and the barn cleared out. Then a note comes down she'll use the ballroom after all. And *you* complain.'

She whirled around and left him so quickly he had only time to call her name before she was away, furious because he had lost understanding, but astonished too, as if God had. Back in the Kitchen she saw a footman writing something on the blackboard, and then his announcement for those who couldn't read:

'Tonight. Ten o'clock. Ghillies' Ball. Prepare: One hundred dozen meat pies ...'

The little, crusty minced beef and mutton pies, gallons of pickled onions – the rest left to the Master of Cellars. Mrs. Newlands had no need to declare the Kitchen in a state of emergency. Linty forgot Sheena in the rush to do her part, first chopping onions, then rolling and shaping the pastry, and not a sound around but the shoveling of coal in the ovens or the whish of poured salt in the buckets of meat. The Queen spoiled? No – cruel, to dump this whim on tired people near the end of the day. They would miss their dinner because there were three others to prepare as well as the pies, and it would be a marvel if Duff and Macose and their assistants could manage.

'When you're so tired,' Jenny said, peeling pot after pot of dinner vegetables, 'it's all a kind of blur.'

At nine o'clock the day blurred to an end, with only a quick pie and a cup of tea before late staff took over. Mrs. Newlands murmured something about eightpence extra for them all and she knew they'd all enjoy the Ball after they'd freshened up.

Linty waited until Sheena had gone before she ventured out with Jenny and Elspeth, the thin rain wakening her from the steam of hours. They all took different directions home and had parted in the courtyard when Ian Wyness came out from Upper entrance.

'Will you come to the Ball with me, Linty?'

Johnny hadn't asked; besides, he'd probably be Master of Revels. A fine time to pay back indifference by flirting the night long, but she said, 'Ian, I'm that tired – you take some-one else.'

'I'll take you home,' he said.

He was understanding, and silent, except for saying that Sir Thomas had told him any pupil servants not now dismissed were considered as staff. 'So we are safe. I thought you'd like to know.'

'Aye. Safe? We'll talk at home.'

Jean and Torquil were above stairs as honeymooners should be. They called out welcome, and told them to finish the stew.

Ian hung her wet cloak on the hook, stirred up the fire and then removed his own cloak, spreading her shawl to dry on the inglenook seat. He was in the kilt, dressed for the Ball, each sideburn glossy-dark from pomade, so smoothly shaven you might take him for gentry, and his long hands so nice. Handsome except for that forehead beginning to want hair. Handsome and kind, because he sat her down on the woolly-covered mattress they called a 'couch' and made her tea.

'You're more than tired,' he said.

So she told him about Sheena. 'I've never hurt her – but she's wild to hurt me. I said to Johnny long ago, when she was a wee girl, that she was daft about him, but he wouldn't have it.'

'Even a little girl can love like a woman. Is she simple?'

'I never thought so. No, I'd say she's clever after what she did today, setting us all on edge. I think she's a witch.'

He didn't laugh as Johnny would have. 'There are people like that, not witches but evil, poisoning clean air. Your

97

housekeeper will find that if she's any sense.'

'But what do I do until she does – if she does?'

He came to sit beside her on the rug. 'In the Bible it says "Resist not Evil." Did you ever hear that, and wonder?'

'I never heard.'

'Stand naturally, and let it go over you like a big wave, bending as it strikes. Just take it calmly. The thing is, you're not relaxed, and so she makes impact. Do you see?'

Maybe she did. 'Just ignore her?'

'Aye.'

'But with Sheena, I'm afraid, *afraid*.'

'See that she doesn't know it. Are you afraid this minute?'

'No. Because you're here, and talking and explaining how to be.'

'I'll always be here when you need me.'

Silence, and the shadows pushed around the ceiling by the firelight.

She wished she could shed her weariness, change from her crumpled best dress and go to the Ball. But there was no strength in her and Ian knew it. He asked where the blankets were. He'd cover her and leave her to sleep.

He left her so quietly that she didn't hear the door close, only the stir of turf as it crumbled and the pat of rain on the thatch. Sometime during the night she had a dream of Sheena clawing at her face, and she called out, 'Ian!' which was strange, when it should have been Johnny.

All the staff lined up that morning to cheer off the Royal Family, in a din of barking dogs and pipers and Duncan shooting off guns that shied the carriage horses, and caused the Prince to signal a stop to it. The Queen, in a gown of Balmoral satin and a gray cloak, looked sulky. The sun had come too late and everyone knew she hated to leave – or so she had said.

Spoiled child, Linty thought. If I were Queen I'd smile, even if I was going back to my duties, just as I'll summon a smile at my own chores because there's my living to make. *She* doesn't have to clear up the mess after the Ball. Instead she will have a lovely ride, cushioned on velvet, to a yacht.

The Queen nodded curtly to the few remaining Uppers, to Mrs. Newlands. The ghillies came forward, bonnets in hand. She looked at Johnny and smiled, and said something, and smiled again at his reply.

'What was it?' Linty asked him at their long-delayed breakfast, when she sat closest to him of the women at table.

'Och, she just said goodbye in Gaelic.'

'And called you "Mr. Brown"?'

'Of course not. It's been "Brown" for months.' He poured milk on his porridge. 'I stopped by last night.'

'What?'

'You were asleep. I just poked my head in and left. It was about three.'

So he had cared enough to take the walk, to see to her, to hope for a talk. Never mind Sheena glaring down the table. She would take Ian's advice. Yesterday had been daft; today she was herself again.

And so it was, because Sheena was put to the clean-up of the Ball with other Lowers, and Kitchen relaxed because Mrs. Newlands had left off her corsets and bulged a little and ordered elevenses for everyone like a celebration. Aye, and it was back to Dinner mid-day, and High Tea at six, and only two of each for Mr. Duff to cook, and him so joyful he made a little Scots flag of sugar and planted it in a tea cake at four.

A wonderful day, and somehow Sheena back from Upper made no difference, as if a wasp is there but you don't really notice. Then Upper came down (well, two footmen) to linger a moment and gossip about what a shambles it was in some ladies' and gentlemen's rooms – discarded paint pots (if Her Majesty knew *that*!) and cigar butts in the fireplaces, and empty bottles under beds. Well, the gentry were only human, weren't they, and some cooped up for days on Her Majesty's order because she was afraid they'd mate in the garden, when it would have been easier right here, except they were English. Oh, such *lovely* gossip, like a dresser overhearing a Duchess say, 'It's a wonder our line's extant; my mother on her wedding night asked my father to kneel by the bed and ask God's forgiveness, and hers, for what he was about to do.'

'I couldn't have done it then,' Duff said, and the idea of him with a Duchess got him teased 'till the end of the day. Yes, a good day, with only one little flaw at the end, when Linty found Ian waiting to walk her home and had to say to him, 'I promised the evening to Johnny.'

Jean and Torquil greeted him but went upstairs to their own hearth. He took his favorite place on the rug and was quiet so long that Linty was sure he had something important to say.

'God, I feel sorry for him.'

'Who, Johnny?'

'The Prince. Working himself to death here on "holiday." What will it be like back in London? And no matter how hard he tries, he can't make a dent in the people.'

He had tried, Johnny said, because he wanted to be popular for the Queen's sake. That was why he had the idea for a big exhibition at the Crystal Palace in London in '51 and brought together all the finest things in Britain – paintings, silver, and new things, like a submarine-boat even. People came from all over the world to marvel; but despite the work he put into it, the people still thought of him as that German puff. 'He isn't!' Johnny said in a kind of rage. 'Clever she may be, but he's her very backbone. The light burned in his study until all hours when hers was out long since. She should start learning now to stand on her own feet, because when he goes . . .'

'Is he going somewhere, then?'

'Not too soon,' Johnny said softly, looking into the fire. 'But yes, too soon. He's tired out. And royal stud as well.'

'Johnny, what a thing to say! As if he was a farm animal!'

He went on talking as though he hadn't heard her. 'Nobody knows that man's torments or maybe ever will, he being so strict with himself. They say he doesn't smile. Why the hell should he? Public smiles would freeze on his face, and him only wanting a little sport and rest to be the ghost of himself?'

'Does he love her?' she asked softly.

'He will die for her – if that's love. But not as a hero – as a worker bee to a queen.' He turned from the fire and looked at her. 'Now, what's wrong with you? Fretting over that Sheena?'

'No. It's what you said about the Prince.'

He shook his head and the red waves were ambered by firelight. 'Och, I'm glad he shot his ptarmigan; it's little enough ... What's in the larder, Linty?'

Like old times, him always hungry; and because she and Torquil were both at work, a nice meat stew to heat. But she was puzzled about Johnny, telling her just so much, then drawing a cloak on his talk. Even the whisky later didn't loosen his tongue. She said, 'It's a fine new flask.'

Red morocco leather with two golden letters on it – J.B.

'Was that a gift, Johnny?'

From Her?

'I'm well paid,' he said, and smiled.

But he couldn't have bought such a case from Braemar or Ballater, and he'd not been in Aberdeen for years. It must mean that she approved of his drinking, perhaps had shared it; yet she was so almighty stern with her own guests that they had to hide their bottles under the bed.

'Johnny,' she said, 'I don't seem to know you any more.'

And as he put down the flask, listening, she wanted to say: Why are you here and what is it you want from me, because it's a long time since we were children together. I am twenty-five years old and I need a life with bairns, like other women.

Johnny Brown, she thought, you don't play with human souls, not you – kind and generous and concerned about hurt animals. What about me, speared but not taken? Do you not care at all that Ian is paying me so much attention?

She wondered what he would have replied, but just then thunder grumbled along the hills and seemed to shake the cottage, and the rain came down. 'My God,' he said, getting up and peering at the window, 'there's holes Torquil didn't see. Now, get a pan and then rags and I'll see what I can do ...'

There he was, behaving like a husband again.

'She's got great plans for improving tenants' cottages,' he said. 'New thatch, new timber. When spring comes just see what she'll do.'

She, spoken like God. Furious, Linty said, 'We're not tenants! We own this cottage clear! She'll do nothing for us!'

'She will if I ask.'

He turned from the window sill, wiping his hands on a rag. 'There's things I'd like to say that I can't. You'd think I was fou, or bragging. But I've things to teach the Queen, in my way, and she's eager to learn.'

'Books – you?'

'Did I say books?' He was angry now. 'I shouldn't have spoken. Why must you push so, Linty?'

That did it – the old, old accusation. She snatched his flask from the table and hurled it into the fire, hearing the shatter of glass on wood, seeing the fine leather curl and darken and die.

'I am pushing now,' she said, too furious to care about the anger she had aroused in him. 'I am pushing you out of here, for good and all! Keep your damn secrets. Go to London, Windsor, Osborne. Go to hell! Just keep out of my way!'

A step on the stairs and Torquil called, 'Linty?'

She whirled. 'Go away, Torquil, this is between me and Johnny. I need no help.' Now she faced Johnny again. 'Get out. Now. Fast.' She went to the door and flung it open to the rain.

An odd thing: she thought he sighed as he went past her, and walked almost like an old man, as if part of his life was over – as it was. No more coming here as he pleased, sure of warmth and welcome, of solace. He would remember, not the days they had spent together since childhood, but the smell of burning leather and her shrill voice.

Of course they would meet at Castle meals, but the table was large and they need not speak. And when that was noticed, why, folk had more important gossip after the speculation died.

When he had left, closing the door quietly, Linty thought: If I were keeping a journal I would say, if I could write, *I died tonight.*

Chapter Three

There was no asking or seeking of forgiveness. It came about at High Tea next day when Linty, serving, passed seed cakes to Mrs. Newlands. Sheena joggled her elbow. The cakes flew to the floor.

'Of all the clumsy—'

'No, Mrs. Newlands,' Johnny said from his end of the table. 'Sheena tripped her arm.'

'Aye,' said Duncan, 'I saw it too.'

'It's true, Ma'am,' Elspeth said, picking up the cakes.

'I'll get more,' Linty said, and went into the kitchen, so full of gratitude for Johnny's speaking up for her that she wanted to cry. Rejoining them, it wasn't seeing Sheena sulking under Mrs. Newlands' coldness that calmed her, but hearing Johnny say, 'I've a thing or two to say to you, Sheena, when the work's over.'

'Mr. Brown, you do not take upon yourself the discipline of my servants—'

'No, ma'am. This is not a Kitchen matter.'

Since the corridors were banned to them there was no other way out for Sheena, but the door that led to the courtyard. She went out through this door, looking defiant; nobody had spoken to her since tea.

In pairs or threes the other girls left, until finally Mrs. Newlands locked the cupboards and the tea chest and extinguished the lamps. For a moment she and Linty stood at the window, watching the full moon beyond the tall pines. Mrs. Newlands said, 'What does he have against Sheena?'

'It's not right to tattle, Ma'am. I think it's private, as he said.'

'I won't have lovers' squabbles brought out at table.'

Let her think that, then, though how could she have got it so twisted?

'You'd better go. You've oil?'

'Yes, Ma'am.'

She picked up her lantern in the corner, but she needed no light, for the moon was full. Outside, the smell of autumn came in a gust of sweet plants dying and flowers and wet leaves. Torquil's trees – or so she called them – were like spice after the long rain. She came into the gardens and Johnny was waiting.

He opened his arms and she went into them, crushed close, close, and not a word said. He kissed her and she felt his tongue for the first time, tasting of tobacco, and met it with her own, and she was like a drowning woman.

'I love you,' she said, lips muffled against his beard.

'No matter what?'

'No matter what.'

'I'm not fair ... it may be a long time to wait.'

'I'll wait.'

He was stronger, wiser than she. Had they gone to her cottage, she'd have bedded with him gladly. But, his arm around her, her lantern in his hand, he took the road to the Inver Inn, where there were people and safety.

'Sheena?' she asked finally, on the way home.

'She will not fret you again.' He said it, not bragging, just stating a fact, 'She had a kind of love, I think. I had to kill it.'

It was the darkening of the year, and she had to tell Ian Wyness that he could be only a friend. He should find another woman – and wasn't that Margaret upstairs pretty? Och, aye, very pretty. But ... was Linty promised to Johnny?'

'Aye.'

No ring, no plans, just a long time to wait, and she knew it had something to do with the Queen, his being in permanent service. She might have commanded that he shouldn't marry, for some reason, Johnny being unable to say so, or too proud to admit he'd had to take such an order from a woman. Or perhaps the Prince had commanded, though it was all such a mystery why a ghillie and a maid shouldn't marry, and the family away for months.

Torquil saw it differently, 'It's something in Johnny says "wait." So, wait.'

But if her body longed for his, what of his own needs? Some wench at the farm whom he didn't care about, perhaps? A visit to that widow in Braemar or the merry house in Aboyne? You heard these things of other men but you didn't shudder because it was part of life; it wasn't love, any more than the coupling of animals. So suspicion was snuffed like a candle.

Only a tiny stub glimmered through the winter when she was overtired or restless in the night: that no other woman mattered to him – except Victoria.

Another spring, and the Queen bending to touch a puppy, reaching to tilt a white cherry blossom, watching the lambs snowflake the fields. Its snowcap melted from Lochnagar and the streams were in spate, rushing towards the Dee. *Fishing Picnic for Six Persons* went up on the Kitchen blackboard, and so meal was provided for the fish to be rolled in, and butter and bread, and salads and sweets, and the makings of tea.

Johnny knew calm streams and secret places – the eerie rain-forest on Farquharson land, a dark cathedral of mosses and tall pines that never saw the sun. And the Queen would climb to remote heights in mud-slippery shoes, sure of Johnny's care of her, rewarded by the sight of eagles. Fifteen-year-old Bertie – out of his sailor-suits and into the kilt – accompanied his father on shoots. 'But,' Johnny said, 'there's no fun in it. It's all too strict, like a lesson, and he already knows the rules. Poor little bugger. Just now allowed to order his own food and making the most of it.'

That spring Prince Albert made the most of his passion for improving things. He had derelict cottages razed and new ones begun, farm offices put up, roofs mended or thatched, fences repaired, wells cleaned. Dr. Robertson, as factor, was in and out of shielings and huts, and the Queen set about nosing into every cranny where she might find an old lady to give a red flannel petticoat or a warm shift. You couldn't believe the tales you heard of her, walking into Mrs. Grant's, accepting tea, and putting a bundle of Bertie's wet socks to dry by the fire. Advising young Mrs. Menzies how to raise her bairns – and who should know better, with eight of her own? Except that Johnny said she only did her duty by the children – damned if he didn't think they bored her much of the time. It was Prince Albert who took the brunt of them, though sometimes she'd go out with them at twilight and hunt moths or play fox and geese on the lawn.

So little changed during the months, the years. Albert was created Prince Consort, but to Crathie folk he had always been that. The proud little telegraph man rode from Ballater with news of the Indian Mutiny. Miss Florence Nightingale visited, shocking everyone but the Queen with her short hair. And more and more the Queen was alone at night, Albert closeted with his equerry-secretary, Colonel Ponsonby.

But there would be Ghillies' Balls. It seemed the Queen never tired of them, and now, for the first time, Linty saw Upstairs – the vast ballroom.

Battle-axes, stagsheads, a huge fireplace backed in carved oak, chandeliers winking hundreds of candles from the beamed ceiling. She had thought it would be gold and white and ladylike, but no; Johnny said it was more like a fine hunting lodge, or a baronial hall. The Queen, dressed in white tulle and pearls with a wreath on her hair, danced first with Prince Albert, he not so good at the reel as she but as if his mind was far away beyond her bare shoulder; and then Johnny was summoned, and he danced with her. Linty, with Grant, joined in with all the others – ladies, gentlemen, Upper and Lower, all in the skirl of the pipes.

It was hot, with too many people – and by the look of them, some hating it. Ladies in satin, a rainbow of color in gold and pink and crimson, lace skirts whirling, jewels sparkling – faces grim as they flung in and out among the ghillie partners, the foresters, the footmen, the stiff black-coated gentlemen who took the rough, red hands of the maids in turn. Flowers fell from hair and button-holes, were stomped underfoot, and beyond the wild cries of the ghillies, the howl of the castle dogs.

It was all wrong, Linty thought, smiling at Ian during a whirl. It was all wrong because who could be herself – but the Queen? It was a great nonsense to think you could mingle with Upper or Lower without fear, unless there was strong drink in you. And what had those poor gentry had but a little wine at dinner? Even the gentlemen were hurried from their port after fifteen minutes, because She didn't approve of those long sessions away from the ladies, and the temptation to smoke.

Yet She was so free tonight you'd never think she was nearly forty – plump, aye, but with such smooth skin and hair still gold-brown – like a feather passing among the men, then coming to rest by the tired Prince and smiling and looking up to him on tiptoe, like a child for approval. But oh, he was more like a tall white statue, unable to bend except for a bow stiff from his shoulders.

She stayed on until after midnight, after he had gone away, taking other gentlemen – perhaps to sit in his study and figure out the world. Linty said to Johnny on the way home: 'Look, his light still burns.'

'Are you thinking he does all the work, then?'

'Isn't it true?'

'No. The work on paper, yes, but it's She who has the cleverness to know when to reject, to accept, when to stand firm. Prime Ministers are foisted on her and she must work with them willy-nilly with three duties – to warn, to encourage, to advise. She can't mix in politics, and when things go wrong she's blamed, and when things go right it's the Minister takes the credit. I'd not like the tightrope *she* walks, and Europe a chasm.'

'But she has the Prince to help.'

'Aye, but she must learn not to lean. If ever there was a time—' His voice trailed off. 'I think there'll be frost tonight.' As time went by it seemed that Johnny was getting bolder. He spoke his mind to young Bertie and took no nonsense from him. 'So now he detests me plain and has some respect.' But it was upsetting to hear people criticize Johnny for his sharp tongue – ordering an Upper footman not to fiddle about his stables: didn't *he* know the Queen's favorite saddle? But he never minded when her skirts and boots were brought him to be cleaned of mud. And he loved what she called 'The Great Expeditions' into the wilderness that lasted overnight.

From one of them he came back chuckling. 'The Queen was fair pissed off at me and Grant . . .'

Well, it had been a strenuous trip, the Queen and the Prince with General Grey and Lady Churchill in the sociable to start, but then they'd had to change the ponies at the Linn of Dee, and finally, bogged, all had had to walk. They eventually got to a coaching inn at Granton. ' "Now remember, Brown, we are travelling incognito as Lord and Lady Churchill and party," she told me as I handed her down, and I said, "Yes, Your Majesty" and a groom heard so she was saluted. Well! That wasna so bad, but when they got to their rooms she asked the maid to come and tell me and Grant to serve at table. Well, now, how could we? We were already well into our bottles in the Commercial Room. We are *not* indoor servants. So I sent the maid back to say we were too bashful.'

'You didn't!' Linty said, fearful for him.

'Next day she said, before we started out again, that she didna like strangers serving and peeping, and that we should have served the breakfast too. I just said, "Grant and I were bashful, Ma'am," and she looked at me very stern, but with a kind of twinkle and said, "I never heard intoxicated called bashful before, but I suppose it's a prettier word," and then she turned away. I thought she wouldna speak to us again, but just the orders for the rest of the journey. Only an hour later she was so merry, asking me to point out the different glens. Why, she'd forgotten her anger like a child does when it has a new thrill, which is new mountains.'

She doesn't want to lose you, Linty thought; no matter what you do or say, she won't lose you. 'And Prince Albert? Didn't he chide?'

Johnny shook his head. 'He's too tired a man to chide these days. Bertie's a great disappointment to him, I think – just the opposite of himself, you see, smoking cigars in school and wearing slang clothes. I can't abide the lad, but he shouldn't be tattled on. Damn spies, I say – he's a right to his own young life.' He paused. 'I told her Oxford would straighten him out.'

'*You* said that?'

'There's lots we talk about when I'm leading her pony on the narrow trails. If it's a thick haar I think she likes the sound of a voice, just trusting to me and the pony and listening to talk. I've been educating her in what happened to our people, is still happening in the far hills.'

Yes, the homeless ones and those in the grind of poverty, little better off than those of Clearance times. Torquil had seen them in his wanderings and blessed them, for there was nothing else to do but help with the burying. 'What I said to her of the old days that started it all: the sheep coming. She wanted instances; I didn't spare her. I told her of the old woman, ninety-nine she was, alone in her hut when the bastards came for the land. "She's lived long enough," they said, and set fire to her hut. And the old man whose mill was spared, living in hiding and licking the grain-dust from the boards. Such a rage got in the Queen, it's made her more human to know all this. She said, "Brown, I can't stand the 'fashionables'" – that's the English who sit about the gaming tables and do nothing else with their money earned from all the misery up here. She said, "They resent it that I don't ask them up for shoots, but this is my home and I shan't." I think she suffers in London, Linty, where she can't avoid the fashionable without causing hard feelings, since it's politics come in.'

I am beginning to like her a little, Linty thought. At least I'm not jealous now. When we marry . . .

But come to think of it – and the stardust of that night gone a little – Johnny hadn't said one word about marriage, had he?

In March the telegraph brought news of the death of the Queen's mother, the Duchess of Kent. Mrs. Newlands waited for word as to what to do – the staff should pay some respect. But Sir Thomas merely wrote, 'Wear black, and see that all are in church Sunday.'

Linty had never seen the duchess, but some had served her

at nearby Abergeldie where she sometimes visited — a pleasant, sweet-faced old lady, fond of music and dogs and whist. Johnny had been to a couple of dances she had given for the staff, but to Linty it seemed odd that he took the death hard. Alone with her in the kirkyard, he said, 'I'd like to do something for the comfort of the Queen — this will be the first, terrible rip.'

'Because she loved her mother so?'

He kicked at a stone. 'No! She had a terrible time getting out of her domination, to try to be Queen on her own at 18 — hard enough, I'd say, without a mother clawing her back to the cradle. But she'll be full of remorse. I think she loved and hated — like lots of us.'

'Did she talk of her mother to *you*?'

'Not like I'm telling you it. But things like, "Brown, see if the Duchess would like to drive out today, but tell her I'm in my work," (when there she was preparing to ride with Grant), or "Inform the Duchess I am too busy to—" Oh, the excuses she had. And then the guilt — sending over strawberries, and little notes, and promises to see her, which I'll say she kept. But if her mother hadn't been her mother — no love, believe me.'

'Then she'll not mourn, really.'

'You dinna ken the Queen. She'll do, and feel, what's expected. I shouldn't be surprised she was sick over this.'

Sheena came around the side of the church with Michael Wright, the Bush shepherd. Ignoring Linty, she said, 'Johnny, we're just betrothed. You'll come to our wedding in three weeks Sunday?'

It was a queer way she said it — defiantly, triumphantly, not smiling like a girl should be with the banns posted. And that Michael wasn't bad looking: a dark foxy face but with fine blue eyes, and known for a hard worker, with a hut of his own.

'You'd not have a wedding so soon in the Queen's mourning?' Johnny asked.

'What's it to do with us?' Michael asked.

'Respect,' Johnny said, 'I'm surprised Mr. Anderson agreed.'

'Well, he did,' Michael said.

And Linty knew why. Sheena seemed slender as always —
from the waist up. At first, hidden by the wide kitchen aprons,
she hadn't noticed the swelling or the thickening waist and
breasts.

Perhaps it would settle her, Linty thought, take the wild-
ness from her. Except for kitchen talk like, 'Here's turnips,' or
'Mrs. Newlands wants gooseberries picked,' she never spoke
to Linty if she could help it.

'Three weeks Sunday I dinna ken where I'll be,' Johnny said,
'but I wish you well.'

'Well!' Linty said in surprise and relief as Sheena and
Michael walked away down the hill, 'she's just in time before
the gossip . . .'

Only Johnny wasn't listening. Because he said, 'She'll have a
rare hard time of it this summer. I wish she could come home
where she belongs.'

And of course he was miles away in thought about the
Queen. Like a parent fretting about a child? Well, it was best
to think of it that way.

He took from his sporran a little dried wisp of white
heather. 'I gave it to her before she left to bring her luck, and
she gave me this half back for my own.'

On a June morning, when Linty went to the kitchen as usual,
Mrs. Newlands said, 'You're going to Upper for training.'

'Oh *no*!'

'You should be grateful. It means more money, and a nice
black dress and apron.'

'But why me, Ma'am?'

'Sir Thomas wrote and asked me to choose, and you're deft
now. I'll take you up to Mrs. Hayes.'

Up, up carved staircases, but in a different part from
the ballroom. In the corridors all the wallpapers were tartan
printed, and also the soft carpets they walked on. Everything
smelled of polish. They passed rows of linen cupboards, open
at the moment for the maids to be sprinkling rose leaves in —
such neat maids, with their hair up, coiled fancy, in those
black dresses with aprons that sizzled with starch. She could
never look that way, with her hair always crowding her cap —

and *their* caps sat their hair like ruffly butterflies.

Mrs. Hayes' office was all white except for a tartan carpet and window hangings. As she rose from her desk and nodded to Mrs. Newlands, Linty saw that she was dressed like a lady, in black bombazine with maybe six petticoats underneath. Dozens of keys corded her waist. Her face was flat and pale under a fringe of gray hair. Her eyes were small and cool and gray, and when she spoke Linty knew she was English because of the crispness.

'Linda,' she said, repeating the name. 'I must say that's odd. Anyway, if you suit you shall be called Clarke. Do you know what spotless means?'

'Yes, Ma'am. Absolutely clean.'

An approving nod. 'Well, think of that as your goal – and keep yourself that way. You will wear black aprons for fireplace work, white for chambermaid. You're fortunate now that no guest is in residence so you may practice in the various rooms and get to know them. Your meals, as you know, will be taken downstairs on second shift. Are there any questions?'

'Is there a chimney sweep, Ma'am?'

Both housekeepers laughed. 'Your work is to *polish* the fireplaces. The lower footmen bring up the logs and hot water.' Mrs. Hayes pulled on a bell rope. 'Stewart will show you today's work, and give you your clothes.'

Well, as she told Jean and Torquil that night, it wasn't so much heavy work as damnably delicate work. She'd seen only a few public rooms so far, but her head was dizzy with Balmoral tartans and Royal Stewart tartans, Highland targets on the walls, and everywhere stag heads and great masses of curlicued oak – chairs and tables, loveseats, screens, cabinets and desks, in that twisty oak that was so hard to polish because dust caught in the niches. To get a piece of furniture really clean would take you half an hour, using cotton wool cones to get into the dirt. Then the wallpaper had to be brushed – it was tartan or thistle pattern everywhere – using a ladder. The footmen did the cornices and polished the candelabra and chandeliers, but you never worked in the same room with them at the same time, so she only saw Ian Wyness at meals.

'It's like they don't trust men and maids in the same room

together,' she said to Jean. 'My God, I had a great mantelpiece clock to dust and polish and had to move it to clean the marble under, and called to Stewart to ask what to do. She said leave it for a footman. And will you believe it, there's one uppity footman does *nothing* but fill the ink-wells when the family's here, and see to the candles? Right now I'm sort of a roving maid, Stewart tells me — she's nice — learning it all; but later I'll be "positioned" if I suit.'

'It must have been a wretched tea,' Jean said as Linty ate leftover venison from their meal. 'You're so hungry.'

'I was nervous, and at luncheon too. I'm the lowest of the low up there. I made the mistake of saying "Hello" to Ian, and I know he wanted to smile back but Mrs. Hayes was watching. He's Upper now; he'll be waiting on table to the royal family. We're not supposed to talk except like gentry: "May I pass you the parsley sauce?" It's supposed to be higher than "Can I?" And I shouldn't have said "Hello"; it's "Good day," or "Good evening." '

It all seemed very odd to Jean.

Linty explained. 'When later on some Duchess's maid comes to visit, or a Lord's valet, we're supposed to know how to act.'

'I'm glad I come home for meals,' Torquil said, 'or take my food box. The la-di-da would kill me.'

Jean giggled. 'Maybe it's part of the training if you have to speak to the Queen, Linty.'

That wasn't funny; as she'd known for years, the terror of working at Balmoral was the possibility of coming face to face with her or the Prince. Now she saw the alarm-system — bells on each landing. There had been practice, as Ian said, almost like lifeboat drill. At the time the Queen left whatever room she was in, a bell rang four times, pressed by a dresser or a lady-in-waiting. The staff scurried for cover. It was easy enough now, with all the empty bedchambers, but when they were full you dashed for the linen rooms or the broom closets or, yes, even the men's privy if the women's wasn't handy. Just anywhere to be out of sight.

'And what would happen if we were caught?' Linty asked Stewart.

'I don't rightly know. I don't like to think about it.'

Chambermaiding wouldn't be so hard except for all the knicknacks to dust in every bedroom, the prints and pictures that almost covered the walls, the tiny china ornaments that crowded every table. Lovely little things of purple glass, butterfly paperweights, and every kind of vase you could imagine, to be filled with late roses when the Queen came in autumn. There was talk that she had had a 'breakdown' because of her mother's death and didn't go out on her public duties, that Dr. Jenner was with her as if she'd been dying herself, and other doctors called in. Somehow, in all the secrecy that was like a web about the family, news came that Prince Bertie, visiting Germany, might seek the hand of the Danish Princess Alexandra. Those things, Johnny said, were what the poor Queen had to worry about when she should be here enjoying the September sunshine.

But she didn't come. The household, poised for news, received none. It wasn't until more than a year later that Johnny learned, from the Queen herself, that Bertie had got into a scandalous scrape in Ireland when some of his Guards friends had smuggled a young actress into his quarters. The matter was hushed up but the Queen could not forgive him. 'His very presence was abhorrent to me.' And, in this same autumn of her first deep mourning, she was worrying about whether to join the Confederates in the American War.

The household didn't know that. It could rejoice in its freedom, restricted, of course, by keeping the castle cleansed and warmed in case the family came. The eighteen ponies were exercised, the guns cleaned and ready. But when the first frosts bit the hills, and snow fell, Johnny said, 'I knew somehow she wouldna come. There's a terrible dark on her.'

Linty was sharing a dram in the warm stable, sitting on straw at the end of the day. 'She'll get over her mother.'

He tapped his pipe ashes into a bucket. 'That was only the start. I can't tell you what's keeping her south, Linty, but she's in terrible fear. I think it's Prince Albert. I can almost ... see it is.'

So far across the cold mountains he could see, and even feel, because his voice had tears in it. 'It's a big silvery room she's in. All in black. The younger children are there, playing, and Bertie in uniform — handsome he is. She says she can't bear the sound of his voice, and tells him to go to his room. She puts her hands to her ears and motions him out like he was — the smell of rot. Only I think the rot is somewhere else, and my face is burning up, Christ, and my body!'

'Johnny, you're fou!' She jumped up and faced him, frightened, for his eyes held a queer shine. Gently, she shook him. 'Come out to the air.'

It was as if she'd awakened him from a bad dream. He blinked. 'What?' he asked. 'What's wrong?'

She wanted to say: You had some sort of fit. Instead, she said, 'How much have you had to drink today, Johnny?'

'Why, most of my bottle.' His eyes were natural now. 'Did you call me fou just now?'

'Aye.'

'On not even a *bottle*? Why, then?'

She could see he was sober. 'I think,' she said slowly, 'you sort of went to sleep on your feet and had a dream and talked in it.'

'What did I say?'

She repeated it and he shook his shaggy red head. 'That's the way it was,' he said, 'a kind of thought I must have said aloud.' Then, briskly, 'Come, let's see to the cat,' and led her to the far corner to bend beside the nest of rags and tell the young cat, softly in Gaelic, not to fret, her kittens would be safe. Strange, she thought as they bolted the barn and walked out into the snow, how he tends things — or needs to. But without a thought to fathering his own, and him nearly thirty-five.

Nor could she safely wait too long for children, as Jean reminded her. It was a shame, Jean said, that Johnny made her wait on and on. There seemed no good reason now, with the Queen likely not back until spring.

But as always Linty was too proud to ask.

Torquil stretched out by the fire and said, 'When a man wants to wait, he has reason deep in him. Just as I had to wander, he has to bide his time. And Linty has six, seven years yet.'

'But it's so unfair!' Jean said. 'The pleasure of bairns while you're young that he denies you.'

Jean, who did not seem able to have children, was happy just being married to Torquil, free from pain, able to do her chores with only just a ripple of a headache now and then. For Linty, children would have been a happiness, but as it was she shared so much with Johnny – except his bed. She did not yet belong to him.

And there was the Queen....

Oh, she respected her. She could see how, under her care, and the Prince's, things were so much better in Crathie. They had brought in machines and new ways of working the farms. You didn't hear of beggars on the roads, or leaky roofs, or cattle disease. You knew that every old woman in the farthest glen was snug (how much of this was Johnny's doing?); there was a library at Balmoral even, free to the people. The school now had two masters for different ages, and a separate privy for the boys and girls, not in the bushes as it used to be.

Aye, the Queen had been good to the parish, but as Linty got to know the Upper maids better and listened to their chatter during their free fifteen minutes, she learned that there was another side to Victoria. Visiting a library down south, the lady in charge had presented her young daughter to the Queen who, ignoring the deep curtsy, said, 'I am here to see the *library*,' and turned her back. Here, her guests had little fun unless they were asked on the shoots or permitted a pony, and she must approve beforehand whether a lady and gentleman might stroll together in the gardens. Worst of all for everyone was her selfishness at table. Just ask any Upper footman ...

For the Queen reckoned that one half hour was sufficient for dinner – aye, even a state dinner at Buckingham Palace. She raced through each course – gobbling – and you had to keep up with her or find yourself still with the fish when she, through with her dessert, was rising. After fifteen minutes she wanted the gentlemen back with the ladies, too, and they had to stand in the corridor – damn drafty it was – and not talk until talked to, and then all stiff conversation about the weather.

Johnny said the Queen could be a rare scream, though without knowing it. Knowing he'd a bit of education she'd asked him if he had read *Hamlet*. 'He was a Prince of Denmark,' she said, 'but I had no use for him at all – he *pottered*.'

As for young Bertie, all of Upper knew that his mother terrified him – too strict one minute, then sentimental about his curls, then ignoring him or saying how much brighter Princess Alice was. You couldn't but be glad the boy was at university and maybe to be married, for he must surely want his own household to be away from Mama; besides, Princess Alexandra was supposed to be beautiful.

By now Linty had learned to make the great beds just so, or at least the test bed in the blue room, which was considered the hardest to manage, being off in a corner. Chadwick, the butler, allowed her to see the fine china kept in Upper pantry, but no one but himself washed it, nor the silver, which was polished once a week. There was so much of it that it kept him busy for two whole days. He gave her little tips for the future: newspapers must always be ironed before given him to present to the royal pair; the lowly Boots must remove all shoelaces for ironing, which might be her task in the press-room. There was no knowing just where she would be 'positioned' so it was best to learn everything.

Mrs. Hayes, using the test blue room, brought in traveling bags, stood at the door and said, 'The Duchess of Atholl has just arrived. She is being greeted downstairs. What do you do?'

Die. Faint. 'I – oh – I move the luggage so she doesn't trip?'

'Good. Now?'

'I ring for hot water and light the fire?'

'Good.'

'Then I unpack?'

'*No!* Should she see the room strewn with garments? You wait. Then she appears. What do you say?'

'Nothing, until *she* says.'

'And then what?'

'I curtsy and say, "Your ladyship, I'm Clarke." '

'*No.* "Your Grace, I'm Clarke." '

117

It was then that Her Grace was supposed to say which of the cases should be unpacked first and what she'd be wearing for tea or dinner. Usually they wanted a bath first after the long, dirty journey, so she must ring for a footman to fill the tub down the corridor; and while the Duchess was bathing she would unpack the essentials and lay out the dress and undergarments and shoes. Every lady would have a jewel case, to be placed on the dressing table. It would always be looked after by the lady herself.

'And then?'

'The lady's own maid takes charge to dress her and do her hair. But you must know that *very* rarely a lady comes without a maid. In case it should happen, you will know about the unpacking and you would help her dress, but you are not expected to do hair.'

Oh, for the Kitchen again! The many bedrooms were familiar now, even to the creak of their doors or the way a curtain balked; but to think of them peopled was frightening. Never mind, the valets in training felt the same way only they said that their job was even worse, what with the bloody snobs swearing at them if things weren't just right. They said the higher the gentleman's rank the more he thought it manly to use bad language. Prince Albert, though, was different. Ian said it was because he was so sure he was a man.

Ian flirted with some of the girls but he was slow about taking up with anybody. Whenever possible he was near her, and she thought he did not discourage easily – and was sorry. One day during their fifteen minutes of freedom they stood together in the common room, by the window, apart from those who were having tea. He said, 'Sheena has quit work to have her baby.'

'I hope for good,' she said, 'I'd hate to have her sent up here for training.'

'Not likely. She hasn't plagued you lately?'

'No. But I feel the hate's still in her. It's not Michael she loves – it's Johnny.'

He said, 'Why aren't you marrying him, Linty?'

As if it were up to her! 'He's not ready.'

Ian said, 'Long love's a sad thing. I should know. I think we're two of a kind, you and I,' and left her abruptly.

That night in her cottage Johnny had a dark mood on him that the drink couldn't lift. What was wrong? He growled at her that why should anything be wrong? Couldn't a man be silent if he felt like it? Was he to turn somersaults and tell jokes? If she thought him dull company, he'd leave.

So she was quiet. Snow fell, slow and steady, and the wind rose. It would not be an easy walk tomorrow, across the drifts. At the window she could see the woodpile like a white hill. Lucky they had stacks in the indoor shed.

She thought of the quarters Johnny shared with Grant above the coach house. 'Will there be a fire in your room?'

'How the hell should I know? Do you want me to go and see?'

'Ah, Johnny, I just meant if Grant is out somewhere it will be a fearful cold thing getting to bed, after a cold walk. You could stay here.'

'No.' He got to his feet, took his heavy jacket from the hook and put it on. 'Goodnight.'

She handed him his lantern, opened the door against the push of the wind, and closed it as soon as he was through. At the window she saw him plodding through the snow, shoulders bent like an old man.

Torquil awakened Linty. 'Tea's ready. I'll walk you to the castle.' Usually he left for work an hour later than she for his winter chores in the greenhouses. 'You'd never get through those drifts on your own, Linty.'

The sky was black when they got outside, and they needed both their lanterns. Suddenly, from very far off, they heard the sound of bells.

Not sheepbells – deep bells, tolling. 'From Ballater Kirk,' Torquil said.

And now the nearby bells of their own kirk joined in. 'It's likely a bad fire,' Linty said.

They hurried on as best they could, plunging through the drifts, and finally reached the inner courtyard. The bells still tolled. Torquil left her and she ran upstairs to the common

119

room, where the maids were hanging their cloaks. They agreed, it must be a bad fire, midway between the two parishes, where new barns, all dry wood, were going up.

Then Mrs. Hayes came in. She stood just below a gas jet and its green shade made her face a terrible color. She said, 'We have had a telegram. Prince Albert is dead.'

He wouldn't have liked the way things went that day, Linty thought – except for the whole staff gathering in the dim-lit ballroom to pray for his departed soul, and for the Queen. Whatever you thought of her, it was terrible to lose your mother and your husband within ten months. He would have thought the prayers proper, but the household was so upset that nobody did their work except Duff and the kitchen staff.

Mrs. Hayes seemed all to pieces, not chiding the maids and footmen for gathering in the common room to wonder, to speculate. Some rumors had already seeped in from God knows where – that he'd been assassinated by the Chartists; that he'd taken a bullet meant for the Queen. It was only late in the day that the Reverend Anderson drove over and asked them all to assemble – again, in the ballroom. Linty stood beside Johnny. He must have forgotten the coffee grounds, for he stank of whisky.

'We shall have a special service for Prince Albert on Sunday.' Mr. Anderson paused, as if he was choked up. 'But our prayers mut be for Her Majesty and the family in their devastating loss. He died of the fever, at Windsor. That is all we know.'

He looked about at the black-clad servants, still in mourning for the Duchess, 'I think the Queen would wish the white aprons removed, and black ones put on. No one has told me what to do.' His voice cracked. 'Perhaps I am presumptuous to suggest what she would want, but those of you with children should dress them in black if you can – certainly not colors. My wife has suggested to me that he – the Prince Consort – was father to the realm, as the Queen is mother. Think of that and let it guide you. You are mourning a father.'

Linty glanced at Johnny and saw tears trickling down his cheeks. Some of the maids were sobbing quietly.

Mr. Anderson looked at the pipers in their Balmoral tartans. 'That is right for you, but with black jackets. We will want pibrochs on Sunday, outside, after the service. Now, we will pray.'

Poor man, he could scarcely get through it. Afterwards, the housekeepers took him into a parlor for tea. Johnny said, 'Linty, let's get out. There's no work today.'

She took her cloak and followed him downstairs and out into the dusk. He led her up the coach-house stairs to the room he shared with Grant. Whitewashed walls, two beds, two chairs – and the remains of a fire. He poked it up and added logs. 'Sit down,' he said, 'I'll get drink.'

And she needed it; she wasn't so much sad as stunned, or in some kind of dream. He brought her the mug and lay down, as he liked to, on the hearthrug. It was nice and new – or had been – in the Balmoral tartan; but his boots had dirtied it.

Johnny had turned away from her, looking into the fire, and she thought: The same mood is on him as last night. Only he wanted her here.

He said, after a sip of his drink, 'When I think the first time I saw him – a puff, I thought. I learned better. He was more than half of her. *More than half.* So what's to happen to her?'

'Why,' Linty said, but timidly, 'she was born and raised to be Queen, wasn't she?'

'He raised her from the age of 21, when they married. He made her like a sculptor moulds clay. She could fall apart now. Everything smashed, she could fall apart.'

That was just drink-talk, but she listened because he seemed to know.

'She's not what you'd call a steady woman, Linty. The inheritance isn't good, not good at all. Madness is too close in the line. George Third. She knows; she must know. And what they called a breakdown when her mother died; now this. It's not good.'

How much he must have had to drink today, repeating himself. He turned to her and she saw the tears streaming down his face, and came down from her chair to hold him close. His arms around her nearly knocked out her breath. His kiss tasted of the salt from his eyes. He pulled up her skirts with one hand, flung away the mug with the other, and ripped open her waist as if the buttons weren't even there.

'Oh, my God,' she said, 'not here, Johnny. Grant—'

But it was the hell with Grant.

It was the hell with everything she'd ever thought was love. It was a terrible pain, and blood on the rug, and no softness or kisses, or lovely words, or promises. How often she'd thought of it – in her own herb-sweet bed, by the light of the moon, or candles set by the door, and she in her white lawn gown with the blue ribbons. But this – on the hard floor, her clothes and herself ripped and then not a word as he turned off her and lay beside her . . .

She sat up. You couldn't call it rape, because she hadn't tried to free herself. She had done as he wanted. Like a cow to a bull. Oh, she'd not forgive this. If he'd have said, 'I love you,' and kissed her, it would have been all right.

He turned, leaned on an elbow and looked up at her. 'I should say I'm sorry.'

She stood up, the pain still in her. 'You'd better mop up before Grant comes in.' There was a mirror in the corner over a washbasin and she pulled a comb from the clutter of razors there. She tidied her hair, found her cap on the floor, and put it on. She reached for buttons that had rolled off and gathered them up into her pocket. 'Mop up the blood,' she said. And then, hard and vicious, 'Grant'll think you stuck a pig up here.'

He sprang to his feet. 'How dare you say a thing like that?'

'Because I'm not caring what I say. You're not God.'

Oh, but he had been the very height of her world, and someone to trust even beyond loving. Like God, he'd had mysterious ways, like keeping her his without promising marriage. But she'd believed in him.

She swirled on her cloak. 'Aye, you're tall. You can stand and bar the door to me and look down at me – but I'm out of you, out of anything you can say or do. Because you're dung.'

'Linty—l'

'Let me by.'

'Linty.' He blocked her way. 'I was out of my mind – I was that upset—'

'Do I care one good goddamn about the Prince and the Queen? Should I? Should I be used because *you're* that upset? Why don't you ride to Ballater and use that telegraph thing and tell her you're coming? But remember – a *lady* wants *kissing*.'

She slapped aside his hand, so sharply that her own was hurt. 'I'll never see you again. Och, aye, by chance, but never by meaning to. I'm not telling anyone why.'

He knelt and gathered her close, pillowing his head on her waist. Such an abject way for a big man to be, murmuring for her to forgive him, saying 'I love you' over and over, running little kisses along her cloak. When he stood up she couldn't leave his arms until thought of Grant pushed her away.

Johnny tended to the hearthrug with cold water, then turned it over. 'If you want to think it never happened, Linty, then it never did. I'll not touch you again until we marry.'

Even now she could not say, 'When will that be?' She only said, 'Get some sleep, Johnny. You'll be by tonight?'

'Aye,' he said, 'and sober. I shall never take another drink until after the darkening.'

Torquil asked, 'Where were you? I waited to bring you home.'

'Johnny was upset – I was with him.' She took the mug of tea Jean offered and sat down. She wouldn't reveal Johnny's roughness, but there were no secrets here and she wanted them to know. 'I lay with him,' she said, and smiled.

They didn't chide, they cuddled her, for this was an event in a woman's life, not a shame, because love was in it. After tea Torquil heated a big pot of water for a bath, and though the drafts in the shed were murderous, she felt like a bride afterwards in the warm blue dressing gown, blue ribbons in her hair and Jean's lavender water sprinkled on her skin. Blackberry wine was brought down from its stone crock and poured through muslin; it tasted of summer.

'I'm not sure he'll want to bed tonight,' she said, 'but you don't mind if he stays?'

Och, no – had they not been lovers? And if a baby started,

why so much better to hasten the marriage. That Johnny, Jean said, had wasted time enough.

'It's odd,' Torquil said, poking the apples that sputtered on the hearth, 'how the Queen has got some bee in her bonnet against men and women acting natural. I can remember when the clergy weren't all so set against such things. Right here in this parish babies were blessed to a couple that hadn't married, and no scandal any more than the lambs would be. But I ken big towns are different, and the Queen got her ideas from big towns, which are nasty.'

'She puts long skirts on the tables at the Castle,' Linty said, 'as if they were ladies' legs.'

'And she's birthed nine – with God knows how many tries!' Torquil shook his head. 'Is she a sham, I wonder – a hypocrite? Did she love the poor man or just use him?'

'She loved him.' Jean and Linty spoke together. Why, even in a crowd you could see the way she had looked at him, looked up to him.

'Do you know,' Torquil said, 'I think toward the last year here he was preparing to go. We never spoke much, of course – but once he knew I'd healed the old trees he would come out by himself and wander around as if he was meditating, paying no mind to me at all, touching the saplings. I'm not saying he was sick – I'm saying a great sadness was on him, and a tiredness. Once he made a little joke, or tried to, about the Japanese cherry. "That is not politics." '

'If he was sad,' Jean asked, 'why?'

'Because for all he tried, the country never took to him. You can do good and be good, but if you don't catch the people's imagination and are a foreigner to boot – it's no use.'

Johnny came in, tossed off his wet cloak and sat in the inglenook. 'There's a little more news,' he said. 'They're not saying just what kind of fever he had, but from the way it sounds – like my brothers and sisters had it – it was typhoid. All the close family got there in time. But it's all very secret the way the newspapers are about the state of the Queen – like a curtain drawn.'

'It should be,' Linty said, surprised that she could feel for

124

the Queen. 'Who should be peering and prying?'

'Right. But secrecy's not so good as a clear statement when folk wonder if she's ill too – or in her mind.'

'Rumors?' asked Torquil.

Johnny nodded. 'All this way from Windsor and we get the red spray as if a whale had died, but nobody tells us how *she* is.'

Jean said, 'There, now, Johnny – blackberry wine?'

'I'm not that drunk I'd drink lady-brew.' But he smiled at her as he uncapped his flask. 'I kept my promise, Linty – after the darkening.'

The apples were eaten, and cheese, and then Jean and Torquil went upstairs to their own hearth. Johnny beckoned Linty into the inglenook and she snuggled against him.

'I love you,' she said. 'And it's a new feeling that I belong to you, too.'

He said nothing. His silence grew long. She turned to look up at him.

'Did I say something wrong?'

'No living creature "belongs" to another. That's woman-shit.'

Furiously she moved away, pulled his cloak from the hook and threw it towards him. 'Get out! Go!'

'I'm sorry I used the word—'

'It's not the word, it's the thought behind it! It's the dead-cold way you said it! You'd think I wanted to *imprison* you – well, I don't. Because I don't want you.'

'Come back here, Linty, and stop lying.'

'Why should I? You ruined a lovely feeling I had – the belonging. I didn't say *you* belonged to *me*.'

He laughed and came out of the nook to pull down her hair and kiss her dizzy. He lifted her and carried her into the bedroom in the path of the firelight and teased her with lips and hands for a long time before he shed his clothes and locked himself into her.

Sleet cracked against the window. Far down the glen a dog barked, and the sound rejoined her to the world. Close in his arms, on the rim of sleep, she heard other dogs join in. A fox ... and because she loved all things in that moment she hoped it would be safe, aye even it, snug in its lair with its mate.

There had never been so dark a Christmas. Black candles at the Castle, everyone in black, and there was no tree, nor even spruce branches laid on the mantelpieces. Mrs. Hayes received instructions that the Prince's rooms must not be touched, but locked. In Crathie Kirk there was only the pibroch of the pipers on Christmas Eve. No carolers sang from house to house. It was as though Christ had not been born because Albert had died.

But Hogmanay — you could not keep a Scot from celebrating the New Year. The first foot in one's door after midnight must always be that of a dark man — for luck — and Ian Wyness led the First Footers on their rounds, bearing coal as the symbol of warmth for the year, oats for plenty, and whisky for cheer. Despite the snow, no croft was too distant to visit, and each had a welcoming fire. The old ladies, hair covered in their best mutches, served shortbread, gave and accepted drams, bestowed the ancient Gaelic blessings. It was a time for renewal of friendships and the patching of quarrels. And so Linty must welcome, among twenty others, Sheena Wright and wish her well, and inquire of the baby.

'He is well.' The pale, frigid eyes stared from a plumpening face. Then she turned, swaying a little from new drink in the heat of the fire. 'Johnny — Johnny Brown! Come kiss me for old times!'

What else could he do but come and bend down to her, but Linty saw the tongue, swift as a snake's, dart against his mouth. He drew back, but she twisted herself against him, her snow-wet hair glistening his face. Again she turned, facing Linty, her hips grinding against him, both arms around his neck — smiling.

'Fou as a blue hare,' Johnny said, and tossed her to Michael as if she were feathers. Both men laughed. Ian, behind Linty, caught her hand and held it, and drew her toward the door as if he knew she needed the cold air beyond the reek of the peat.

'I'll not be sick,' she said, answering a question he hadn't asked. 'It was disgust — and fear.'

'I know. But I'm here.'

He had never laughed at that fear, as Johnny had. She said, 'Until she's out, I'll be staying right here with you. It's like evil she wants to spend.'

'There, Michael's getting her shawls, see? They're all footing off, and myself too.' He looked down at her. 'It's not the time to say how I feel, Linty – I know you're bespoken – only if there's any time you need me?'

She wanted to raise and kiss the hand she held. 'I've nothing to offer you but my fear.'

Then they were swept aside by the swarm of people leaving and singing, kissing and wishing a happy new year. Jean and Torquil went up to their room.

Johnny said, smooring the fire, 'Duff gave me a bottle of brandy that "got lost." We'll drink to our own new year.'

On top of all the other cheer people had brought – whisky and beer and rum? Still, the worst that could happen was that Hogmanay head tomorrow, with no work to fret it at the Castle. She shivered into her long flannel nightdress and joined Johnny in bed by the fat candle, sipping from his mug.

She wanted to speak of Sheena, but he would slap off the subject like a fly – besides, a new dawn should start happily. She thought of the many things to be grateful for – Jean's health, the headaches so rare now; her own work and Torquil's, that bought shoes and boots and material for clothes.

Johnny drew her close and she lay back on the dark red frill of his chest curls. Curly he was all over, so that sometimes it tickled her to sneezing and him to laughing. But now was the solemn time for a New Year's wish, and she said, reaching up for the mug, 'To your dear health.'

He kissed her and took the mug, and she waited for his wish for her. One wish only, and so it was only prudent to ask health – against typhoid, cholera, consumption, the terrors that choked or burned.

'May God help her,' he said, and drank.

She came in May in her black widow's weeds, the veils hiding her face and her carriage like a hearse, black horses plumed in black, the children and attendants in black, with only here and there the sparkle of a jet jewel among the ladies. Straight to her apartments she went and then asked Mrs.

127

Hayes for the keys to the Prince's. She asked no guests to dine with her.

Upper servants had separate dinners that night – the first for the Castle maids and footmen who had worked all day, the second for the visiting footmen, valets and ladies' maids, whom Linty caught a glimpse of in black evening dress. Her last chore was to prepare these maids' beds for the night with hot stone bottles, then to lay out their night things. Imagine a *maid* with a nightdress trimmed with lace, a silk dressing-gown. Only here in privacy was mourning discarded; the gowns were flowery or white, or pale blue. Rows of scent bottles stood on the little dressing-tables.

Free to go home, she stopped by Mrs. Hayes' office with a question. 'What shall I call myself, Ma'am? Is there a chamber-maid-to-the-maids?'

Mrs. Hayes, who looked tired enough to cry, said, 'We'll sort it out later. With so many guests you'll be working both for gentry and maids – just wherever you're needed. But you need a niche, don't you?'

Aye, that was it.

'There's the small linen room between servants' quarters and gentry. Tomorrow after breakfast you go there and stay there until your bell rings, then you go to whatever room summons you. And you always go back to where you can be found for the next chore. That is, unless Sir Thomas – but I can't bother him now. He's all to – well, it's trying when Her Majesty gives no orders and the *real* Master is gone.' A wan smile. 'We just do the best we can until the house settles down. And you're all trained for emergencies.'

That awful, frightening word. And what it meant in Kitchen and also meant up here was simply that, whatever happened, Her Majesty must be pleased.

Johnny came by briefly that night, but in one of his strange, mute moods – and seemingly only to deliver the message that he might be off to Loch Muick for a day or two. The Queen was so depressed she might need an outing to be reminded of happier times. She was very white under the thin crepe veils, she had lost weight and wasn't too steady on her legs.

It was creepy going up to work that morning, the sky rain-dark, the gaslights in the corridors so faint you had to grope up the stairs, and the girls with you in cloaks like black crows, or their heads shawled. They tiptoed past closed doors where shoes stood polished, on up to where gentlemen's boots glistened in the first light. Another bend in the corridor and they were safe in the common room, where they could remove their wet garments and dare to whisper or cough. At the long oval mirror they put on their black aprons and caps, tidying one another, then trooped down to the dining-room, which Kitchen had just left. Breakfast consisted of eggs and gammon and jam, as befitted Upper, but everybody was scared, even the footmen at the far end of the table.

Oh, for the safety of Kitchen, Linty thought, with its hot fires and chatter, and where She would never come — at least without good warning. Mrs. Newlands had made conversation possible, but Mrs. Hayes had that kind of Engish silence you didn't break in on unless you had to ask for more tea or sugar. Not that she was a cruel woman, but all nerves, so that she jumped when Jenny touched her shoulder in passing the oat-cakes. 'I am sorry, Ma'am,' Jenny said softly, but with a crack in her voice that made it loud. It was so bleak that even the tea tasted flat, and the food like ash. Nerves. As if She was some huge monster who might jump out at you upstairs be-fore you had a chance to escape.

The little linen room was too close to the Royal wing for comfort, but with the door shut Linty felt safer. When she told Johnny about it later he called it a 'ladies' battle station', for besides the wardrobe of linens it had all manner of remedies — a table and iron for pressing clothes; a sewing basket; a little chest of refreshers like Florida Water and Vio-lette; vials of smelling salts. There was a large silk box of various kinds of buttons — all black — frogs and tassels and braid. There was a chair by the window, and Linty sat in it timorously, waiting for the bell to ring, in the gloom of a still-gray day.

Mrs. Hayes poked her head in. 'Quick! You can help clear up the ladies' maids' rooms while they eat . . .'

That was not so bad, but the maid of the Duchess of Rox-burghe was ill, and so she must help that lady dress at eight-thirty. The lady was tall and slender and helpless as a child; she had done nothing but put on her stockings and black chemise for modesty, and even then had got the seams all wrong. She said nothing to Linty but pointed to piles of pre-arranged clothes: the first petticoat of padded silk; the short steel and whalebone corset that extended to the hips; the long-legged drawers; the starched, braided black cotton petticoats trimmed with lace; the black satin overpetticoat; the black poplin dress with its wide frilled sleeves edged with braid; the dozens of jet buttons to fasten. Then the Duchess sat down on a chaise and extended her feet for black kid shoes. She spoke for the first time.

'My hair.'

'Oh, Ma'am – Your Grace – I don't *do* hair!'

'Then ring for someone!' She seemed as frightened as everyone else. 'For the love of heaven, call someone!'

It was like that all morning, emergencies, from room to room, and the gentry in trouble for fear She might want them and find them lacking. In a way it was funny, all these fine ladies as scared as the servants, only for reasons like a lost butterfly bow, spaniel curls flopping, a broken fan. As if She, in her grief, would notice just how everyone looked. As if she cared.

There was a little pause at eleven. Linty was alone in the linen room. Ian Wyness burst in with a gentleman's button for sewing on a jacket and Linty said, 'Och, that's nothing to look so spookie about. Here, I've the thread—'

'It's not that,' he said, standing while she worked. 'It's what I had to do this morning. You won't believe it. I had to bring up the Prince's shaving water.'

The needle jabbed her finger; she didn't notice. 'Are you daft?'

'She is. She said, "Each morning, as usual, you will bring the hot water to his dressing-room, as the night footman will do before dinner." Linty, my God, his razors are laid out, just as they were . . . and she said, "A clean towel each morning, of course." And I said, "Yes, Ma'am," and backed out of there as fast as I could.

'It wasn't only just what she *said*; it was her eyes, quiet and steady and not a tear — as if it was all normal. I got to wondering if I hadn't imagined it all and spoke to Annie MacDonald, her wardrobe maid, who's been with her all through the death. She said, "You heard right. Our orders are like that wherever she is. Each night a clean nightshirt is placed on his side of the bed. It's all rumpled and wet with tears when I awaken her." '

And that was not all. Annie said that a photograph taken of the Prince's corpse on his deathbed under a wreath of evergreen was hung above his pillow in whatever bedroom she occupied. Her only interest seemed to be in the vast mausoleum she was having built at Frogmore, and in statues and memorials to Albert the Good. She called Johnny and Grant to her apartments to ask them to recall the exact spot where the Prince had shot his last stag — there would be a stone to mark it, as there would be for his last shoot at Windsor. There would be a great cairn on a mountaintop — Craig Lowrigan — a pyramid of stone high above the Dee he had loved, high where the golden eagles soared.

That afternoon a photographer arrived from Aberdeen and spent hours in the Prince's apartments photographing every object there in its set place, so that whoever dusted might always restore the exact order of books, pen, paper-weight, inkwell, everything on desk, dressing-table, night-table. If he had left so much as an antimacassar askew it should never be straightened, for there on the lace his dear head had rested.

The following day she summoned Johnny again to discuss which ladies and gentlemen should have the ponies, and she herself went to the stables to look them over. 'Linty, she couldna bring herself to ride out in company, but she had me harness Lochnagar to the little cart and drove it herself a way up the river, with me riding ahead. A wind whipped up, and I saw her draw rein and pull to a stop, and fumble for her shawls. I put two around her and she said, "You are handy, Brown. He thought a great deal of you, you know. He chose you for me."

'I said, because she looked so forlorn, just eyes looking out, with the black veil blown back, "Is there anything he would want me to do I haven't known of?"

'She was quiet a long time and then she said, "He would want you to stand by at any time of need. You are handy even with shawls." Then she turned her head and I think she began to cry, because it was always him who shawled her. Like a child she was, trying hard to be brave with her father gone — for I think he was that, Linty, as much as husband. And then she turned to face me again, with her lip bitten in and a big tear down her nose, and she said, "I like to think he is always with me, that he is here now. But Brown, I can't fool myself. He isn't. If only I had a way — I reach out at night — I touch what he touched, wore, felt — and it's all hollow. I hear the comforting sermons, the poems . . . afterlife. I believe because I must. But how can you know what is real and what is a dream?"

'Well, what could I say? I've a blunt way about me, no fancy thoughts like poets and ministers. I just said, "If he's here he'd not want you cold and miserable, so keep those shawls about you." I gave her a nip from my flask — just a wee one. She looked up at the hills all about and took a deep breath and said, "It's as close as I can get," and she meant, to him. Then she started up Lochnagar with her little whip and we came back. There were the doctors, Jenner and Clark, all upset because she'd been out. My God, that woman can take the weather, and I had her shawled, but they chittered like a couple of old maids. They'd like to *keep* her ill is my view. And just what the hell good are they when they didn't even know his fever was typhoid? They called it "gastric" or something. Anyway, to my mind they're a couple of fools. Her three hours out did her more good than staring at the bloody walls, or having tea with a bunch of women afraid to talk to her.'

Linty thought, gratefully, that he wasn't afraid to talk to her about the Queen, as he used to be — perhaps because now she and Johnny were almost like man and wife, without secrets. Aye, she could really be sorry for the widow who had so little privacy except here. Here she would surely recover.

You couldn't help but hear the ladies-in-waiting talk — loud-voiced, authoritative women who tried to whisper but somehow couldn't. The dear Queen was *ill* with grief. In the six months since the Prince's death she had become *worse*. 'It is the full realization now ... the cushion of shock taken from her. Remember, it had been such a *love* match. So who can blame her for her – well – *odd* behavior?'

Rarely did she breakfast with her children, who were all here but Bertie. She was busy over the Boxes in the mornings, or in consultation with General Grey or Colonel Ponsonby, who served as secretaries. 'The queer thing,' Ian said, 'is that she keeps us hopping to them with notes when you'd think she could save herself hours of work with a conference. It's as if they were all the way to London, not along the corridor.'

From Paris came a dressmaker and milliner to extend the mourning wardrobe. It became known that the Queen had burst into tears because the Prince had always chosen every single cap, bonnet and gown for her. 'I have no taste – *he* had.' She ordered dozens of black handkerchiefs dotted with white to represent teardrops. Offended by the bright metal ear-trumpet of an elderly dresser, she had had it covered in black crepe and lace.

The eight maids-of-honor could be recognized by the miniature of the Queen surrounded by diamonds which they wore tied in a bow on their left shoulders. Linty overheard scraps of their conversation – how eerie it must be to sleep with the plaster cast of a husband's hand above one's pillow, how flushed she looked after meals, how nothing seemed to give her comfort, not even the children.

Her principal comfort seemed to be journeys into the hills, along the coils of the Dee. One June afternoon Johnny guided her, with General Grey and Lady Ely, into the heart of Ballochbuie to its waterfall.

'She summoned me to walk with her apart from the others, and och, Linty, she looked like wax. She said, "I have been very close to suicide."

'My God – to tell *me* that! I was that shocked I didna know what to say, and then she said, "I've good reason to fear madness."

'Well, so I just said what was sensible. I said, "Nonsense, woman."

'She stared at me as if she'd kill me – and then she threw

133

back her head and laughed, right from the belly. Only the tears were close after that. She talked about the Prince being too good and pure for this miserable world, of how she had to live and rule as he would have wished, how every decision was made with his approval in mind, of how she'd not be dictated to by any minister of state or church but by the spirit of the Prince. I said that was rare good sense but to use her own, too, and she laughed again. Then she told me Bertie is coming to visit next month and that she dreads it. "He is the opposite of his Papa ... He caused his death by a scandal with an actress ..."

' "Och," I said, "don't blame the lad for a caper; it was fever killed His Highness." But she went on about Bertie being idle and wild and making his father so unhappy, and maybe ruining his chances of marrying Princess Alexandra. I never heard such an outpour – and to me – as if I was a friend.'

Linty said, 'Maybe it's easier to talk to you than all those politics people because you wouldna try to twist things round. Like they say, you've no axe to grind.'

'Maybe.'

It pleased Linty that it never even occurred to him to say "Don't repeat these things." He seemed to know she wouldn't, not even to Jean and Torquil. It took away all of her jealousy of the Queen. Early the next morning, as a tiny tribute the Queen would never know about, she gathered the first pink roses from her garden and took them to Anne Mac-Donald to place in the royal apartments as a wee offering, but please not to mention who had brought them.

Prince 'Bertie' came in July – plumper, a little red-faced, very stylish even in his black. Arrogant, the servants whispered, as if he thought himself king already, the way he treated his brothers and sisters like nothings. Evidently the Queen couldn't stand him and had him packed off to Birkhall, at Glen Muick. But he was present at the ceremony August 21st when the Queen and her family drove to the top of Craig Lowrigan and placed stones as the base of the cairn: 'To the beloved memory of Albert the great and good, Prince Consort. Raised by his broken-hearted Widow.'

She did not seem to improve in spirits and left Balmoral as

sadly as she had come, but Johnny said that at least Bertie's marriage had been assured. 'She thinks a wife is the steadying he needs.' Without the court, the household relaxed. Sir Thomas wrote the housekeepers that white aprons and caps might now be permitted, and white cotton stockings for the footmen. The children of Crathie began to wear colors again.

It was a hard winter, with cruel winds and the beat of sleet. Johnny still said nothing of marriage, but Linty was content to be with him nearly every night. Odd that she wasn't with child – but then, such matters were mysteries. She was happy enough.

In January she was thirty-three – but she didn't frown in the looking glasses she polished. Her hair was still fair and she had learned how to part it and coil it and use an iron for spaniel curls as the ladies did. With the money she and Torquil had saved there was enough to buy material, and she and Jean sewed dresses of blue and gray poplin trimmed with ribbon, flowery muslins for the summer, and they made up hats with daisies and cherries and other frivolities Johnny brought from Ballater. Aye, he was like a husband, thinking of everything – except marriage.

Rarely did she see Sheena, except at the Inver Inn, where folk gathered on a Saturday night if the snow was polite. Sheena never spoke – she glared. It was hatred so raw, after all this time, all these years. Johnny still took it as a pesky joke – 'Och, she had the hots for me, that's all,' – but Linty sickened at the stare of those pale eyes and finally said she'd never go to the Inver again; even with all of the people, the pipers and the fiddlers, she felt unsafe.

Only Ian felt with her what he called 'the malignancy' – Jean and Torquil, loving as they were, thought it all fancy. Daily in their free fifteen minutes at work she grew closer to Ian in friendship, able to tell him anything except the Queen's confidences to Johnny, for those were sacred. And he could tell her anything, too – love affairs without love in them, and though he was careful not to mention the names of the girls, she knew. You could tell from the way they looked at him, those Upper maids; but they were not jealous of her because everyone knew she was Johnny's.

135

Johnny showed her a photograph of the President of the United States, Abraham Lincoln, and said, 'Now, who does that look like?' Why, it was Ian, except Mr. Lincoln had a beard and was older, with ruts in his cheeks. A fine stark face they both had, deep eyes – tall and proud looking. But all the footmen would have felt prouder if those cotton stockings were silk; it was one of Prince Albert's economies, which, of course, the Queen would never change.

Margaret Stewart, who helped train Linty, was promoted to be Cleaner of the Prince's apartments, and she hated it – partly for fear of breaking something or shifting an object, though she had the photographs to study, and partly because she said it was too creepy to describe. On his desk was the blotting book open, and his pen on it. His watch ticked. Och, no, she didn't believe in ghosts, and yet when you worked up there in the light of dawn you'd swear you weren't alone. Once her garter had come undone, and she was embarrassed to raise her dress and fasten it because he was maybe there.

Nobody envied Mrs. Hayes the job of the Queen's bed-chamber, with the cast of the arm above the pillow and his deathbed photograph. But she didn't say much. However, she always had Forbes stand in the doorway until she had finished, giving as an excuse that she might need more cloths or polish.

Maids gossiped freely about what they'd heard – that the Queen was most partial to the widows among her ladies and bitterly resented the mere idea of remarriage, so that she would not accept some ladies in England who had taken second husbands. The Queen would wear mourning to her own grave, but was allowing gowns of gray, mauve, lilac and purple in honor of Prince Bertie's wedding.

This took place on March 10th at St. George's Chapel, Windsor, and the newspapers were full of it – but how it was more like a funeral, with the Queen sitting up in a queer little cage with purple velvet curtains, made so that she could pull them back and forth according to her emotions; sometimes she hid herself to weep, and other times peered out to watch the ceremony. The journalists reported the dazzling beauty of the Princess Alexandra and the fine looks of Prince Bertie, but it was the Queen who dominated from her lonely stage above the Choir.

In the autumn the Queen returned to Balmoral with Mr. Gladstone, whom, Johnny told Linty, 'she couldna take to at all. She told me she tries – she must work with him – but by God it's hard, so she likes to get out away from him.'

Fiona, a night maid, was ill, and Linty was asked to do double duty on the evening of October 7th. The Queen had been up to Glen Muick with Princess Alice, who took along Willem, her negro page. Johnny and Smith drove, and Kitchen had provided the Queen's picnic whim of broth and boiled potatoes.

Since she was not back by eight, Kitchen began to worry about what to do about her dinner and Mr. Gladstone's. The pâté of pheasant and grouse would keep, but the roasted chickens would be dry. If she were not back by nine, should Mr. Gladstone be served? Sir Thomas thought so, but it was taking a lot upon oneself to make the decision.

Shortly after ten o'clock Johnny carried the Queen in from a pony and called for Dr. Jenner. She was taken to her bed-chamber, rumored to be dying. Linty, waiting in the linen room, was tempted to seek Johnny, but she dared not leave her post.

And then Stewart came in, smiling. 'Smith was drunk and overset the carriage in the dark. The Queen is only bruised, and with a cut on her head; she's taking soup and steamed fish. But your Johnny's a hero!'

Och well, he said later, it was nothing. Smith had been nipping at a flask, got the carriage onto knotty ground and overturned it. Johnny had jumped out and pulled the ladies and the page to safety, released the horses from their traces, and sent Smith to get ponies – 'he was sobered up fine by then.' There was a long wait but Johnny had claret, which soothed the ladies, and they all rode back on ponies. 'What a woman! Her head rubbed into stony ground but not a whimper. She didn't even scold Smith; she just dismissed him, poor bastard.'

Two days later Ian, who had been serving the Queen and the Princess and Mr. Gladstone at dinner, said, 'You should have seen him gape when Her Majesty poured whisky into her claret. And like everybody else who eats at a normal pace, he was still chewing his cutlets when she'd finished her cherry tart and cream; so up she got, with the Princess following, and left the room. He asked what time he had to finish and I told him fifteen minutes. He had salad and a tart but let the coffee go, and the brandy. Then he was out to join the two ladies in her drawing room.'

Gordon, who passed chocolates there, carried on the story. 'Her Majesty said, "Is it not a warm evening for October?" and Mr. Gladstone said "Yes, Ma'am." "As warm as London, I should imagine," she said, and he said, "Yes, Ma'am." Princess Alice said nothing until her mother asked if the stars were out, and she said, "Yes, Mama, very bright." Then the Queen had me open the windows wide, saying she needed fresh air, and believe me it was bloody cold, but she went over and took deep breaths while those two stood shivering – there wasn't a fire, of course. Then she went to the door and said "I assume you're as tired as I am," and that meant "get to hell out of here," so they all said goodnight. Well, when I got home to my peat fire and stretched out on the rug with a hot gin toddy, what my wife said about making rowan jelly seemed like bloody brilliant conversation.'

As it neared time to leave Balmoral for Christmas at Osborne, the Queen told Johnny, 'I shall never again take up residence in London. I must have the peace of my country homes. I must be where his heart was. If I lose the sense of his presence, then I lose everything.'

In the spring the Queen returned still in her black, but sometimes she wore a white cap of lace that fell in folds to her shoulders. She had grown plumper but was still so sad and subdued that it was a relief when she was off again – not even Johnny could make her smile. Torquil said it must be that she'd set herself too deep into mourning to pull out.

It was a hot, dry summer and Crathie worried about its crops, but gentle rains came in time, so the harvest was safe. And in October Linty thought she was pregnant.

In November she was certain, from the swelling of her

breasts and a sickness early one morning. Now she could tell Johnny. Now the banns could be posted.

At the end of the day she sought Johnny in the stables to ask him to walk home with her, but Grant said he was shooting on the hills. He might not be back for an hour or two. Bringing game home in the dark could be a long job, and if he were tired he might not come to her, when she wanted so to celebrate, and Jean had collops simmering.

Oh, but she *had* to see him tonight, so she told Grant she would wait up in the room they shared and he laughed and said not to mind him, he was off to the Inn till midnight.

Lying on Johnny's bed, his pillow behind her head, the little oil lamp aglow, she thought of how to tell him. She turned it over in her mind and decided that such wonderful news did not need dressing up.

A Christmas wedding? No, just a few days before so that everyone would be free to come. She would need white muslin for her dress and blue bows would be pretty. If there was enough sun she might lay out her mother's wedding veil for bleaching, or buy some tulle if it wasn't too costly.

She dozed, then jumped awake as she heard Johnny say, 'Come in for a dram,' and there was Duncan behind him, both of them bloodied and muddied.

Johnny paused in the doorway. 'Linty! Is anything wrong?'

'No,' she said smiling; but Duncan might linger on an hour or two. 'I came to say Jean is cooking collops – but have your drams first.'

Johnny poured for the three of them and they talked of the day's shooting. There was enough deer to last through to Christmas, Duncan said, if Johnny didna have the appetite of six giants.

'Well,' Johnny said, 'the fact is – I won't be here.' He spoke in a rush, not looking at her. 'The Queen – I mean I've been sent for to Osborne.'

Linty had no words, only a terrible chill up her spine. Duncan said, 'What for?'

'Well' – he still avoided looking at Linty – 'it seems Dr. Jenner wants her to keep up her riding and she doesna like strange grooms.'

'Lucky bastard,' Duncan said. 'When did you hear?'

'A week ago.' He looked at Linty now. 'I didna like to say until I had a telegraph back making it all official.'

What he means is, he was afraid to tell me, and now he tells me in front of Duncan because he thinks I'll make a fuss about Christmas.

'I'm sorry, Linty,' he said, shame-faced as a little boy. 'But she needs me.'

'Yes,' she said.

In the old days in this village, if a woman couldn't marry right away nothing was thought of it. But the Queen had changed all that; and if she found out that Johnny had got Linty pregnant she might sack him – or both of them – and then where would they be? *God, how I hate her, hate her, hate her.* She maybe doesn't know I exist, but she's ruining my life. She has a whim to have Johnny – I have a desperation.

Duncan looked at her and said, 'I'll be going along now.' He downed his drink, the nice man, and left.

Johnny said, 'I am sorry, but what can I do?' He came over to the bed and sat beside her. 'Likely we'll be back in the spring.'

'And in the spring I'll be seven or eight months pregnant with your child.'

'*What?*'

'Aye, you heard me. I came to tell you.'

He pulled her to him but she broke away and stood. 'When do you leave?'

'Next week, to be there before December 14th, as that was the day the Prince – Oh, Christ, and no time for the banns.'

'So you're there to comfort her for the anniversary. A dead man is more important than I am—'

'But I didna *know*.'

'Suppose I had told you last week. You'd have still agreed to go to her?'

He hesitated. 'It's a command.'

'You'd not have your head cut off.'

'That's not the point. If I don't go, why – she's lost so much, Linty. She's in a wavery kind of way, and if I fail her—'

'Never mind me!'

He stood beside her. 'But I do, little hen, I do. If it weren't three weeks for the banns. Suppose I posted them in London, and you come to me there?' But then he shook his head. 'I'd have to tell her to get the time off. It would likely upset her, so—'

'So I stay here.' She flung away from him to the door. 'I'm not ashamed to bear the child – I'm ashamed of you. Deep right to the inside of me, I'm ashamed of you. No, don't say a word, not another word to me, ever.'

Alone, on the way home with her lantern, she knew this was the very end. Too grieved for tears, she told Jean and Torquil. 'It is not just a row – it's the finish.'

Rightly, Jean said; but Torquil could see Johnny's point of view. 'You do not fail your sovereign, Linty. In his way, he is right. She must come first.'

'Not to me! The child comes first. Even Michael Wright had the goodness to marry Sheena in time.'

The smell of the collops was sickening, her stomach was all upset like her thoughts, so she went into her room and closed the door. It would be a relief to cry, but anger held the tears back, and her disappointment in Johnny.

Jean came in. 'Ian Wyness is here. I'll tell him you're in bed if you'd rather not see him.'

'I can't refuse – it might be a message.'

Not from Johnny, of course, but from Mrs. Hayes. She tidied her hair and went in to the fire. Jean and Torquil excused themselves.

'I heard about Johnny leaving,' Ian said, 'and I thought you might need cheering – as he's at the Inver.'

'Celebrating the Queen's summons,' she said bitterly.

'I doubt that. He set off like a black cloud. Besides, it's not the Queen's summons. Dr. Jenner and Sir Charles Phipps sent for him as a kind of Christmas gift – a surprise to cheer her up.'

'He said it was her command!'

Ian smiled. 'A white lie, Linty. A man can brag—'

'Oh, no,' she said, 'that's not the reason he lied. But how do you know who sent for him?'

'The telegram came to Mrs. Newlands, only she promised

141

him not to mention it until he did. She's that proud that some-one from Lower should be so important to Her Majesty, she said. Linty—'

'He lied about her commanding him to come because he *wants* to go! He doesna have to! He could have made some excuse to Dr. Jenner, and if it was to be a surprise, she'd never have been the wiser! He wants to go at the very time—' She broke off, and added lamely, 'I mean Christmas.'

'But it's an honor to him. You wouldn't want to stand in his way, would you?'

She brought him a dram from the bottle Johnny always kept in the cupboard, poured one for herself, then sat across from him. As she raised the glass to her lips, she thought: If Johnny is drunk tonight at the inn it's not for mourning me; and if he looked like a storm-cloud when Ian saw him go, it's anger at me. But whatever he feels can no longer matter.

'I don't stand in his way,' she said. 'Nothing does, nothing can. It's over between us.'

'You don't mean that. Just to miss Christmas, to be a few months away—'

'It's not that. It's far more than that. I told him tonight I'm going to have his child—'

'Ah, Linty.' He came to kneel by her chair.

'He tells me this lie that she's commanded him; he could easily have refused Dr. Jenner. He's willing to leave me to everyone's pity while he rides about with her and plays comforter – or more.'

He took her hand. 'You don't believe there's more.'

'I don't know what I believe. I'm that upset I can't even cry. It's as if I was dead.'

He clasped her hand more tightly, then brought it down to his lips. 'I love you. I would ask you to marry me except for two things – you'd think I asked out of pity, and you'd think I've taken advantage of your being so miserable.'

She shook her head, withdrew her hand to her lap. 'If I agreed, it's I who'd be taking advantage. I couldn't give you love, only the friendship we already have. A man like you deserves more than that.'

'I've lived on crumbs for a long time – just to see you, to

142

hear your voice. And you won't believe it, or maybe you will, but each day that starts I say to myself, "I might meet Linty, she might want to see me in her free fifteen minutes," and when that happens I remember at night every word you've said. And to be blunt – you are the woman in my arms, in the darkness, until she speaks and ruins the dream.'

She stretched out her hand to touch the dark, thinning hair. We pity one another, she thought, but I mustn't say that. He is too dear to hurt. He caught her hand and kissed it again and she said, 'There's always said to be some way out, only I've had no time to think.'

They were silent for a while, and then she said, 'In the old days, a woman had a choice.'

'But not now. You have got to marry, Linty, or go away.'

And that was impossible. There wasn't enough money to settle in a new place like Aberdeen. And she'd be terrified there, seeking service with strangers, until the child was born – never coming back here to Jean and Torquil, unless she told lies about some husband who had deserted her.

There was a pound on the door, and Johnny came in. Ian sprang up. Linty, from her chair, said, 'You're fou.'

He stood, swaying a little. 'Aye.'

He didn't even seem to see Ian, only herself. 'I've things to say to you.'

The things he should have said earlier this evening. She looked at Ian. 'Thank you for the dram,' he said, and left. Briefly, as Johnny sat down on the hearthrug, she thought how selfish one is in happiness – but time enough to think of Ian later.

'It wasn't exactly a command from the Queen,' Johnny said, his words slurred. 'I'm to be a surprise to her.' He fumbled to light his pipe. 'Linty, I told you she fears madness. So do the doctors. So do many people. Anything that can be done to cheer her – shouldn't it be done? Isna my first duty, and yours, to our sovereign, next to God?'

She was chilled again. 'Isna a man's first duty to his woman and child?'

'I'll marry you the day I return.'

'In the spring! It could be June, and the baby already born!

143

Do I, did I care for such things years ago? But now I must. You'll marry me in three weeks or not at all.'

'There's no way to stop in London and post the banns. There's no way for me to get there without telling her why I need time off. And if I did tell her – God, her mind's upset enough—'

'Without learning that her favorite is marrying another woman! Well, you can tell her just that, Johnny, and join her for the new year. Or you can go to hell right now.'

'Jesus Christ, don't you understand? The Prince died on the fourteenth – it's her worst time; I *must* be there before then—'

'Then go.' She went to the door and opened it. 'Go now. We've said all we have to say.'

He tried to pull her into his arms but she fought him off, because even a kiss could hurt too much, and a kiss would lead to bed and worse hurt later. 'Get out,' she said, and spat in his face.

For a moment she thought he would strike her, but he lowered his arm. He was gone.

Alone in bed, the wind rattling around the little house, she prayed to be able to cry; but no tears came.

Chapter Four

Two evenings later, on a Sunday, Torquil came in with the snow on him; Jean shook out his coat and put his boots to dry near the hearth while Linty brewed tea. He said, 'We'll be digging ourselves out to work tomorrow if this keeps up.'

'Aye,' Linty said, putting bannocks on a plate, buttering them. She brought them with the teapot to the table Jean had set, stared at the cold meat and rushed from the room to be sick.

Sick again and again but, she was sure, not of the baby – of her hurt. Back with them, she said, 'I'm sorry. But don't ask me to eat.'

'For the child,' Jean said, 'you must.'

'It might die.'

Torquil turned on her in a rage, the first she could remember. 'So you'd let Johnny cheat you of that? Of the love you'll have the rest of your life? Aye, I know you're sick to the very core of you, but you will nourish this child – *our* child – *do you hear?*'

He was right, of course. Meekly she accepted the mug of milk, managed to swallow a gravel-tasting bannock. Snow floated down against the window and hissed on the logs in the hearth.

Johnny was leaving tomorrow on the early stage from Inver. She thought of him having a farewell dram with Sandy and Mariad before the coach left. Folk had asked her if she wouldn't be there to see him off on the long journey. She'd used the excuse of work, though if she had asked, Mrs. Hayes would surely have granted her an hour. Grant and Duncan might suspect a rift between her and Johnny, but no one would know for sure. One thing to his credit – even in drink he was close-mouthed.

Another month and she must start lacing tightly, wearing one of those costly corsets, or Mrs. Hayes would surely notice; it was she who would have to decide whether Linty might stay in service. Perhaps she herself would not mind – but she'd have to write Sir Thomas and he would reflect what the Queen would think, probably not bothering Her Majesty about it but just saying, 'Get rid of Clarke.' But gossip was such that surely Linty Clarke and John Brown would be associated, and if the Queen were to know – my God, it would be the end for him.

Why should I care? He can always come back to farm at Bush. But it will be a struggle for Jean and me, and if the Queen is so shocked about 'sinners' then maybe even Torquil would be dismissed because he's my brother-in-law. So then where are we, the three of us, and a baby too?

Torquil came up behind her and pressed the back of her neck with his long, strong fingers as he did when Jean had the ghost of a headache. She went limp, letting the fingers slide up and down, back and forth, and the terrible tightness seemed to ease from every muscle. Jean said, 'Just bring your head down . . . that's right. You'll sleep tonight.'

But she didn't, not until she heard Jean moving around to make the morning's porridge. A few minutes later, when she could have slept forever, Torquil knocked on the door.

The black sky, the black day to get through, and the snow.

Och, yes, she said to the maids in Upper, she was gey proud that Johnny was off to Osborne. Only too bad he had the journey in such weather. By the sea, was it? Then it would be lovely in springtime. Of course she would miss him – he'd been such a good friend; aye, from childhood. In love with him? Had they thought *that*? Well, to tell the truth, they'd become too used to each other – maybe it was a good thing he was gone so both of them could look around corners.

It was like walking a tightrope, wondering if she was saying the right things, wondering how much they all suspected.

146

They'd never come out and questioned her before, but now Johnny was important, the first of them ever sent to the Queen – and Lower at that.

So many lies she told, and she got so little sleep that her wits weren't about her. In her free fifteen minutes she shut herself into the linen room and dozed until Stewart came in to awaken her. Then work through the late afternoon and High Tea, with Ian watching her from his end of the table. When she started home he was waiting in the courtyard with a pony borrowed from Grant.

'Up you go,' he said, and swung her gently onto the saddle.

She clung to him as they rode through new-falling snow in silence. At the cottage, the pony tethered, Jean welcomed them, then went upstairs to Torquil.

'I won't stay,' Ian said, 'You're tired to death.'

'Aye,' Linty said.

Tired of lies, of fear for the future, of love itself. Tired of this long enchantment she'd been living in that was like a spell she had to break.

'Ian,' she said, 'will you stay with me tonight?'

He put his arms around her. He was as tall as Johnny; she had to stand on tiptoe to kiss his cheek – the long sideburn rough as Johnny's. Then the tears came in a flood she couldn't stop.

He latched the door and carried her into her room, lit the lamp and undressed her. Then, when she shivered into the bed he sat on its edge and said, 'I'm staying,' and patted at her tears.

But he didn't undress; he dragged a blanket over him and lay beside her and stroked her wet face and her hair. She told him to take the pony to the shelter of the wood-shed and before he came back she was asleep.

Sometime during the night she awakened from a dream of Johnny, reached out and felt warm wool – an arm. Ian was still lying on top of the covers and as she touched him he said, 'Awake?'

'Aye,' she said. 'Ian, Ian, I don't love you. I never will. Only I do in a little way because there's nothing I can't tell you, you know?'

147

'I know.' He turned and held her.

'I'm glad you're here.'

'I'm glad to be here.'

'You must be cold.'

'I'm dressed, and the blanket.'

She looked into the blackness of the room, smelt the dead oil of the lamp. 'I slept, you know.'

'I know.'

'So you haven't slept?'

'No. I didn't want to.'

'Tomorrow *you'll* be tired.'

'Tomorrow be damned.'

She cuddled her head into his shoulder. 'This isn't fair to you. Only I feel so—'

Safe. At peace.

'– much better. I don't mean happy, just that I can face things.'

He was silent.

'I think, I think I can face things.'

'You say you love me in a little way. That would be enough. And the truth is between us. How many couples have that?'

'I don't know. Johnny and I didn't lie – that is, until lately. Only, in a way I deceived him. I never came out and said I loved him until last year. I was too proud.'

He chuckled softly. 'That wasn't deception, Linty – and you had to keep your pride. But with me you can shed it.'

'I have.'

'Will you marry me, then?'

Oh, but he deserved so much more than she could give. And wouldn't it be deception when she gave her body and pretended pleasure in his?

He caught her thought. 'I wouldn't expect passion. Maybe I'd never rouse it. But a man always hopes.'

'You mustn't hope even. Do you want me that way?'

'Any way.'

She lifted her face, and they kissed, but her tears came salt on his mouth and he drew away gently. 'Go back to sleep, darling.'

It is the right thing to marry him, she thought drowsily.

Jean and Torquil would be pleased, the little family made safe. She would be a good wife, tending his needs. Never again would she see Johnny alone. There could be no temptation if she avoided him when he returned.

She wondered where he was at this moment — some coaching inn. If he had gone to bed drunk. If he were wakeful, thinking of her.

The banns were posted that afternoon and by dusk all of Crathie knew. Nobody came out and said, 'But we thought you'd marry Johnny'; still, as people said, 'How wonderful ... all happiness to you,' she saw question marks in eyes. Let them think what they pleased — that she and Johnny had quarreled. Since the baby would come early she and Ian contrived a little ruse: Och, they'd been courting in secret for months. No one must ever guess that the child was Johnny's.

The Scotts invited them to the Inver that night, and half the parish was there, despite the snow. Weddings, funerals, christenings were big events, and the surprise of Linty's engagement to Ian provided extra excitement. Over and over she managed the proper sly laugh, 'we fooled you, didn't we' kind, clinging to Ian's hand as though it were a raft at sea.

Then Sheena and Michael came in past the fiddlers and the pipers, and she clung closer to Ian in the old terror. He understood instantly, leading her into the next room through the press of people. But Sheena followed, making her way to them.

Even in a small room reeking of liquor, Linty could smell the gin on her, and the pale eyes were glazed. She said, 'Everyone's surprised but me. You settle for what you can get, don't you?'

Michael pushed her aside. 'We wish you happiness. Sheena, come, we'll have a dram for the road.'

But as he dragged her away she said, 'Johnny never loved you.'

'Drunken slut,' Ian whispered. 'Forget it, darling.'

Only it was true. If he'd loved her he'd have married her years ago.

149

That week she and Jean sewed the white bridal gown. Taking the last few stitches, Linty pricked her finger with the needle and blood spurted on the hem.

'Oh God!' she said.

Jean pretended to misunderstand. 'A bit of cold water on wadded thread will take it off like magic.'

'But it's the worst luck in the world. The worst omen ...'

'Don't be a goose.' Jean brought water, worked on the spots. 'Now – Mama's veil just won't do. I'll get the coach into Ballater—'

'No. I don't need it – the expense. I don't *want* it. We'll just make a little frill for my hair.'

Jean argued but Linty was adamant. Why should she have a veil when Jean hadn't? Anyway, a bouquet was no problem, for Torquil got permission to use greenhouse flowers, which Mrs. Hayes took responsibility for. She'd certainly not write to Sir Thomas for permission on such a minor matter.

But Ian had to write to Sir Thomas for permission to move from his castle room to Linty's cottage. It was granted. And since Sir Thomas was at Osborne, what would be more natural than for him to mention the wedding – or would he think it too trivial? So perhaps Johnny knew.

Linty tried to sweep aside the thought that there was still time for him to interfere – to return, even. Then what would she do? No, she couldn't hurt Ian – she couldn't do that to him.

Until the very morning of her marriage she had the feeling that it wouldn't take place. Even as she made her vows at the altar there was a dream quality – it couldn't be real. This was someone who looked and spoke like Linty Clarke, but the true Linty wasn't there.

Again a revel at the Inver – for the house was too small for so many people, and it was filled with gifts. There was blue and white china, a fine plump turkey, a pretty linen tablecloth, a tray to hold pipe ashes, a calendar, a knitted muffler, a shawl, deerskin slippers for them both – all the things people had made, or grown, like the barrels of apples and cider and potatoes from Johnny's folk at Bush Farm. He *must* know – one of them would have written to him.

At five in the morning Linty, tired again, and to exhaustion, put on her new white nightdress and crept between the freezing sheets as Ian undressed. But before he put out the lamp she made herself smile, made herself ready to endure it all.

'Darling,' he said, getting into bed, 'you'll forgive me – I'm so damned sleepy.'

She knew it was a lie – the first between them. And she blessed him for it.

When he did make love to her it wasn't the way she had feared it would be, partly because he was gentle and tender and – well, deft. Partly because, again, it wasn't quite real – she was miles away under his body, his kisses. She hoped he didn't know that, but she dared not pretend because that would hurt him too much. Passively, and with affection, she accepted.

She could say to herself, as she said to Jean and Torquil, 'I love him – not as I should, but it's more than liking.' And he didn't try to play master of the house any more than Torquil did – they shared the tasks of wood-cutting and snow-shoveling like brothers, merry together. They planned the building of a new room, with a fireplace, at the back of the house, for when the baby grew older the cottage would be too small. Aye, it could be done for very little – and there were Ian's savings and earnings to help, so that when it came time to stop her work there would be no great worry about money. And after the baby was born Jean could care for it if Mrs. Hayes took her back into Upper.

When her pregnancy became apparent she asked Mrs. Hayes if – say, in August – she could resume work and was told, 'Of course.' So all was well.

On the second of March Linty received the first letter of her life, given her by Jean when she returned with Ian from work. It could only be from Johnny. 'Read it to me,' she said, still in her cloak. It was Ian who read it.

'My dear Linty:
I could not at first disturb the Queen with anything, for she is disturbed enough. I have been promised a cottage of my

151

own at Balmoral, for I told her I wished to marry; or she said if I wanted a cottage here in the south I might have it. My wage is to be 120 pounds. From now on I am called "The Queen's Highland Servant," attending her both outdoors and inside and taking no orders from anyone but herself.

You said the baby would be born in June. Her Majesty need not know anything of this. I don't think she even knows your name or that you work at the Castle. When I return we will marry – as if you were a widow? You will know best. Meanwhile, my love to you and do not be angry. I could not help it. I have much to tell you.

Johnny'

She took the letter from Ian, controlling the urge to weep and laugh at the same time.

When Torquil came in Linty said, 'Read it again, Ian.'

When he had finished Torquil said, 'He either wrote that drunk, or tending a madwoman has turned him mad. How in God's name could he suggest that Linty should masquerade as a widow? It makes no sense.'

Ian said nothing, looking at her, and she managed to smile. 'We'll just forget about it,' she said. 'Toss it into the fire where it belongs.'

But when they were alone in bed he said, 'It's a terrible irony.'

'Irony?'

'Aye, the offer coming so late.'

'I suppose his conscience suffered.' She settled her thickening body on her side of the bed, knowing he would not make love tonight – as if Johnny lay between them. 'Tomorrow you must write him for me. Just say: "Linty and I were married in December. We congratulate you on your new honors." '

'Coming from me it would be cruel.'

'He knows I can't write.'

'Then it must be: "Linty asked me to write you and thank you for your letter, but we married..." I wonder who he thought would read this letter to you? Indiscreet as it is?'

'Maybe you – he knows we were friends. But I can't think about it.'

I mustn't think that he loves me; it will break what small content I have.

No, not so very small – she was at peace with Ian, and what more could she hope for? He was a good husband, a protector, her dearest friend.

'Goodnight, darling,' she said. They kissed and he moved to his side of the bed.

It was an hour before she slept, and when she did she dreamed of herself in Johnny's arms in a wee house shawled in honeysuckle and wild roses. She could even smell the fragrance as she awakened in the dark to reality.

Her tears were silent. Ian mustn't know. So already she was tricking him, and when Johnny returned, what then? Then she must trick herself that Johnny meant nothing, nothing at all. She must be prepared to lie to him, to herself, that love was a cold corpse, deep-buried.

Linty was in childbed the day the Queen returned with Johnny and her retinue. Jean and Mrs. Groves, the midwife, helped with the birth – and Torquil stood by, more comforting somehow than any doctor. In the intervals between the pains he sat by her bed and she clung to his hand, but not in fright – more in faith that since he was here, all would be well.

Into agony she went and then up again, like climbing a ladder to peace; plunged down, she screamed through blood-bitten lips. But at last she heard someone say, 'A boy,' and soon she was holding the baby to her breast.

Perfect, plump-toed. A spattering of reddish hair, and blue eyes. There was no question but that his name would be Ian.

She was in bed for a week, too happy for love of the child to think beyond feeding it, this marvel of silky skin and warm mouth. Ian had borrowed an old cradle; he rocked the baby, singing to it. If the red hair saddened him, he never mentioned it. Likely it would change and darken.

On the day before she returned to work, in mid-afternoon while she and Jean were having tea in the main room, Johnny knocked on the door and came in.

Jean said, instantly, 'Och, you'll excuse me, I've work to do upstairs,' and left them.

He looked just the same except for fine boots, and perhaps his curly beard was trimmed more neatly. He wore the kilt as he always had – his own. But there was something different in the way he stood shyly near the door instead of taking the hearthrug, or the stool, or the inglenook.

'Sit down,' she said.

He looked around the little room. 'The child?'

'In by my bed.'

'May I see it?'

She led him in, bent over the cradle and gently pulled the blanket from the chin. 'This is Ian.'

He spoke on a sigh. 'Like I'd thought. Hair, the Brown chin.' He tried to smile, turned away into the next room.

'What color are his eyes?' he asked as she joined him.

'Blue. Lighter than yours.'

She did not add that babies' eyes often darkened.

'Linty, what can I say? Except when Ian's letter came – God! It was like the end of the world.'

'How could you think I'd wait for you?'

'I didna think – I trusted.'

'After the way we left each other, you thought I still loved you?'

'Aye. I felt it. I knew it. I was sure then as I am now.'

She forced herself to say, 'You'd better go.'

'You're still angry, and I can't blame you, but—'

'It's not anger now. I'm past that. All I know is, she was more important than I and she always will be. Besides, there's Ian. I'll not hurt him.'

'But you don't love him.'

He moved forward and she backed against the wall.

'Please, you can't ruin things.'

'My God,' he said, 'are you afraid of me? *Me?*'

'Yes!' she said.

'Och, Linty – we can't lose each other. It was love long before we bedded. It could still be.'

'So you ask only friendship?'

'What more can I ask? No, I'm begging. Will you believe that I have no true friend anywhere?'

She sat down. 'Except Her Majesty. So why do you need me?'

'Partly *because* of her. I've got myself in a hell of a situation because I didn't have the wit to stay a ghillie. I haven't a friend at court except Ponsonby, her secretary, and that's only because he suffers me as a kind of jester, a comical fellow able to amuse her or soothe her. The others are affronted, furious that they, the nobility, should have to call a servant "Mister." She's aware of this, although of course I'd be the last to tell her, and now she's making me more hated by ordering Dr. Robertson to trace my ancestry and puff it up, trying to make a gentleman out of me. At Osborne she even tried to make Prince Alfred shake hands with me. He refused, and who can blame him? Except she does ... But who can I talk to but you? With honesty?'

'You could leave her service.'

'I've thought of it; but it would be like deserting a great ship that's making a dangerous voyage without a captain. My duty is to keep her on course.'

She understood that need of him made him do daft things, even in childhood. Risking his life to save a sheep in a blizzard was 'only my duty,' or fretting to find a wounded bird that would die anyway in the high hills. He had never quite grown up to realize that there was firstly duty to oneself.

'Is she mad, Johnny?'

'No, but to fear madness is a terrible thing. She feels alone on a peak with only myself to guide her. Och, I can't explain it, why she leans on me instead of Palmerston, the Prime Minister—'

'You brag, surely.'

'No. She doesn't consult me on politics, but she will ask advice on little things. It is important to her how she appears to her people and I tell her all she needs to do *is* to appear, not hide. I'm frank about rumors that she'll never open parliament again. I even argue that she must return to Buckingham Palace. She's turned her social duties over to Bertie and Alexandra, and folk resent it. They want a Queen, not the Prince and Princess of Wales. The newspapers are cruel – Ponsonby

155

tried to hide them from her but I took in the worst to show her, to try to waken her from what Jenner calls "torpor." Not that I get much help from him or anyone else; they're too afraid of her.'

As she was silent, he said, 'See, I've spewed out some of it and feel the better for it. But there's much more. God, I'm not just for treks outdoors, I'm like a bloody maid, shawling her and seeing her bonnet's on straight, and once I had to tell her to change her mouldy old black gown for something decent; she'd spilled food down it, and none of her women were bold enough to tell her.'

'I know it's hard,' Linty said, 'but it's your new life, and I have mine. You can't come here even in friendship without it hurting Ian.'

And to have to sit so carefully far from him, longing to stroke the glossy hair, to kiss away the frown. 'You see,' she said, 'it hurts me too.'

'I'm asking too much. I'm selfish. But I need you.'

Abruptly, he left. The sound of the door shutting brought Jean clattering down the stairs. The baby began to cry. As she fed him, she told Jean there was no reason to worry. Johnny had poured out some problems, that was all. Odd, though, that he'd left in such a hurry.

She didn't know until later that night that he had sought out Ian after work. 'He promised me on his honor that he would never touch you. He explained a little of why he needs to see you sometimes alone here. I said it was up to you.'

'He has no right to ask anything of me.'

'He knows that, darling. But it's a kind of desperation, I think. As he said, you're the only one he can confide in. You've no idea how he's resented. Why just this morning Sir Thomas ordered him to saddle two horses for the Duchess of Atholl and her groom. Johnny said he took no orders but from the Queen, which is true. Gossip has it that she sends for him at any hour of the day or night, has given him a room near her own suite. She seems bent on a scandal.'

'If she is,' Linty said, 'I'm not. I won't have folk saying that he comes here, mocking you and our marriage.'

'Because you're afraid?'

'Only of gossip.' Now she had lied again to Ian.

'You needn't fear. I'll be in the house.'

'You think, then, I should see him?'

He took her into his arms. 'You'll be doing great kindness just by listening. And how could I begrudge so small a part of you?'

How terrible to be trusted, she thought.

Back at work she heard the Queen's ladies whisper against 'that awful, uncouth Brown' who thought nothing of popping into their drawing room and without so much as a bow, saying, 'You, you and you for Her Majesty's dinner,' *pointing* at them. Never in proper court dress but in that indecent kilt, and always reeking of whisky whatever the hour. Someone must warn her dear Majesty that there was atrocious talk – but who dared repeat it?

Johnny repeated it to Linty when he came by twice a week to sit by the fire in the small new room Ian and Torquil had built of pine logs. Always Ian welcomed him, then left them; and this very trust strengthened her resistance to a glance, to a chance touch of hands as he handed her a glass or a dropped bit of sewing. 'The Queen has trouble sleeping,' he said. 'At midnight one night she sent Annie for me and of course the fool had to talk. All I did was sit in a chair near the Queen—'

'*Sit?*'

'Aye, she always asks me to sit. And by God, she said, "Smoke if you like but raise all the windows or I'll choke." It never occurred to her that her bedchamber would reek of tobacco in the morning, she's that damn innocent. What she wanted to talk about was Bertie and how marriage seems to have made him more responsible; but she worries he's going with a flash set. I just tell her that if she'll get back to London and take over her duties from Bertie – but she interrupts and says "*Nobody* understands," and looks over to all those things of the Prince's above the bed and begins to cry. God, Linty – so I go over and pat her shoulder, and then she says there's nobody but me and her Uncle Leopold she can really depend on, and he's so far away in Belgium – he's King there – and then she sits up straight and dries her eyes and talks about going to Coburg to unveil a statue to the Prince and then visiting King Leopold on the way back. She wants me to go along. . . .'

If I had married him, Linty thought, he'd scarcely ever be with me. Four months a year at Balmoral, but on almost constant duty, and at all hours.

He looked at his watch. 'It's time to get back. She's upset if I'm not in the Castle, within call.' He got up from the stool. 'Linty.'

He would say something hurtful about loving her or missing her in Germany. Swiftly she went to the door, opened it and called to Ian to bring a farewell dram for Johnny.

They went out into the night together, Johnny and Ian. Torquil said, 'You married a saint – or a fool.'

'It's none of your business,' Jean said, 'so long as Linty's not hurt.'

'It's all right,' Linty said.

And it was; for a while, at least . . .

It was a long while before Linty learned that the visit to Coburg was disastrous. Duke Ernest failed to provide a room for Johnny next door to the Queen's, but placed him in a separate wing of the palace with other servants. Insulted because her personal attendant had been insulted, Her Majesty stated that she would never again visit Coburg.

Then, in December, Balmoral was plunged into full mourning again when news came of the death of King Leopold. White caps and aprons were exchanged for black. Folk said December was always a terrible time for the Queen. Just four years ago, lacking four days, she had lost her husband, and now her beloved uncle. Might the new year cheer the poor soul.

But it brought further newspaper attacks. *The Times* hinted that she should abdicate in favor of the Prince of Wales since he had borne her public duties for four years; a Swiss paper suggested that she and John Brown were secretly married.

Of course not, Linty thought, she would never marry beneath her, and she was still so deep in love with the Prince. As

Ian said, it was just the newspapers wanting to sell copies. You couldn't believe a word in them.

She remembered the story of his being summoned into her bedchamber; but perhaps the Queen felt about Johnny as she did about Ian. You could bed with your dearest friend and still love someone else. One thing was certain: if Johnny was bedding the Queen he'd never tell a soul on earth. Not even me; especially not me.

She pretended to herself that Johnny was no more than a special sort of servant, for the idea of him lying with the Queen was somehow revolting, as if he'd been commanded to do so – or, just as bad, if he used his body to curry more favor. She dared not believe that of Johnny, always so independent, so honest. And yet – all things were possible since that lie he'd told her.

Because she was guilty about her love for Johnny she was more tender toward Ian, in a kind of play-acting she hadn't wanted to do; but if he found it false, it pleased him just the same to think her passionate. It was the least she could do in gratitude for his goodness.

To her astonishment he called the child 'John' and she said, 'But we named him Ian. It wouldn't do if folk began to wonder—'

'Nonsense. It saves confusion. Ian and John are the same in these parts, and nobody's wondering.'

The real excitement, that year of 1866, was that the railway had reached Ballater – a miracle for this remote area, celebrated with frolics at the Monaltrie Arms and all the inns to Braemar and beyond. The Queen had not permitted it further for fear of ruining the scenery. At Balmoral the ladies gossiped about Her Majesty's beautiful water-closet at the station, with pretty flowers painted on the enamel bowl. Linty learned that most of them dreaded Balmoral, having to accustom themselves to the Queen's passion for fresh air, shivering at scant fires in their bedchambers, hoping they would not be selected to accompany her and 'Mister Brown' on those 'arduous' jaunts into the mountains. They compared colds as once they might have compared jewels. They complained of indigestion from having to eat so quickly if invited to the Queen's table.

They hated those Hallowe'en bonfires, watched outside in the biting wind, and those Ghillies' Balls. Wasn't it a bit *odd* for Her Majesty to be in deep mourning but dancing with common folk and making her ladies do so? Of course she was still 'disturbed' and must feel that the dear Prince was most alive here where he had been happiest.

'Never talk in front of the servants' was an old rule, but servants always knew. What Upper didn't know, Lower did. Often the Queen couldn't sleep and whoever was on duty in Kitchen was sent up with oranges, pears and big apples, to be received at the Queen's door by Johnny Brown. In the morning the cleaning maid would take from a lady of the bedchamber *two* empty glasses which smelled of whisky, and a plate of fruit peels and seeds. It would be bloody cold in that room, the maid said, with all the windows open.

To let out tobacco fumes, Linty thought. But why weren't they more discreet about the glasses – unless it *was* innocent? Or unless Johnny was too fou and the Queen too sleepy to think about them. Och, it didn't make sense.

It didn't make sense that Her Majesty was so forgiving about drunkenness. Upper footmen who had been with her at Windsor remembered that one of their number had dropped a lighted lamp which tumbled down the stairs, him being fou at the time. Sir Thomas had made out a report for her on his bad history of drink, but instead of sacking him she had written in the margin 'Poor man.'

Mrs. Hayes, as puzzled as any, said that things had sorely changed since the Prince's time. When Ghillies' Balls started at seven o'clock some who waited on table were not quite steady for the Queen's Dinner at nine, and Ian reported how she'd talk against the sound of fallen crockery in the corridor. 'Many a guest has wine spilt on him, or her, but Her Majesty never seems to notice. She just whispers to me. "Wyness, replace that man," and smiles as if it were all serene, and the next day Petrie or Gordon or whoever offended is chided by Sir Thomas – but not sent away. It seems as if she is really sorry for the underdog.'

Linty was sorry for Ian that autumn, having to work late, helping the butlers and other footmen through the race of dinner. 'Just to think,' she said, 'after all those years I've never seen her but from a distance. Would you say she's still beautiful?'

It was a jealous question, for some men liked plump women, and perhaps Johnny...

'No,' he said, 'but there is something seems to make her so. Her eyes and her perfect skin. Her voice and her posture.'

She tried to word another question without rousing his suspicion. 'Would she still be attractive to a man, do you think – I mean, if she wanted to marry again?'

He laughed. 'What you mean, darling – would Johnny be her lover if he had the chance? I'd say she'd be a challenge to any man.'

'Even you?' she asked, making it seem a joke.

'Why not? I'd be curious. But if she weren't the Queen it would be no adventure.'

So, from a man's view, it seemed that Johnny could be attracted, and the thought was the more upsetting when he said, casually one night, 'The Queen's going to build another wee house up at Glasalt burn as a kind of hideaway.'

'But she has the little huts, Johnny.'

'They remind her too much of the Prince, she says.'

Aye, Linty thought, she couldna be happy with Johnny in a bed shared by the Prince's things; perhaps he himself had complained. But in a new place she might take a new love without guilt.

It was hard to be with Johnny – she left the door partially open into the main room, furious at her own restriction, at the way it wasn't natural not to so much as touch his hand on parting but lead him in to the others for the road-dram. When he left for the winter in Osborne she was careful that their last hours were spent at the Inn surrounded by people.

He never wrote. Before he returned in the spring she determined that she could not endure their private talks. Friendship was too much to ask because it was too little. They must drift apart, cut the last link. So she would tell him I am content with my husband and son, with Jean and Torquil. You must go your own way, find someone else to confide in.

But when he came to her house on the night of his arrival,

161

she didn't have the heart to say so right then. He looked tired, thinner, the first gray in the fire of his hair and beard. He had to see their child at once, cuddling him, making him laugh, presenting the gift of a teddy bear, and for Linty a paisley shawl with matching slippers. So, because Ian was waiting on the Queen's table, they were alone, Jean and Torquil visiting the Scotts.

'He looks like me,' Johnny said, as John was put to bed. 'His eyes are mine, his chin, his nose—'

'They change,' she said, bringing whisky to the fire. 'And Johnny, I have too.'

'No. You're still a girl.'

'What I meant was—'

'If ever I'd think you changed it wouldna be the same world. My world here . . . I canna make you understand what it's like outside. What's the sea to the mountains – just a flat nothing. London's a horror and we avoid it, we hate it.'

'We,' as if he and the Queen were married.

'But she's been nagged into reviewing troops in July, in Hyde Park. I told her she should; and she's been avoiding things too long and this is important. I had to beg and coax, and finally she said she would if I came along with her, but the Earl of Derby says she's got to go it alone because of the newspapers making a scandal.'

He downed his dram and reached for the bottle. 'It's got so she won't stir outside without me, so she told the Earl to hell with the troops, and it's been one long argument. The funny thing is, she really feels for the soldiers; every one of them's a hero to her. She can get all weepy by hearing that none of them would want to return medals to be inscribed for fear they weren't the ones she herself presented, touched with her own hand. Christ, she's so sentimental one minute and hard as flint the next. She claims she's too weak to make public appearances but she's often up at dawn, then working on her boxes, then riding her pony or out with me, but never where folk can see her. She's not too weak to do what she wants to do – and that's with more energy than a dozen younger women. The doctors – I hear them talk – they don't know what to make of her.'

'Maybe the change of life,' Linty said, 'but she's only forty-seven.'

He hesitated as if he didn't know what she meant – or maybe because a lover would know for sure.

'What I think,' he said finally, 'is that she's going to keep this grief for the Prince just as long as she can, and I'm not saying it's not real enough. Always visiting his tomb, raising statues. I've told her the cost of all those memorials would keep ten thousand families alive, but she says the people need these reminders of their dead father; she forgets they never loved him – only we at Crathie even respected him, and that took a while. You don't stuff a German down British throats, or any foreigner, but she can't see that. She only sees what she wants to see, like they say about an ostrich putting its head in the sand.'

He lit his pipe. 'The queer thing, she really feels she's mother to the nation, but when I say, "Well, then let them see you," she bristles up and says they know she's *there*. But they want her in Buckingham Palace and out in the carriage among them and opening new buildings. There are awful rumors that she *is* in the Palace but locked up, mad, and the prime minister her keeper, with myself the strong man to prevent her violence. I come right out and tell her these things, but she laughs and says it's just maniac talk, that the nation trusts her. And to prove it she hauls out a huge box of letters of sympathy from grieving widows like herself. Then she makes things worse by dancing here.'

'So she's not really grieving?'

'She is. But it's like she's two people inside herself. Sometimes it seems to me as if I'm talking to a stone throne draped in black; at others she's a girl of eighteen, ready for any lark. And you'd never believe what she laughs at. I tell her a dirty joke and she howls if it's not too raw; but let the French Ambassador say something she thinks is "risky" and she freezes like ice.'

That's because she loves Johnny, Linty thought, whether she knows it or not. Yet who could be more different than the Prince she mourns and Johnny Brown? Except each gave, and gives, his life to her.

'Did she freeze like ice when you told her you wanted to marry me?'

'Well—' He shifted the stool from the fire, fussed with the pipe, 'I didna exactly say I wanted to marry you – that is I didna mention your name. I just said I wanted to marry, which I'd need time off for. She seemed all upset at first, saying wasn't my duty to *her*, and we had a hell of a row – didna speak for two days. Then she sent me a stiff note to my quarters saying she would give me a cottage here or south as "reward for past duty." I had a footman send a note back thanking her. Then I wrote you. When I got Ian's reply I told the Queen I'd changed my mind about marriage. She thought it was for her sake and raised a lot of tears and called me "my dear good Brown" who had sacrificed for her.'

And took him into her bed as a reward?

He must have read her thought in that strange way he had, because he said, 'I'm not much for talking about love, but you know I love you.'

'I can't go on with you,' she said. 'It hurts too much, and it's too dangerous.'

Right at this moment it was dangerous, for if he was to touch her she'd not think a moment ahead.

'I'm selfish. I told you before, I can't lose you.'

'You will,' she said, 'unless you promise to be strong for us both.'

'I know. It's hell for me, too, but worse hell if I had to dam up all I'm thinking and feeling and worrying about. It's said the Queen's on a lonely pinnacle – but she has her whole family to confide in. She's forever writing letters to her daughters, her journal—'

'Do you still keep yours?'

He nodded.

Ian came in, greeting Johnny like a brother. Perhaps, she thought, the things you fear most never happen.

The Queen got her way against Lord Derby – her insistence that Johnny accompany her to review the troops in Hyde Park was providentially prevented by the execution of Emperor Maximilian of Mexico by a firing squad. Although a distant relative, the Queen ordered deep mourning. She could not possibly attend *any* function, she said. And what utter nonsense, she told her equerry, Lord Charles Fitzroy, that the mob would have overturned her carriage had she appeared in the Park with John Brown!

In May, Crathie readers were shocked by a publication called *The Tomahawk* hinting that the Queen was totally idle. In June they printed a cartoon, *Where is Britannia?* showing an empty throne covered by robes of state and behind it a British lion asleep. The accompanying short commentary indicated that if the Queen could entertain the ghillies and old wifies of Crathie, then why not her own nobility? In August there was a cartoon of Johnny, *A Brown Study*, showing the jeweled crown in a glass case. The British lion has awakened and is rampant at the feet of a kilted Highlander who casually smokes a pipe, his back to the throne. Wicked, Linty thought, vile. Then someone told Mrs. Hayes (who was too discreet to say who) that a nasty thing had come out in *Punch* last year, a pretended Court Circular:

> Balmoral, Tuesday
> Mr. John Brown walked on the Slopes, He subsequently partook of a haggis. In the evening, Mr. John Brown was pleased to listen to a bag-pipe.
> Mr. Brown retired early.

MacLeod the postie had got hold of the terrible *Pall Mall Gazette* last year but hadn't wanted to show it to anybody — only now at the Inver, with a good many drams inside him, he talked about how foreign people thought the Queen had married Johnny, and read from the *Gazette*: 'The Hon. Mr. Harris, British Minister at Berne, has addressed a complaint to the Swiss Federal Council against the *Lausanne Gazette* on account of an article in that Journal containing calumnies against Queen Victoria.'

It was said that people in London — 'the fashionables' — who'd been offended that they were never invited to Osborne or Windsor, and who missed the parties at Buckingham Palace, made jokes about 'Mrs. Brown being too busy to receive anyone.'

Of course Linty knew that none of it could be true; but it

seemed that the Queen herself was recklessly bent on scandal. Everything she did provoked more. At Balmoral Johnny complained of overwork, of being up at all hours with trifling messages footmen should be delivering. Because he didn't like the late chore of cleaning up the smoking-room, the Queen ordered that it should be closed by midnight to all gentlemen, including Prince Christian of Schleswig-Holstein. A servant had become more important than a royal personage.

Johnny told Linty on his next visit, 'She never lets me have time off, and my feet are swollen with all the running on piddling errands, so we've had it out; but I'm well hated by everyone but Ponsonby, who knows on which side his scone is buttered.'

'You're getting above yourself,' Linty said, teasing. 'You think you can do anything?'

He flushed red as his hair. 'What do you mean?'

'What do you think I mean, Johnny?'

'Och,' he said hastily, 'that I'm tactless. Well, I have to be to keep her from all the toadies that bore her. I'm glad she's got a chance to escape to Glasalt.'

The shiel was complete now, in its remote woods near the water. Besides stables nearby and a keeper's cottage was the Queen's hut – a sitting-room, bedroom, maid's room, dining-room and kitchen all on the ground floor. Above were rooms for Johnny, Grant and the cook.

Linty, with all the rest of the Balmoral servants, was invited to the fire-kindling in October. The little house could hold only a few at a time, but she saw its comfort, its snugness before, with the others, she spilled outside to join in the whisky-drinking. It was Grant who made a welcoming speech to the Queen, but Johnny who filled her glass and stood beside her. In the torchlight, in her black gown and heavy fringed mantle, she looked tiny beside him, and pale, but she was smiling. Her hair, under a lacy veil, was graying, but the great eyes glowed as fiddlers started up and Johnny led her into a reel on the carpet of grass and fallen leaves.

The Queen did not return to Balmoral that night when the party ended at eleven. She and Johnny and Grant remained with a maid and a cook, and next day it was rumored that the men had stayed up very late drinking and singing – which must have disturbed Her Majesty, who slept below. But she had made no complaint. 'The little passage near my room shuts off everything,' she told Mrs. Hayes that evening. 'But the sad thing is – it is the only house I have ever built as a widow. I fancied my husband was there, and blessed it.'

The shiel beside the Loch of Sadness became too cold even for the Queen that month, when snow fell on the mountain tops. In Crathie she attended christenings, partook of cakes and hot toddies, visited old Mrs. Grant, who was ill, discussed farm business with Dr. Robertson, showing interest in every cow and sheep that ranged the vast properties. She liked details, Johnny said – what had happened to that lost ewe, had the shepherd been to blame, and should Jenny, the barn cat, have another litter of kittens?

Surely the Queen was happier now; but now her ladies whispered that she spent part of each day communing with the Prince, seated by his white marble bust as if it were an altar, a shrine.

If that were so, Linty thought, she cannot be in love with Johnny. Or else she loved them both – one as God, the other in passion.

Balmoral clattered with its March cleaning – the tartan carpets were taken outside and pounded, the windows washed, the rooms scoured. Linty was checking linens when Mrs. Hayes came in and said, 'They want a younger maid to help in the Queen's apartments. I've suggested you.'

'Oh, no!' she said. 'Please, I'd be too scared!'

'It's an honor. And six shillings extra—'

'Thank you, Ma'am, but surely there's someone else could do it better.'

'A new broom sweeps cleaner, they say.'

Sir Thomas Biddulph had been replaced by Sir John Cowell as Master of the Household, and it was said he was stricter. One mistake, and she'd likely be sacked. 'I just can't, Ma'am.'

'I can't force you. But there's another post you might consider – all-night maid. Annie is getting too old, Beth has just married – what would you say to that?'

'What would it mean, Ma'am?' she asked.

'All of your days free until seven at night, when you'd start duty here in the linen room to tend any lady who required you. It could mean mending, as you do now, bringing smelling salts, any service needed. After midnight you'd usually be free to doze off – the bells are not likely to ring.'

It would be marvellous to be with little John throughout the day, and she would be free of Ian's lovemaking. Not that she really disliked it, but it would mean that she wouldn't have to go on play-acting night after night. Mrs. Hayes said her Sundays would be free, and of course the extra pay was important.

'Would the Queen be wanting me?'

'It's possible, but not likely. And you could find whatever she asked for; you know your way about.'

So it was arranged, and Ian took it better than she had hoped, saying that with the extra money she could have a new Sunday dress and little things she needed. Why, with the family savings mounting, they might even have a holiday in July – all the way to Edinburgh, if she liked.

She began her new job a week before the Queen arrived, so as to test how much sleep she'd need during the day. What she had not counted on was the queer way the castle seemed to be when everyone had settled to sleep, and most of the servants were in their quarters.

Someone was always on duty in Kitchen, but to venture down there for a cup of tea and a sandwich at midnight was creepy. The faint gaslight made shadows, and if you looked at a stag's head on a landing it seemed to be alive. Back in the linen room there was too much silence, as if the world had stopped. Or a sudden creak would be heard in the corridor when nobody could possibly be there.

If only she could read – she would learn with John when Ian began to teach him – time would pass more quickly. In the lamplight she knitted mittens; she would knit shawls. Perhaps in time she wouldn't be so uneasy.

It was impossible to sleep even had she permitted herself to.

The maids' lavatory was only just down the corridor, but

she found herself tiptoeing for fear of being heard, or seen. It was daft, but once out of the linen room she always felt watched.

The night before the Queen's arrival Mrs. Hayes stayed until nine to check all of the rooms. One next to the Royal Suite, hitherto used by a lady-in-waiting, had been converted, she said, to accommodate John Brown.

'Mister Brown,' she added hastily. 'We must always be very careful to address him as "Mister."'

'Johnny wouldna care.'

'But the Queen would.'

It was after midnight when Johnny came into the linen room, started toward her, then mindful of his promise, sat down near the door.

'You shouldna be here!' she said.

'And why not?' He tossed off his jacket and pulled out his flask. 'How are you, hen?'

'All right. But if you're found drinking in here—'

'She doesn't follow me about; I follow her, and she's tucked in safely.'

'But suppose she rings for you?'

'Not tonight she won't; tired to death she said – and looked it. Have a dram, Linty?'

She shook her head, watching him drink. 'How has it been with you?'

He shrugged. 'A little easier on my duties because I made such a row about leaving last month, and meant it. On call every damn minute, not enough sleep, no holiday since I started – and she's no better in her mind. She's gone in for Spiritualism . . .'

Not that it surprised him, Johnny said – she'd been reaching out for the dead Prince all these years. 'But the trouble is – *I* am the contact with him.'

It was a weird tale. A young Englishman, twenty years old now, named Robert James Lees, had been psychic since the age of three when he saw a vision of a Highlander in a kilt sitting by his bed. Later, at thirteen, he held a seance in a fashionable London house, and while in trance delivered a message from the Prince to the Queen. Hearing of this, she sent two courtiers to him, incognito, to test his worthiness. He wrote down the secret pet name by which the Prince called her, and sent it to her in a sealed envelope. She was convinced that he could help her reach her husband, invited him to Windsor and there held seances in secret. 'That was before I came to be her Personal Attendant. She asked him to take a permanent post as Resident Medium, but the lad seemed unwilling to visit often, saying he wasn't what they call "professional" yet. I think he's honest enough, for the Queen's grief would have made her credulous, easy prey. Anyway, two months ago, when she summoned Lees again asking that he take a permanent post, he said "No, Ma'am, my spirit guide won't allow me to devote my time to one individual." She told me she cried, but he said not to despair because someone very close to her would help. He described me, the Highlander he had seen in his vision.

'She summoned me from my room while he was still there and he nodded and said, "That is the man, Ma'am. He can do as much for you as I can." '

'Oh, God, Johnny — but it's horrible!'

'It's only a different kind of service.'

'But when I said you had the second sight you always laughed.'

'You told me I said things I don't remember. "Trance" Lees called it.'

'And do you go into these trances for her?'

'The queer thing is, Linty, I don't know. We sit in silence, the two of us, beside the Prince's bust. I seem to sleep in my chair but I can hear myself speak with his voice; then, when she turns up the lamps and I wake up, I don't know what I have said. She is always in tears, but happy tears, and she no longer talks of suicide. She feels that he is guiding her, through me.'

'And what do you feel?'

'A terrible tiredness when it's over. I told her, twice a week is all I can manage.'

'Doesna she think it a sin against the kirk?'

'No, because the Church believes in the hereafter.'

'But not in ghosts—'

'She feels he is real, is there, is with us, and calls it a holy thing. All I know is, she's more content. She talks of opening parliament again – of appearing in public more often.'

'As you want her to. How do you know you're not speaking for yourself in a dream?'

'I don't know.'

'You said she was no better in her mind.'

'I meant, she leans. Her own mind should be clear of the Prince, but it never will be.'

'You're helping to keep him alive to her.'

'Better that than her despair. If we can bring her out of retirement, as she says he wants, why then, it's worth it, isn't it?'

I don't know, Linty thought; I don't know what to believe. It seems to me this meddling with the spirits isna right, but then Johnny could never be evil or tricky.

'Some night this week,' he said, 'she will ask for another seance. You can be there and hear for yourself.'

'You're fou!'

'I'd like a witness present. She will never repeat to me what I say, but you can, and I want to know.'

'How on earth could I—'

'I'll ask for the library. You can stand behind the draperies—'

'And sneeze and be discovered!'

'Small risk, but if you are, many a maid has been trapped in a royal room dusting; she'd think nothing of it if the hour is right. Say Wednesday at five, just after her tea.'

'Small risk,' she mocked. 'Just me being sacked.'

'You forget,' Johnny said quietly, 'that if it came to your being discovered, I can protect you. What I demand, she will grant.'

She was careful not to be seen entering the Castle early. But, safely behind the full tartan draperies in the library, with its dim rose-shaded lamp, her very breathing seemed loud, and the thump of her heart. She was mad to do this. She held a dust cloth, and it *might* seem that she had been at work

171

here and scuttled for cover at the sound of Her Majesty's entrance.

Someone came in – she dared not look – and she heard the rustle of skirts, then a voice: 'You may go, Annie. Send for Mr. Brown.'

It was a beautiful voice, clear and soft and young. How could she have such a voice at her age, nearly fifty?

Minutes passed. Somewhere a clock ticked.

There was no knock on the door, but the beautiful voice saying, 'Come in. Sit down. No, here, close to him.'

To the marble bust on its pedestal.

A few moments' silence. 'Is he here, Brown?'

'Aye.'

A soft sigh, then silence again. Suddenly Johnny said something in German – *Liebchen*, it sounded like, and then more German words in a stream – he who didna know a word of the language. And his voice wasna his at all.

'Gladstone,' he continued in English. 'You must put up with him, work with him, not against him. He is a good man, always was. I have told you: guard against emotions, see the man as he is – capable. Remember, encourage, consult and warn; take no sides. Do not give Bertie power beyond his small scope; he was my failure; I tried. Prepare yourself for trouble with Bertie but do not panic. Do not heed letters from the public; they are all emotion. So often have I told you, against emotion guard.'

Another silence, long this time, and the sound of heavy breathing. 'Benjamin Disraeli – there is emotion, yes. You thought nine months of his power too brief; you were disappointed, but he will come back. On this, take heart for the future – it is radiant. I am with you always, never doubt. Do you question?'

The lovely, silvery voice. 'What will be the trouble with Bertie?'

'A woman.'

'Not Alex?'

'Another woman. Prevent, you cannot. His nature it is. Alex will help you; she is true to him and to you.'

A sob. 'When may I come to you?'

'When time it is, *liebchen*.' The voice was fainter. 'I am very tired but you are strong; you will grow stronger. How are my trees?'

'Oh, so many! Can't you see them?'

Silence.

'The first buds are coming out, early this year. The snows are still on Lochnagar.'

'I feel cold. I am very tired.'

Silence.

Johnny's voice, drowsy: 'I fell asleep, I'm sorry.'

'It's all right.'

'What time is it?'

'Twenty past five. Have you had tea?'

'No.'

'You may have some here.'

'No, I'll be off. You're weeping?'

'Well, he spoke to me of things. His – your voice now. I should not like to be alone tonight.'

'He wouldna want that, would he?'

And just what did *that* mean? And why had he never called her Your Majesty, or Ma'am?

'You can't disappoint folk at dinner. He wouldna approve. Come, I'll take you to Annie and get you set to rights.'

Such a very long silence before Linty heard the swish of silken skirts, the closing of the door. Peering out from the draperies, she saw the soft rose lamps, caught a faint fragrance of lilac. She was free to leave, and to wonder.

She was so sure that Johnny would come by to the linen room that night, if only to hear what he'd said in his trance, but he didn't. *I should not like to be alone tonight.* Oh, it was all so confusing; she wished she hadn't been there. Why hadn't the Queen called the Prince 'my darling' or 'beloved' or by the pet name in German – only 'you'? Well, you didn't call God by pet names either.

It was cruel of Johnny not to come to her tonight, when he must know she needed to talk. But perhaps he really was tired. She was convinced that the Prince had spoken. Even if Johnny had somehow learned German, how did he get into that

173

special, unforgettable voice? How would he dare to predict things, like Mr. Disraeli coming back and the Prince of Wales getting into trouble with a woman? Even forseeing logically that such things could happen, how had he known years and years ago that the Queen would come here, of all places on earth? That Balmoral would be razed and rebuilt?

Three years ago she'd have sworn that Johnny was incapable of lying – but she had learned otherwise. And so he could be mistrusted. Was it possible, after all, that he had learned these German words of endearment from the Queen? The thought was hateful, but even if true it would not kill love. Her love reached back into her childhood in utter faith; it could, without faith, reach on till her death.

She had so much to live for: there was wee John, the goodness of Ian, the understanding of Jean and Torquil to whom she could tell anything except the secrets which Johnny entrusted to her. The warmth of her family's love was important to her; but she knew that she would sacrifice even that if Johnny beckoned her into the cold.

The dawn came, cold and pink in first birds' song. She rang down to Kitchen for tea and scones at six. At seven she made her way home through sleeping flowers, snuggled into bed with Ian and lay awake to the soft sound of rain.

Johnny came to the linen room the following evening during the Queen's dinner. He had no memory of what he had said the night before. Concerning Mr. Disraeli, it was odd that the Prince had said nothing against him. 'He never trusted him, thought him a wily imposter. But Her Majesty began to like him when he wrote his first letters of condolence praising the Prince to the sky ... He flatters her, he amuses her, and she doesna care a damn that he's a Jew ...'

That didn't interest Linty. She said, 'Was she – I mean, did she spend the evening alone?'

'Och, she sat with her guests – or rather, they stood – until past eleven.'

'I thought you'd come by here.'

'These trances tire me more than a day in the hills. She's always begging for them but I'm firm. I tell her I wasn't hired for that, and I never know whether what I've said might upset her.'

'If you speak through him, and it sounded like it, you couldna upset her. Do you think it's really his spirit, Johnny?'

'How in hell should I know? Lees thinks so. She does. But the trouble is, she's so open about it. Earlier on in the year Bertie was at Windsor and wanted a pony for a morning ride. She called me in to the morning room and said, "Mr. Brown, will it be all right with you?" But she didna look at me, she looked at Prince Albert's bust, *then* back at me. To make it worse, when I said "yes," she looked at Albert again and nodded. Bertie's jaw had dropped about six inches; he's not so stupid he didna get the point. And of course there's gossip she won't make a decision of any sort without me – a pack of lies. I only tell her what I think if she asks. I say "Don't you go confusing me with the Prince just because you need to lean," and we have a row. Twice this year I've packed up to leave, but each time she pulls me back – and with more money. I'm making two hundred and thirty pounds a year now, and seventy pounds for clothes. I'd be a fool to quit, even if I – thought I should.'

He meant, 'Even if I wanted to.'

'I get blamed for everything. They say that because I don't like travel to foreign parts – and I don't – she doesna travel oftener. I didna like the Swiss and the smells there, but neither did she or Jenner, for that matter. I don't like being stared at because I'm in kilt, or laughed at when I can't hit anybody; and there's plenty can travel with her if she wants to. My orders are to protect her and care for her. I do, but I'm not squirming while I do it. She says she wants to knight me, and we had a row about that. Try as she would she couldna get my ancestry puffed up and I said, "just leave me be." Making the family call me "Mister" sticks in their craws as it is.' He looked at his watch. 'Ring for some supper, will you?'

'But I've had mine. I'm only allowed something at six.'

'I am. Ask if there's venison and neeps, and I'll drink claret—'

'Not here!'

'Why not here? I can eat where I like.'

'Suppose some lady needs attention and finds you here?'

'Suppose she does? Then you're mending my jacket.' He took it off and gave it to her. 'Tell Macose plain boiled tatties, and none of his fancy sauces on the meat.'

It was when he was still drinking the claret and having a sweet that Lady Jane Ely came in. What she wanted Linty never knew, for she looked at Johnny eating from his tray and said, 'Good evening, Mr. Brown,' and hurried out again.

'Good,' he said. 'They know not to interrupt me when I'm busy.'

There was an old bridge over the Dee considered too risky to cross, yet folk still used it at their peril if they weren't near the chain bridge. Linty felt herself on just such a bridge when she was alone with Johnny. Never mind that the linen room was a public place; if he kissed her there it would lead to bed somewhere else. And she would have to leave Ian, who was devoted to young John as if the boy were his own son, and John in turn worshipped him. If it came to leaving Ian and living near Johnny through the years, she couldn't part them. It was hell, and it couldn't be solved.

On his last night at Balmoral before the court left for Osborne, Johnny came in to her shortly after midnight. Offering a dram from his flask, he stood close to her. She smelled lilac and moved away.

A man didn't reek of scent unless he'd been very close to a woman, and this was the fragrance she remembered from the library. He frowned. 'What's wrong?'

She told him, and he swore. 'You know I'm part lady's maid! Forever shawling her or bringing a mantle. So if I smell like a bloody lilac bush how can I help it?'

Her mind did not believe him. Her heart did. It would be so long before she saw him again . . .

'I'll have that farewell dram,' she said.

When he started to leave he moved toward her, then stopped, looked at her for a long moment, hurried out the door.

To the Queen?

Linty was returned to day duty, and so was Ian. Jean cared for John, marveling at his brightness. He had learned to read;

soon he would enter Crathie school, well ahead of his class-mates. Linty dreamed of a great future for him; he would be an important man, like his father, but not enslaved in service to anyone.

As the months passed he came to look more and more like Johnny, the red wavy hair, the nose, the chin, the deep blue eyes were all Johnny's. One summer Sunday, picking berries, he and Linty met Sheena in the woods. She stared at John and smiled.

'You look just like your father,' she said.

'Do I?' John smiled back, puzzled. 'Only he hasn't much hair and he's great big tall.'

'You'll be as tall as him someday,' she said.

Fearful of what Sheena might say next, Linty hurried John away. Long hate, she thought, is like long love. It is never-ending.

In early autumn the court returned to Balmoral. Bertie came for the grouse-shooting and sent his valet to Linty, who had gone back on night duty, to mend a kilt torn on a stile. She had finished the job and placed it in the press when the door opened and a husky young man with pointed beard came in, elegant in black evening clothes, a white camellia in his buttonhole.

She recognized him from his portraits and trembled into a curtsy. 'Your Royal Highness.'

He smiled. 'What's your name?'

'Clarke, sir.'

'My valet's dining. I need my kilt to the Ghillies' Ball.'

She brought it from the clothes press. 'There, sir.'

'How long have you been here?' he asked, taking it over his arm.

'Oh years, sir.'

'You can't be that old.'

He was flirting, ogling, looking at her bosom like – well, like any man. Jolly, he was, and merry-eyed. But he made her feel uncomfortable. She wished he would go.

'I am nearly thirty-nine, sir.'

'I don't believe it. You look twenty.'

'Thank you, sir. I hope the kilt is rightly done?'

177

He must have dozens. Why should he require this one? 'Oh, I'm sure it is. You'll be attending the ball?'

'No sir, I'm on duty here.' She did not add, 'throughout the night.'

'You'll not miss much. I find them a bloody bore. No grace to the dancing – or do you like it?'

'I'm used to Highland ways, sir, but I don't dance often.'

'What's wrong with the lads hereabouts?'

She said primly, 'I am married, sir, and my husband on night duty too.'

Then, thank God, Margaret Stewart came in with a ball gown to be pressed, backed out at sight of the Prince but was waved forward by him – and he left.

Margaret chuckled. 'Did he make a try?'

'Of course not.'

'The way you looked upset – you'd not be the only one. Kathy and Sheila both. They say he's a ram.'

It seemed indecent to be talking like that of the future King. But she couldn't help but be interested. 'What did he do, then?'

'Kisses. They had the sense to make excuses of duties elsewhere, and he didna seem offended. But the strange thing is – have you seen Princess Alexandra?'

'Not even from a distance,' Linty said.

'She looks like a tall, beautiful lily – all in black tonight, of course, but her skin is so white, and her shoulders bare and her hair pouffed up. It's sinful that the Queen insists in mourning. But what I'm getting at, the Princess is the prettiest woman ever I saw. Why should he want anyone else?'

Linty shrugged. It was just manlike, she supposed, to want an adventure. But risky here, with his mother all eyes and ears.

'Of course she's pregnant again, but you'd think he'd show her some respect,' Margaret said, warming the iron on the fire and laying out the ball gown on a board. 'Look at this, Linty – Lady Bruce's. God, look at the ostrich feathers . . .'

All the ladies wore black except the very young ones, who were allowed violet or gray or white. It seemed the Queen was in perpetual mourning, and when folk thought it was about to

178

be lifted some relative died, so that nobody could quite say she carried it on for Prince Albert. Nobody except Johnny, who said she would never change and that her dresses were a disgrace, some rusty with age.

'What's the Queen wearing tonight?'

'I havena heard.'

Two ladies' maids came in with a flutter of requests. The dressing bell rang and there was the usual panic. Between quarter to nine and nine-thirty Linty dared not move from the linen room, for the Queen could be whimsy about dinner. Those few servants who had met her in the corridor by chance, with no means to flee, said that her eyes had been terrible. She frightened everyone, even her family, and it was said Bertie had a dram in his suite before he could face her – and she so small. It was the eyes, like blue daggers; the cruel chill of her voice, if she spoke. Usually she didn't.

You could not always trust a footman to ring the warning bell that meant she approached along the corridor, but Linty heard it at five past nine. She was standing near the closed door when she heard a familiar voice:

'Oh, for God's sake, woman, tie up that bow; it looks like a dead crow had lit on you.'

Johnny.

And a clear, sweet voice, with a giggle in it. 'I'll find a looking glass along . . .'

That autumn was warm and sunny and the Queen was often at Glasalt Shiel overnight with her tiny retinue – and always Johnny. Bertie, in obvious disfavor, was lodged at Abergeldie Castle during his brief stay, though everyone said Her Majesty was fond of the Princess.

Johnny's wages had now been raised to three hundred and ten pounds, with clothes money extra. 'I have so much,' he said to Linty one night in the linen room. 'I've been trying to think how to give you some without Ian knowing.'

'Don't be daft.'

'For the child—'

'We have enough,' she said, not in pride but in fear. 'Dinna upset things; let us be.'

'But he knows I'm the father. If I put some money in a bank in Aberdeen for John's education, would he complain? We're friends—'

'Dinna test it,' she said. 'Torquil said he was either a fool or a saint. We havena fooled him; but he'd feel a fool if you gave money for his child.'

'*His* child!'

'He loves John as if the boy was his own. – He'll not be patient with an insult to his pride.'

'And how long must I be patient?' Suddenly he was pulling her out of her chair and pressing her body to his. 'You belong to me.'

There was the kiss she had dreaded and longed for; but he'd be gone again in a couple of days. She was strong enough now.

She pushed him away. 'We'll call this another goodbye.'

'It doesna have to be. I've got her to agree that I may stay on here each season two days after she leaves.'

'What's two days, then?'

'At Glasalt. We two.'

She was back in his arms of her own will, questionless. If he said Glasalt, so it would be, as if a King commanded. He would know a way. She started to say, 'But Ian—'

'Ian will never know, never be hurt. Trust me?' he said.

They heard footsteps in the corridor and sprang apart. Gordon, a footman, came in and said, 'Mr. Brown, the Queen commands your presence.'

It was nearly one in the morning.

Johnny said, 'Tell her I'll be along in a while,' and lit his pipe as the door closed.

It was all so easy, as if Johnny were royalty. After the Queen left he simply told Mrs. Hayes that the Shiel required cleaning – one maid was sufficient. Linty Clarke Wyness would do, and his brother and sister-in-law would find it a rare treat to help – no pay required. He, Johnny, would stay at Bush and sleep two full days; he was that tired.

Ian believed her so readily, and this hurt. Jean and Torquil worried that the Shiel would be frigid despite its fireplaces, and she was lent Torquil's heavy sheepskin jacket. She said she would walk to Bush to join Johnny's brother and sister-in-law and ride to Loch Muick by pony. She promised to bring John some souvenir of the Queen's, if she could find it – something she had left, be it a scrap of torn paper or a discarded ribbon. In cleaning up, goodness knows what she might find.

She wanted to tell Jean and Torquil the truth, as she always had, but they would worry; they would feel a burden of guilt for Ian. She had arranged to meet Johnny near the old bridge after Ian and Torquil had gone to work.

It was a gray, sunless day, the slopes dark with heather. Johnny was waiting, with a mare provisioned with bags of food. They rode into the wilderness, past sheep that huddled together from the scent of snow, up and around the loch and then to its end, to a cluster of tall pines, where the Shiel, stables and keeper's hut stood near the water.

It was a mournful place, Linty thought as Johnny unlocked the door: rightly a 'widow's retreat,' but beautiful in its way, with the dark, silent water that reflected the full skirts of the firs. Inside the pine-paneled sitting-room, Johnny made a fire. She sat near it while he unpacked the food and took birch logs into the kitchen.

A very humble place for a Queen. It was carpeted in the Balmoral tartan, but the furniture was of simple pine, the fireplace of rock. There were no ornaments except for a small bust of Prince Albert on a pedestal near the window.

As Johnny came in with a bottle and glasses, she said, 'Am I sitting in her chair?'

He laughed. 'She is generally by the window, and the window is usually open.'

He came to sit on the rug by her feet, clinked his glass with hers. 'I can't believe you're here.'

'Johnny, you're *sure* your brother won't make some blunder?'

'Of course not. If someone should come to Bush seeking me – and they won't, because I'm on holiday – he'll say I'm out shooting. If the worst came to the worst, he'd ride here to warn us.'

She relaxed, warmed by the fire, discarding her shawls. It

181

seemed he wanted to wait upon her, not letting her into the kitchen but bringing turkey legs and heated potatoes and turnips. But she could not eat much, nor, oddly, could he. They set aside their plates. He pulled her onto the couch.

It was as if he had never left her body, remembered it like a song. Every cove and cranny known and cherished and then, like a fuse slowly lit, the ending, the kisses that renewed and rekindled the fire.

Later they stood outside watching the sunset bloody the water. They gathered more logs from the woodpile. They fed the mare in the stables and bedded her in straw. He made up a fire in the Queen's bedroom while she brewed tea and cut gammon for sandwiches.

They talked until midnight, but of the past, avoiding serious things. Remember when you pulled me out of the pond, Johnny, then hit me for swimming too far? Remember how we wished on the chestnuts at Hogmanay and you burnt your hand getting yours back? Remember when I took the looking glass down Mariad's cellar steps on Hallowe'en to see the face of my future husband and you asked why I'd done it? Remember, Linty, when we saw the eagle over Lochnagar, like a shaft of gold? Remember, remember . . .

It was creepy in the Queen's bedroom; she tried to ignore the death photograph of the Prince, the plaster cast of his arm above the bed. It seemed proof that she had never slept with Johnny – how could she, if all her beds were like this?

But she wouldna think tonight, this night of such loveliness. At dawn the trees arched like a white cathedral. The snow had come.

Johnny washed windows; Linty scrubbed, swept, dusted. Under the Queen's bed she found a button, and mindful of her promise to John, said, 'Is it off the Queen's dress?'

'Aye, I'd think so,' he said. 'If it's black, you can be sure it's hers.'

She put it into her apron pocket.

They cleaned out the stables and the keeper's hut. The Shiel was warm now from its three fireplaces, and at dusk Linty used the bathing tub and changed to her blue wool

182

gown. In the kitchen she cooked leek and potato soup while Johnny bathed. The remaining turkey would make a nice cream-on-toast, and she remembered to add sherry, as Macose did. Surely the Queen wouldn't miss one bottle?

Johnny came in wearing a dark-red dressing gown. She said, 'I've opened a bottle of – *oh*.'

A black button was missing from his robe.

'What?' he asked as she stared at him.

It was the same button, no doubt of it. Under *her* bed. He had lost it in that very bedroom.

She went to her apron that hung on a hook, showed him the button. 'I can't take this to John. It's yours, see?'

'We'll find him something else,' Johnny said, pocketing the button. 'Look in the rubbish bin and you're sure to find hairpins or an old pen.'

So innocent he seemed – but did he wear that dressing gown in her room? Of course, if he was summoned late at night, he wouldn't tarry to put on his kilt. But it was awful to think how that button might have come off, her grabbing him . . .

He sat down at the kitchen table. 'Nibs of pens; you'll find dozens in the desk. She writes like a demon to everyone in her family and keeps her journal every day. But why is John so damn interested in her leavings?'

'You're so used to her,' Linty said, calming. 'Y'dinna ken how a child can feel about royalty.'

'I'll post him a pack of things for Christmas if that's what he wants. Good, you've opened the sherry.' He brought glasses. 'I've come to like it better than clary, but I still can't stomach champagne. Not that it sickens me – it's like nothing; just because it's costly the fashionables go into debt for it.'

Later he looked at her nakedness as if it was a marvel to him, twining her hair around his hands, his throat, meshing himself into it. Who spoke of love when one was in it, like a deep loch?

Nor did they speak of tomorrow, when he must leave on the train at dusk to be gone until spring. A special train from Ballater for Mr. John Brown. The same hard winter for Linty

Wyness. But as she sank to sleep in his arms, she thought, I will remember, remember. And I will forget that button.

They worked again that day. Linty found little things for John, and before they shared a last dram at two, Johnny said, 'I must do something about money for things that you and John need, and I've thought of a way.'

'Please – it would be too dangerous.'

'I'm giving my brother a hundred pounds for you. Go to him whenever you need it, for any reason. Each year there will be more.'

She thanked him; it was safe, and John would need to be educated. She might even find a way to tell Ian – but not now. She could think of nothing now beyond this moment of kissing Johnny goodbye by the smoored fire in the clean Shiel.

'We'll go to Bush,' he said, 'and my brother will take you home. He knows what to say...'

Snow fell as they rode around the loch. Soft, drifting snow, like feathers from a shaken pillowcase. Two figures loomed ahead and Johnny said, 'God! Hide your face.'

Michael Wright said, 'Have you seen two sheep up there, Johnny?'

Sheena, coming up beside him, said, 'Hello, Linty,' and laughed.

'No sheep up there,' Johnny said. 'My brother is coming down – ask him.'

Sheena laughed again. She and Michael stood aside to let the mare pass. 'Don't fret,' Johnny said when they were out of hearing. 'I think she was fou.'

Maybe; but fou or not, Sheena would remember.

They lingered at Bush for an hour, having tea and a dram for Johnny's long road south. Then Johnny said, why shouldn't he himself ride Linty home, seeing as it was on his way – and what more natural than to say goodbye to her family?

His family – John.

Ian was still at work, on the day service, but Jean and Torquil welcomed them with more tea, and sandwiches and oatcakes. Linty gave John the Queen's shoelace, pen nibs, a bit

184

of green blotting paper; and Johnny and the boy discussed fox-hunting. 'It shouldna be a sport,' Johnny said, 'but a riddance of pests, a clean shot...'

Then Johnny left to pick up his luggage at Balmoral and take a carriage to the station. No chance for a farewell kiss, but she could feel them and wondered if her lips looked bruised, if Jean noticed. Evidently not, for she said, 'Poor lass, you're tired – did she leave much of a mess?'

'It wasna too bad,' Linty said, hating to lie, but if she said too little it would be suspicious. Stick to the truth. 'It's a simple, cosy place, not hard to clean, not like her rooms in the Castle; but I *am* tired.'

'Tomorrow you can sleep.'

Aye, the Sabbath. 'What's keeping Ian so late?'

'What do they call it – inventory?'

Ah yes, that system of listing that Sir John had started when he became Master of the Household; he was so afraid something had been stolen or left by guests. He said such a list protected the staff, and perhaps he was right.

'I am tired,' she said again, 'I won't wait up for Ian,' and she went into their room.

In bed, she thought, Please God he won't make love to-night. It would put Johnny further away even than he is, and he traveling so fast on that train away from me.

She heard John laugh at something Torquil said, then cuddled into the pillow. Remembering...

She didn't hear Ian come into bed but she heard his voice at dawn when the light awakened her. 'You were with Johnny.'

She sat up on her elbow.

'Isn't that true?' he asked.

Sheena. How else would he know unless Sheena had gone to the Castle and told him?

She could say, 'Johnny came up to the Shiel and travelled home with his brother and me and his sister-in-law,' but her wits were still asleep. It would sound false. It *was* false.

'Well?' he said.

God, his eyes were so hard, his mouth. She dared not lie. She said, 'Sheena told you she met us on the road?'

'Yes, but I didn't believe it – that bitch. It was what you

185

said to me in your sleep, with your hand on my – then I knew.'

Her tears came, but for him, not herself. To seem to seek him in love, which she never had, and then speak Johnny's name . . .!

There was no point in lying.

'I was with Johnny,' she said. 'I will always be. I can't help it. I never could.' She faced him. 'There's the sacred truth. With something else you won't believe—'

'You love me.'

He said it harshly, but as the fact it was. 'Aye, I love you. I'm glad you know that though I'll have to leave you. I'm glad you said that before I did. It's the truth.'

He was silent for a long time. She dried her tears on the sheet and said, 'I'll be leaving. It would be best if I were to leave John here, with you. Only I'd ask to see him sometimes? I mean, just sometimes?'

'You want to live with Johnny, then?'

'He hasna asked me. He moves around so much, and to foreign countries with her. There's no life with him. There's not even a place to live near him, the way he moves about.'

'Then where would you go?'

'London – Aberdeen – I don't know. I've had no chance to think. You should know what I must do, what you want me to do.'

Again he was silent and she said, 'I've no right to ask to see John after I go?'

'It's not a matter for me,' he said. 'People divorce and I think the courts judge that – as to rights.'

'But you could never stay in service at Balmoral if it was known you divorced, even though you aren't the guilty one.'

'How would you live, Linty?'

'Johnny has given his brother a hundred pounds for me to take when I need it.' She swallowed back tears, for Ian looked so bleak. Perhaps he guessed it was meant for the child. 'I can take service somewhere else.'

'You are nearly forty. Work gets harder.'

'So, it gets harder. But I'm healthy. And—'

She nearly said the ultimate truth: Johnny will take care of me always.

186

'And so you mean to leave us.'

'You want me to, don't you?' she asked.

'Did I say that?'

'You spoke of divorce.'

'I thought you wanted it.'

'It would wreck things for you and Johnny both. I can never marry him.'

'Then stay here,' he said. 'I won't have you rootless and wandering like a camp follower.'

She said, marveling, 'But how can you forgive me?'

'I put myself in your place. I know what love is. I can no more help loving you – whatever you've done – than you can help loving him. It's a helpless thing, like an illness.'

'But Ian, when Johnny returns we'll be lovers again. You can't accept that.'

'I'd sooner accept that than lose you, or have you lose John. We both need you.'

She moved toward him, rested her head on his shoulder. He bent and kissed her gently, stroked tears from her face. 'Go back to sleep,' he said.

It was nearly a month before he made love to her and she was grateful that he had waited and, in her gratitude, more than ever anxious to please him. There seemed no falseness in that but a new closeness, soft firelight compared to the blaze of Johnny.

Toward the end of February Prince Bertie provided the press with more scandal; he was brought to court as witness in a divorce case. Sir Charles Mordaunt accused two of Bertie's friends of sleeping with his young wife. Bertie maintained he had written Lady Mordaunt some innocent letters, and paid her innocent visits, but was in no way involved in adultery. There was no cross-examination and Sir Charles lost his case when his wife was judged insane. But Bertie and his Alexandra were publicly hissed when they drove about London, and were booed in the theater. At Ascot, in June, crowds were cold to him until a horse in which he was said to have financial interest won the final event. Cheered by the spectators, Bertie smiled, raised his top hat, lit a cigar and, smiling, said, 'You seem to be in a better mood now than you were this morning, damn you.' Well, Linty thought as Ian read to her, it wasn't too surprising that the crowd cheered him again. He had a jolly way with him – but what on earth would his mother say about the way he was carrying on?

But she herself was again being criticized for neglecting her public duties, for never entertaining foreign visitors, living in Buckingham Palace or opening Parliament. Surely grief for Prince Albert had been respected, but after nearly ten years of seclusion wasn't it time, the newspapers asked, that the sovereign resumed her responsibilities?

Johnny said later that summer that the Queen had been remarkably kind to Bertie over his involvement in the divorce case, but had begged him to be more circumspect and not to travel with such a 'fast set.' But it wasn't too long before Prime Minister Gladstone, exasperated with them both, wrote to the Earl of Granville: 'The Queen is invisible and the Prince of Wales is not respected.'

But on the first of Johnny's nights back at Balmoral, meeting in the linen room, they talked only of themselves. She told him that Ian knew everything. They stood at opposite ends of the little room, not daring to kiss because people were still in the corridors.

Johnny said, humbly, 'Ian – I wish I could thank him.'

She nodded. 'We must be so careful for his sake. I'd hate to have him shamed – I mean, folk talking. And it's a wonder Sheena didna make more of it.'

'Forget her. She had no proof that we stayed together; even Ian refused to believe her. But we must find some place to be together.'

There were the croft houses deserted after the Clearances, but they'd dare not raise a fire. If we were younger, she thought bitterly, any heatherbed or hedge would do; but we need some grace, not just a mating.

He said, 'I dinna like to bring my family into it again, though my brother would help. Ah, Linty, the world up here is too small.' Then, in sudden fury: 'One thing I know, I'm not sneaking to you in some shed. We might have to wait until she leaves – could you get two days off?'

She was owed a holiday. 'Aye, but where would we go?'

'Aberdeen. I could go with the Queen that far, and wait for you. You could come by coach—'

'Everyone would know I'd left – alone, without Ian, all that way. What excuse?'

Forbes knocked on the door, came in. 'Her Majesty requires you, Mr. Brown.'

'Clarke,' Johnny said, almost with a snarl, 'you didna press my kilt right last year. See if you've learned better.' And as she stared at him, he followed Forbes out.

She waited, sure that Johnny would return during the night. But he didn't. If only she had had the time to learn to read when Ian taught John. There was nothing to do but knit and wonder and remember that lilac scent, and that Johnny couldn't be wholly trusted – except, perhaps, by the Queen.

There seemed no possible way to meet in secret; they could only talk in the linen room on nights when he had an hour's freedom. He was on call at any hour. One evening, while the Queen dined with guests, he came to Linty in fury, and deep in drink.

'I've some rights!' he said. 'Four hours sleep I had before she sent for me at eight. I told Ponsonby, "It's the end. What ever do I get but four miserable days a year, and only here?"'

'Quiet,' she said, for he was shouting.

'Why the hell should I be? I told him to tell her what I said, and then I slept again. When she sent for me after luncheon to go to Glasalt, I'd had a few drams and told Gordon to say so, plain out. She hasna bothered me since, but I'm going to pack and leave. Come with me.'

'You're fou!'

'Aye. What's that to do with it? Will you come with me? Divorce? Marry me?'

'I'll not talk to you when you're like this. You don't know what you're asking or saying. If I did leave, I wouldna go *with* you. I've Ian to think of – and so have you when you're sober.'

Before she could protest he had her in his arms, but with all of her strength she pushed him away and he staggered, holding onto a chair.

'For God's sake go to bed,' she said. 'Please, you mustn't be here. You're drunk and tired, and tomorrow—'

'I'll be gone tonight,' he said, and lurched out the door.

Far too fou to pack, she thought. But most surely the Queen would dismiss him in the morning. She couldn't ignore his insult to her through Colonel Ponsonby and Gordon, the footman. A private rebellion, perhaps, for she'd forgiven him before, but this was public.

If Johnny did leave, then Linty would follow – in time, when talk of him had quieted, when there wouldn't seem a connection between them that would hurt Ian. Only, to leave Ian and John would tear her up, tear them as much, hurt Torquil and Jean, and put her beyond all safety.

For Johnny, even though he might have saved money, wouldn't be easily welcome in service to another family. He was a famous man now, but once he had fallen from favor the most he could hope for was to farm somewhere, and it couldn't be Bush if he wanted her with him.

Chatter in the corridor at eleven meant that guests of the Queen had come up to retire for the night. The warning bell tinkled – and she was on the way to her suite. A lady's maid came in to ask where a warming pan might be. Another wanted to press a riding skirt for morning. Then the Castle quieted.

The hours until dawn were so long. Knitting a muffler for John, thinking of him, wondering about the future but unable to plan . . . If she divorced Ian, would the Queen retain a divorced man in service? If not, would the Gordons of Huntly take him back?

At six she went down the corridor to the lavatory. She came out and was nearing the linen room when she saw two figures approaching, the woman in a wide black robe, the red-bearded man in a dark-red dressing gown. Legs limp with fear, she managed to reach a linen press – the nearest shelter – and hurried behind its tartan curtain.

As they came closer she heard the woman say, 'I'm forgiven? You're sure?'

Johnny's voice. 'I've told you. Now go back; I'll bring up your tea.'

'I don't want you out of my sight.'

'Go back, woman, and get into bed. Stop crying.'

190

Whispers, but clear and close. Linty dared not peer out, not only for the terror of being discovered but because she could not bear to know that their long silence was a kiss. Then she heard him pass her, waited, looked out and found the corridor empty.

She could not, in honor of Johnny's former confidence regarding the Queen, tell Ian what she had witnessed, but on the day when they had their late breakfast together in the house she said, 'I canna tell you why, but I'm through with Johnny. I don't want to see him again – or even be near him. Could you get back your place with the Gordons?'

'You mean, to move to Huntly?'

'Yes. Would there be a place for Torquil there?'

'Vast gardens. I wish I could ask – I mean, ask you why.'

'I've a good reason.'

'But if you're through with Johnny, why uproot us all? Four months out of a year, at most. Can't you avoid him?'

She put down her tea mug with a little clink. 'I am just disgusted. I'm sick of it all. I hate my work. And I'm not sure he'd avoid me.'

'I would order him to,' Ian said. 'I'm not Johnny Brown's servant.'

'No, but you see, I can't order myself if I stay on. It would be hell.'

'Then you'll quit work. We won't starve. Smaller wages in Huntly and the expense of moving wouldn't be sensible. There might not be a house there for us, and who would buy this?'

True, houses in Crathie went a-begging.

'Then I'll quit work,' she said. 'But it's not fair when I could be earning.'

He reached for her hand. 'Perhaps it's only a row, darling. Selfishly, I hope it's more, but love isn't easily killed for people like us.'

'It isn't even a row. He doesna know how I feel. Ian, all I can say is, he's been living a lie for years. If he'd really loved me, he'd have married me before he met – before I met you.'

Jean came in with John to stack logs at the hearth. As she poured tea for them, Linty said to Ian, 'I'll be talking to Mrs.

Hayes when I get to work and setting it all straight.'

Giving notice, she meant. Telling Johnny. Ian nodded. You couldna talk privately during the day. You couldna go in to cry, either.

She had wanted to go straight to Mrs. Hayes and give notice on the excuse that she wanted more time with her son, but the housekeeper had left early with duties at Abergeldie, which served as guest house. So she carried on her usual work in the linen room, mending and pressing, aware as always of the terror spread by the Queen.

You heard it in the chatter of visiting maids, culled from their mistresses. If a joke was told in Her Majesty's presence, no one dared to laugh until she did – and often she didn't, freezing and shaming the teller. If she asked a question, the guests must try to reply as briefly as possible; otherwise she'd cut them off. Ladies with naturally high color used French powder to whiten their cheeks lest Her Majesty think they rouged. Through the years she herself had bared her shoulders (though not now) and had never minded a low-cut gown, but she was livid at sight of an ankle. Legs could never be mentioned. It was 'a chicken limb, or roast limb of lamb.' A piano required its limbs dusted – and petticoated ... A piano stool was a piano *seat*.

Yet for all this, they said, who could believe the privileges she allowed Mr. Brown? Last night he was fou – yes, and most of yesterday, according to Gordon. He smoked wherever he pleased – a reeky old pipe, whereas the Prince of Wales was forbidden cigars except in the smoking room! On her foreign travels, John Brown stalked around glumly and glared at the crowds who stared at his bare knees, cut officials short in their welcoming speeches, saying, 'We've had enough.' But most astonishing of all, when she and Mr. Brown were in Switzerland and an English paper said she had gone there to have his baby – the Queen had *laughed*. Well, that's what the Duchess said. Of course the rumor couldn't have been true, but why wasn't she blazing mad?

They scurried away to help their mistresses dress. At nine-twenty the warning bell sounded – the Queen was in the corridor. A few minutes later Johnny came in and sat down. 'I'm staying on, Linty. I've demanded more free time. I've been thinking—'

'So have I. I'm leaving service. I can't stand this – the way it is with the Queen and you. I saw you both early this morning; I had to hide . . . but I heard.'

'So? She wanted tea.'

'What I think,' Linty said slowly, 'I can't say. But for us, it's over.'

'Tell me why.'

She dared not, for if she said, 'You sleep with the Queen to keep your place,' he might turn violent. So she said, 'I have always come second in your life, but I'm first in Ian's and in John's.'

'What can I say, then?' He spread his big hands. 'But you don't understand. If I'd packed up, she'd have gone to pieces, and – you can believe this or not – I'm the one that keeps her on keel. Ponsonby knows it; he's said as much. The doctors know it, and the family. Now she's got this idea I keep her in touch with Prince Albert, it would be like a second death if I left her.'

'I'm not asking you to leave her. It was your idea, last night.'

'But not now.' He looked tired and sad, pale under his sunburn. 'She wanted a seance this afternoon, and I fell asleep in that trance. She repeated the things I'd told her as Albert. He warned that I must never leave her.'

'So *she* said.'

'She can't lie – she leaves that to the diplomats. She told me years ago that from childhood she could never lie, so that she was punished often for some prank she could have hidden. I'd say that truthfulness is like her second skin. She even argued with the Prince that time when he wanted to go to the inn incognito as "Lord and Lady Churchill" – she saw it as a lie, not a protection of privacy. No, Linty, I believe what she tells me I've said in trance. It seems I warned her to expect more embarrassment through the newspapers, that I said she *had* to open parliament – and by God, she says she will, which is a miracle – I told her to work against a match tax – and that made her want to laugh, she said, since I smoke so much, except that the way the Prince put it convinced her it would be hard on the poor. Finally he – I – mentioned Disraeli as coming back to power someday and bringing her radiance.'

'I remember that,' Linty said.

'Aye, she said that was the second time, and Albert never caring for Disraeli in life.'

'It's so queer,' Linty said, 'I heard you say to prepare for trouble with Bertie – it came true. And you don't realize you sound like him and speak German. It's so queer...'

So queer, too, that she had forgotten her anger against him, shed her suspicions as they talked. They made no plans about meeting in secret, but they knew when he left her an hour later that nothing had changed between them.

So she told Ian. 'I am so sorry, but...'

'I expected nothing else,' he said, and held her close.

Chapter Five

They discarded plan after plan for a secret meeting until they agreed on a picnic. It would be a day in the golden haze of the hills after the Queen left, when both were due time off.

'Sheena will be waiting to make trouble – we mustn't go near her house.'

'I know paths she never heard of.'

There was always a vast cleaning-up after the court left, so the lie to Jean of day duty seemed natural. She told Ian the truth, but dared not look at him for the pain she might see, busying herself at the hearth. For a while he didn't speak. Then he said, softly, 'I love you, too,' and came to take the teapot to the table.

As she set out to meet Johnny rain was falling lightly. Never mind, it would clear; the weather here was like a silly girl who couldn't make up her mind between smiles and frowns. But then it really came down. She couldn't walk another half mile in this, and there was no shelter to seek.

Johnny wouldn't be expecting her now; he'd have turned his pony back to Balmoral. Reluctantly she began her way back through a field, then saw him galloping toward her through sheets of rain. He swept her up beside him, put a cloak around her. 'Where are we to go?' she asked.

'To the hut.'

She didn't question this as they rode in what seemed lakes of water. The Queen hadn't used the hut since the Prince's death – it had been merely a pause for shooting parties. Surely it was safe enough now, remote as it was, and no hunter would venture out on such a day.

Up rough, narrow mountain roads, finally they came to Loch Muick. Perched on the edge were two small wooden huts. With his key, Johnny opened the larger one that the Queen had used so long ago.

It smelled of rot, of mice and mildew. Johnny made a fire in one of the two small sitting rooms, and lit candles. Linty could see wet patches of mould on the walls, foams of cobwebs in the corners of the ceiling. He left her alone while he tended to the pony outside. She sat with her steamy cloak and shawl close to the fire and felt no warmth.

There was no feeling of cosiness as there had been at the Shiel. This place on Loch Muick was indeed a place of sorrow. The plain pine furniture was cushioned in dismal brown, with only a tartan carpet for color. A stag's head stared down from above the rock fireplace, eyes tragic. Och, this was no place to make love.

Yet the Queen and the Prince had loved it; their first visit in 1849 had been merry, with fishing on the loch, pipers, dancing. Perhaps it was this rain that made the place so sad.

Johnny joined her with a parcel of food and a bottle. They sat together on the hearthrug, ate and drank, but almost in silence. A couple of drams in him and Johnny usually talked, but not now. He was almost dour, and she saw the start of age in his face, lines at the full mouth, a forehead beginning to furrow. She felt sorry for them both – for her wet, fading hair, thinned of its lushness; for the hands in her lap, with the faintest trail of violet veins. We are no longer young and we cannot grow old together.

He took her in his arms but there was no passion in his kiss, as if she were a sister to be warmed and cherished. She lay back against him and they stared into the fire, still wordless. We must leave here, she thought, as soon as the rain stops. Something here is changing us from lovers to friends. And I canna let him go back, six or seven long months of separation, thinking of me like this – a dear woman in Crathie, whom he once loved hotly.

'What's it about this place?' she asked. 'It's not for us.'

He held her more closely, his arms about her waist. 'It's just a neglected place. If it were cleaned up—'

'That's not it. It's not the cobwebs. It's like a graveyard.'

'Aye. But here is where they were happiest, free. Of a morn-

196

ing I'd make them porridge and they'd sit here on the rug and share a bowl, drink coffee from the same mug. He was a different man here, Linty, laughing and joking and teasing her. One day we caught seventy trout – he whooped like a boy and bragged like one. She would go out and sketch and then show him her drawings, to be kissed for the good ones. They didna seem to notice who was around.'

'I can never imagine her like that – young.'

'She's like two, maybe three people. A child. A woman. A Queen – and always with the feeling that she is mother to her people. She thinks she must always set an example, but it's not always in her nature to be so prim. Sometimes I think she fights herself. Other times, she escapes. When I – the Prince, I mean – told her to open parliament again, she said she would. But that was in emotion. I doubt she will. It can't go on like this; the people won't stand for it. I told her straight out just before she left. Nobody else talks to her straight, so I had to. She said, "I will not be strong enough ... my health." As if she's arranged to be ill – and believe me, the doctors will connive. She twists them around her finger.'

And you, too. A plump, aging woman, yet with some magic that you can't resist. You hate the indoor duties, the queer seances, the foreign travels. You hate it all, but you will never leave her. There's something in you that wants to protect, to be depended on.

She turned her head and lifted her mouth to his, but his kiss slid to her cheek. So be it; she wouldn't want to make love here, like in a crypt – but she wanted him to want her. She wanted to be able to say, 'No,' but there was nothing to say at all.

The rain pattered off, the wind rose and grieved. Still he held her, her back to his chest, her hair against his chin. He said, *'Liebchen, ich liebe dich.'*

'What?' She turned around to face him. His eyes were closed. He had not felt her move; he seemed asleep, but he was speaking in this language that wasn't theirs. A prickle of fear ran up her spine. 'Johnny, don't talk like that!'

'English,' he said, in a strange kind of voice with knots in it. 'Always English. I do the best I can.'

She wanted to awaken him but was afraid to, like you're told not to startle folk who walk in their sleep.

'Johnny, wake up,' she said softly.

'You must waken. You must not be the princess to sleep away the years of the fairytale, but the queen to rule. You shirk. But you are strong. Of your country you are the fabric. It must not tear of neglect. They must see you, our people. It is not enough to study and tend paper matters. You must go among them as you used to do. Visitors you must greet. But you hide.'

'Please—'

'It is I who beg you, Liebchen.'

My God, the voice was so sad, so in despair. And now the room was filled with shadows, and though the fire burned, it was cold, cold. Looking toward the door, she thought for an instant that a tall man stood there in slim-fitting black that curved at the waist. Then, as she gasped, he was gone, and Johnny said, 'Och, I must have slept,' and yawned, stretching, and took a dram from the bottle on the floor.

'Your shawl's dry,' he said, and leaned to put it around her. 'You're shivering.'

She nodded. 'It was cold here.' Her voice seemed a squeak.

'Have a dram, then.'

'No. It's not that—'

Not that kind of cold. It's a cold of the spirit. 'I want to go,' she said, getting to her feet. 'I want to go home.'

'But why? We've hours before the dark.'

'It is the dark,' she said. 'I think we have to face things. There's no future — we're not young to make one. The years have gone too fast and swept you too far. I can't keep up, you're so ahead in a different stream.'

'That's daft. You can't leave me. Because you are me.' He rose to stand beside her. 'There's a lot of rubbish talked about love and how two people are one. Only with us it's true. I'm with you miles away and you with me. That's why I don't mind you married to Ian for your safety's sake, and John's; that's why Ian's not jealous. He knows you don't divide souls, Linty. It's a kind of wisdom he has and I have. Have you lost it?'

198

As she was silent, he said, 'You try to leave me but you can't. Are you trying again?'

She moved away from him. 'I just want to go home. You were in that trance thing . . . the Prince was here. It's all wrong to be here, watched.'

'What happened?'

She told him. 'It's so queer. We became different as soon as we got here, you know that. We didna want to make love. You didna kiss me like you would have if he – she – weren't some-how here. Oh, God, it's like they'd built a cairn and the stones won't roll away – unnatural, awful.'

'But she's alive—'

'Kept alive by you.'

'That's not true,' he said. 'I only help. She's healthy as a horse and eats like one. Likely she'll outlive us both. But it's my duty to see she does the right things—'

'Duty! It's like a religion with you.'

'What do you want me to do then? Leave her? And would you leave Ian and John?'

The same old question with no answer. Perhaps when John was a baby she could have left him, but now, with him at seven, they were so close, and he so snug with Ian and Torquil and Jean. You loved a child more as you helped him to grow up.

'Don't answer that,' he said, 'I think it's a time to ride with the winds, not to fight them. But one thing you must do.' He brought a bundle of notes from his pocket. 'Take this. Use it for John, or for a holiday—'

'Ian would never forgive me! D'you no ken how proud he is? Do you want me to lose him?'

He couldn't argue against that; there was no secret way of using the money or of keeping it. Finally she said, 'I told you we must leave here. Now – please.'

This time he didn't argue, but smoored the fire and went out to bring the pony around. She gathered up the bits of their picnic and carried the rubbish outside to dump in the loch. The rain had stopped, but the water dripped from the overhanging trees. Gray water, gray hills and sky. And a gray mood was on them both as they rode as close to her house as they dared.

He helped her down from the pony, took her into his arms and kissed her as if it were the last they'd ever know, and she clung to him. Then she forced herself to walk away, not turning as he rode in the opposite direction.

Jean welcomed her with surprise. 'You're home so early?'

'I'm not feeling so well. Chilled, like.'

'Then it's tea and a dram in it.'

John came home from school and joined them by the fire. He was tall for his age, and so like Johnny it was odd folk hadn't gossiped long before this. Or perhaps they did.

'You havena a headache?' Jean asked anxiously.

'No. Just a cold starting, maybe.'

John took her hand. 'You are cold. I'll bring a blanket.'

He had watched Ian fussing over her from his earliest childhood, and he wanted to copy him. As he left the room Jean said, 'It's daft the way my headaches stopped when I met Torquil. It can't be just his hands that cured me, or love – can it?'

'I dinna think we should question such things, but just be glad.'

'I am. I never thought to be so content. But you – do you often think of Johnny?'

A part-truth: 'Aye, he was my youth. I am always glad to see him.'

'And I am always so afraid, each time he's here, that you'll go back to him. It's like seeing a swimmer against a strong current—'

John came back with the blanket and tucked it around her, then left them to see to the hens. 'I won't be swept in,' Linty said.

'But I wouldna blame you,' Jean said, 'if you were.'

So there it was, out between them – in a way. But if she confided in Jean she would be placing guilt on her sister, a burden she didn't need, that should be Linty's alone.

'Why wouldna you blame me, then?'

'Because liking and love are so different. I liked Alec, remember? I thought it was love, but I love Torquil. If I had married Alec, and then met Torquil – who knows?'

'But you are afraid I'll go back to Johnny?'

'Ian loves you so. And what sort of life would you have away from us?'

So Jean had been thinking that way too. 'I wouldna have a happy life with Johnny even if it was possible — I mean to live with him. There would be no roots to it. He would never be home, but with her.'

Had she blurted too much? 'I mean, in service as he is, moving from here to Windsor to Osborne, and the foreign journeys — och, any woman would be mad as a blue hare to marry Johnny, even if she hadna a family. You see?'

'I see,' Jean said.

Then Ian came in from work, with Torquil. Seeing her sheltered in the blanket, he said, 'What's wrong?'

She looked up at him. 'Just a chill. I was home two hours ago, not feeling well.'

'Then you should be abed.'

Later, alone with him, she said, 'I'm not going to lie,' and told him what had happened. 'Another place, or a sunny day, and it might have been different. But I wanted to come home.'

He nodded.

The court did not return to Balmoral until the following June, but there had been news of the Queen in the newspapers. She had finally opened Parliament, wearing ermine-trimmed robes and a new crown. But there were nasty comments that in return for this she expected a large annuity for Prince Arthur and a handsome dowry for Princess Louise, who was married in March at Windsor. There were no further public appearances. The reason was understood to be ill health.

Yet, shortly after her return to Balmoral she wanted to climb Craig Gowan: 'Steep and treacherous,' as Johnny said, 'and she ten years older than the last time she did it. Linty, the woman doesna make sense.'

It was their first meeting of that year, in the linen room at midnight, but he had scarcely greeted her and asked after John before he was in the chair with his complaints. 'She's set herself back again — won favor only to kill it again if it's known she's healthy enough to climb. I told her; I said such a thing would infuriate the people. A woman too sick to open a hospital or even drive through London can climb a damned rough hill. But she says she will, though I warn her – she says I warned her in trance – that she will endanger the Prince's annuity, which hasna been voted yet.'

'If you refuse to take her on the climb—'

'She's so stubborn she'll go with Grant, and he's not as spry as he was. I can't risk that, either.'

'Isna it odd she pays no attention to a spirit warning?'

'She pays no attention to anything or anyone who crosses her whims.'

It was three days before Linty saw Johnny again. And it was all over the castle that Her Majesty had climbed the Craig and seemed none the worse for it, driven up to the high mountains for picnics, and stayed two nights at the Shiel. Then, in sudden need for a change of holiday, she commanded the court to Osborne. Johnny wasn't allowed his customary two days of freedom. A brief kiss in the linen room at dawn, and he was gone.

The newspapers reported that fifty-four votes had been cast against Prince Arthur's annuity.

Early in August, Mrs. Hayes received instructions to make ready to receive the Queen again, but on the 14th a telegram reported that she had a bad sore throat and could not swallow food. Yet she arrived at Balmoral three days later. Her ladies whispered that the poor dear suffered tortures with choking sensations in the throat and a sore arm from an insect sting on her right elbow. During the days she slept, and the court tiptoed.

'She's called "wolf" too long,' Johnny told Linty. 'For once the doctors don't believe her. Ponsonby told me Gladstone said her behavior was the most sickening experience in his forty years of public life. But Linty, she's not lying. She *is* sick.'

'How can you be sure?'

'I am in and out a dozen times a day to help her turn in her bed. Her arm throbs; she gulps for breath. The fools let the Prince die – and I'm not so sure she won't, because they dinna believe her. I've told Jenner right out that this is no bid for seclusion.'

202

A few days later the doctors reported the Queen 'seriously ill.' There was an abscess on her arm that wouldn't respond to treatment. It was whispered that she might not live twenty-four hours. Rheumatism had set into her leg. The famous Professor Lister was sent for.

Johnny, gray-faced, haggard for lack of sleep, came into the linen room at two in the morning, rang for tea and poured a dram into it. 'I help her in and out of a kind of tent on her bed. She can barely move without help. Now her foot is gouty.'

'Why aren't her family here, if she's dying?'

'Like Biddulph says, they'd kill her at once. Christ, she's never found peace with her family. They're for writing letters to, not seeing. Bertie alone would drive her mad.'

Five bells rang, and Johnny sprang up. It was his signal to go to her and he rushed, upsetting the tea tray.

That morning Lister lanced the arm abscess. Later a dressing, after use of the new carbolic spray. But gout settled throughout her body. Johnny had to lift her from bed to couch.

Gradually she improved. Prince Alfred, Duke of Edinburgh, arrived. There were petty squabbles, the Queen furious because the Duke shook hands with everyone but Johnny. Grant revived the old feud and refused to deliver a message from the Duke to the Queen because it was supposed to go through Johnny. The Duke ordered fiddlers to stop playing in the corridor, but Johnny, knowing the Queen's need for cheer, ordered them to resume. Deciding to mediate between Johnny and the Duke, Her Majesty persuaded the two men to meet, with Colonel Ponsonby as witness. Coldly, the Duke said, 'If I see a man on board my ship on any subject, it is always in the presence of an officer.' The Queen, angrily taking Ponsonby's part, said, 'This is not a ship and I won't have naval discipline introduced here.'

Johnny, grateful for the Queen's recovery, took the matter as a lark. 'It cost me nothing to apologize to the Prince,' he told Linty. 'Ponsonby said, "I think His Royal Highness is satisfied." I said, "I'm satisfied too," having the last word.'

Then the Princess Royal arrived with her daughter, Princess Charlotte. 'They were with Her Majesty when I came into the room. She said to the Princess, "Say how de do to Brown, my dear," and the girl did.

' "Now go and shake hands," said the Queen.

'Charlotte said, "That I won't. Mama says I ought not to be too familiar with servants." '

Johnny chuckled. 'Bloody snobs. The Queen was on my side, all right. I told her in private her family had gey bad manners and she agreed; there was no end of a row between her and the Princess. It's all to the good; it keeps her mind off her gout. The poor love has lost two stone in weight.'

'Poor love,' Linty said scornfully. 'Is that what you call her now she's so frail?'

He glared at her. 'She is frail. It's nerves now, and no wonder, accused of shamming, of hoarding money – I could kill the journalists who hint that she salts away two hundred thousand pounds a year; and the sarcastic bastards who say she can't afford to drive about London because she has no new bonnet. And that Jenner comes right out and tells Lord Halifax about the nerves, takes it all as insanity.'

She dared not ask, 'Isn't it?' For even among the loyal ladies there was that whisper. Wasn't it more than, well, 'queer' that she allowed that great hulking Brown to lift and carry her at all hours of the night, without her maids present? And hadn't even Mr. Disraeli been quoted as saying that she was 'physically and morally incapacitated' from pageantry, so that the *Telegraph* asked if the former prime minister meant she was mad? And *Reynolds Newspaper* said that she would have to abdicate.

Reverend Norman Macleod was Crathie's minister now and made the matter more public by stating he had never seen 'the remotest trace of mental or moral weakness' which Johnny said, though well meant, was like the kiss of death – God, why couldn't folk keep their stupid mouths shut? Why not just leave her in peace to get well?

On the first Sunday in November she was well enough to attend Crathie Kirk, Johnny helping her up the steps. The ladies were cheered that some of them were asked to dine that evening, that there was music. But Lady Jane Ely told her maid – who told Linty – that the Queen was very unhappy and cried a great deal due to her nerves and her feeling that few people understood that she couldn't go on show like a circus.

Two days later Johnny said that Sir Charles Dilke, a radical member of Parliament, had attacked her in a speech saying she should be made to abdicate. She ordered the Government to repudiate him; she was in a rage. 'Good for her,' Johnny said. 'The tears have stopped. If it had to happen, it couldna have been at a better time. It's wakened her up.'

All this talk of the Queen – never of themselves. But one night Johnny said, 'I've asked for four days off when she leaves, and God knows I've earned it. We'll go to the Shiel.'

It could be arranged somehow – for one night, anyway. Then, on November 21st, a telegram from Sandringham killed the plan. Bertie had a fever. It was thought to be typhoid. The Queen rushed south. Five years ago, Linty thought as she helped the Upper maids clean up, I'd have been angry. Now it seems that no matter what happens it must just be accepted. Ride with the winds, he said. There was nothing else to do.

Black winds whirled about the Queen. The journalists were kinder – there were no more attacks now that the heir was in danger – but spoke of the Queen's terror that the fatal death-day of December 14th would re-occur. Bertie was delirious, one minute joking and singing, the next suggesting the most obscene reforms when he was King. Sometimes he thought he *was* king – but that didn't come out until later.

While he hovered between life and death, the Balmoral servants talked of his hot temper, his arrogance, and a valet who had once tended him at Abergeldie told of his visit to an elegant country house. 'At dinner a footman lost his grip on a spoon while serving His Highness and a spot of creamed spinach landed on his shirt front. The Prince leaped to his feet, red-faced with rage, then plunged both hands into the spinach tureen and spread it all over his shirt-front. "I may as well make a complete job of it!" he said, kicked back his chair and ran from the room. What astonished people even more was that he came back shortly afterwards, cleaned up and affable. A queer man . . .'

And hating Johnny more bitterly by the year, as Linty knew.

There was the day at Windsor when he came unexpectedly to see the Queen, who had just retired for her afternoon nap. Johnny asked bluntly, 'What do you want?' and was haughtily told.

'Well, you're not seeing your mother until three o'clock. You'll need to go and amuse yourself for an hour.'

Aye, it was like Johnny to dismiss anyone who tried to meddle with the Queen's privacy or comfort. None of the Balmoral servants would forget Johnny's tangles with the pompous military men who had visited there. General Sir John McNeil, an equerry, was furious when Johnny leaned over his desk as he wrote out an order for carriages. 'Go and wait outside,' he said. 'I'll call you when I'm ready.'

'Don't you be abrupt with me!' Johnny shouted. 'I'm not one of your private soldiers.'

After a hot argument Johnny slammed out of the room. That evening he brought McNeil a letter from the Queen offering him a military command in India of such small consequence that he realized he was being demoted.

Then there was General Sir Lyndoch Gardiner, prissy and curious as a cat about everything that went on in the household, and so precise about the smallest matter that Johnny called him a niggling old lass behind his back. One day he arrived at Balmoral and asked Johnny to tell him at once about the Queen's health.

'The Queen's all right,' he said. 'It was only the other day she says to me, "there's that damned old fool General Gardiner coming into waiting and I know he'll be putting his bloody nose into everything that doesna concern him!"'

If they thought that Johnny and I were so close, they wouldna talk about him so freely, Linty thought, or speculate on just how much he meant to the Queen. Some were sure he shared her bed, others said he was only a clown who amused her while caring for her. Gordon remembered a feud between the Duchess of Roxburghe and another lady of the Bedchamber, and then hearing Dr. Reid suggest to the Queen at dinner that the Duchess might visit again, being so pleasant a person.

'Oh, dear no,' the Queen said laughing, 'there would only be what Mr. Brown calls Hell and Hot Water!'

They all agreed, even those who didn't like Johnny, that during the Prince's illness he was the one who could help her most, for it was no secret that when the huge family gathered, as they were gathered now at Sandringham, she was somehow at her worst. On the night of December 13th Mrs. Hayes received a telegram to say that the Prince's crisis was at hand. The Reverend Macleod asked Crathie folk to pray through the night and all the next day that the tragedy of ten years ago might not recur. Linty, knowing more of the truth than the others, thought that if Bertie died the Queen might well go mad through guilt. And if that happened, what would Johnny do? Become her keeper, as it had been rumored he was at Buckingham Palace long ago? To stand by in the twilight of greatness, running to the cackle of a madwoman's need, to her scream, her sobs?

That night she prayed that Bertie would recover, not for love of him, or even respect, but for Johnny's sake.

On the evening of the 14th a telegram announced that the Prince had passed the crisis and was better. Two days later, the newspapers carried the story of his 'miraculous recovery.' The Queen wrote a letter of thanks to her people for their sympathy. Later, the Government held public Thanksgiving at St. Paul's Cathedral, where the Queen raised Bertie's hand and kissed it, to cheers. The newspapers stated that Mr. John Brown sat on the box of the open carriage.

But evidently Her Majesty wasn't so popular in some circles, for the very next day there was an attempt on her life by an Irish revolutionary, Arthur O'Connor, who had pointed a pistol at her as she drove with Prince Arthur. The Prince tried to jump over the carriage but was slower than Johnny, who seized the boy. The pistol proved to be unloaded and so the sentence was only a year's imprisonment. The Queen had him transported for fear of another attempt. Johnny won from her public thanks, a gold medal, and a twenty-five pound annuity. Bertie insisted that his brother had behaved just as bravely, but he was given only a gold pin.

'There'll be no living with Johnny when he comes back here,' Gordon said one evening at high tea.

'For all he knew there might have been no living for the Queen,' Ian said.

Walking home with him, Linty said, 'You are wonderful to defend Johnny.'

'He is wonderful to defend her.'

You are so above jealousy, she thought. Or do you bide your time, knowing that we all grow older and that someday the flame will die? I am forty-three, Johnny forty-seven — there is little time for us as lovers. And so little time together, ever.

He didn't return in the spring, but accompanied the Queen to Baden-Baden to visit her half-sister, Princess Feodore, who was dying. But in the autumn the court came to Balmoral. At the Ghillies' Balls the Queen danced with no one but Johnny, and her ladies were shocked that she would so neglect the gentry. They were shocked, too, that she revived the ancient title of 'Esquire' and bestowed it on him in November. It meant that he was himself now a member of the gentry, ranking just below a knight.

Once again, circumstances prevented a secret meeting. Ian fell ill of typhoid — mild, thank God, but the fever was slow to leave him. There were only brief talks in the linen room, catching up on months of news. He said that despite her relief that Bertie was alive, he might as well not be, for all the rifts between them would never heal. 'She says Bertie is close to a libertine, going about too much again with that flash Marlborough set, and he says what on earth can he do when she goes about so little? But I don't fret for fear we'll have a King on our hands.'

'But someday he will be.'

'A long time off.'

'Do you still have those seances?' she asked.

'Aye, when she insists. She was radiant when the last one ended; again the Prince's voice spoke of Disraeli as coming to power. I don't know; it's not second sight or wishful thinking, and God knows I wouldn't try to play at politics. My enemies — her family, that is — think I advise her. I do not. I only keep her on an even keel as best I can.

'Why do you frown?' Johnny asked. 'Ian's not worse, is he?'

'No,' she said. 'He'll be back at work next week.'

And you with her, at Osborne by the sea or merry at Windsor for a tree-sparkled Christmas. John Brown, Esquire, a great personage famed throughout the world.

Gruffly, as if his throat was sore or choked, he said, 'I love you. Remember that.'

Like remembering to breathe.

On a frosty January day John was late from school. Linty, home by six from her day-duty, worried that he might have had some accident on the road, but more likely, Jean said, he'd been kept in by the schoolmaster for some mischief.

But when Ian and Torquil came in half an hour later, Linty was frantic. Mr. Ingram would never keep a child so late, even as punishment, to take the black roads home.

Ian was about to relight his lantern and go out to look for him when the boy came in. His left eye was a darkening purple and a front tooth was missing, but he was grinning as he spat blood on the floor.

'I whipped 'em,' he said. 'They won't try *that* again.'

'Who?' Ian asked, as Linty hurried for a poultice.

'Some of the boys.' He was made to stand still while Jean bathed the eye and the swollen mouth.

'But who? Why?' Torquil asked.

'I don't tattle,' John said, 'Besides, some girls started it. Girls!' He spat again.

'What girls?' Linty asked, sitting him down and bringing raw beef to the eye.

'Sheena Wright and her sister.'

Sheena's children! 'What did they do to cause a fight?'

'They won't call me by my right name.' One clear blue eye looked up to meet Linty's. 'They call me Johnny Brown. They say Wyness isna my name. One of the boys — I won't say who — began laughing with the girls and I let him have it, and two others pitched in, outside in the garden. You should see the way *they* look. I chased one clear to his house . . .'

'But it was the Wright girls that started it?' Ian asked.

'Aye. Little snots.'

'Why would anyone call you by a wrong name?' Jean asked carefully.

'Maybe they're jealous I know Johnny Brown better than they do. Maybe I bragged a little, saying I'd met him, and they called me a bastard and I pitched in, like I said . . .'

Thank God he doesn't know what was meant. 'Johnny Brown's a famous man,' Ian said, 'and I think you're right, they're jealous. But you shouldna brag to other children. Do I brag that I know the Queen, serve her, have even touched her hand by chance when pouring her wine? It doesn't make a man any bigger to boast.'

'I didna boast!'

'Let it be,' Torquil said. 'Let's eat.'

But after tea, Ian said, 'I think I'll take a walk,' and nodded to Linty. She put on her heavy cloak and they went out into the icy starlight. It would be a long walk to the Wright cottage, he said. But he felt he must go.

'I'll go too.' She had two lanterns alight.

'No need. I'll just have a word with Michael. He's not a bad sort.'

'There is need,' she said.

As always, she dreaded facing Sheena. How many frolics had she missed at the Inver Inn just because Sheena would be there? She had been a coward; now she couldn't afford to be; this was something that had to be cleared up.

She had forgotten how dismal these slopes could be in the dark, how remotely a shepherd lived among the hills. The house, faintly lit, perched in frost-whitened bracken. Dogs ran out to them, and as Ian cuffed them down the door opened and they saw Michael on the threshold.

'Come in,' he said.

God, he had aged, Linty thought – the dark fox-face lined and rutted, his shoulders slumped. Little Sheena and Maggie stared curiously at the guests and were told to go to bed. Evidently Michael sensed this was no talk for children.

'Will you take a dram?' he asked as he took their lanterns and seated them.

'No,' Ian said, 'Is Sheena in?'

'In bed with the infant. She is – not well.'

The little room was filthy. Tea mugs and earthen plates were piled at the hearth, unwashed. Small, dirty clothes steamed and smelled from their place on the hearth screen. Up in a loft hens rustled, and there was the rank stench of goat.

Ian came straight to the point. 'Your wife, I think, is responsible for what happened today,' and told him.

Michael was silent for a long while. Then he said, 'She is not responsible as a normal person would be. She is not in her right mind, Ian.' It seemed that each word was wrenched out of him. 'Her last pregnancy – it unhinged·her.'

Linty sat quietly, her hand against her nose for fear the goat stench and the clothes stench would cause nausea.

'I don't know what to do,' Michael said. 'The children love her. I can't take her from the wee one – and me on the hill all day. If I call in a doctor, it can only be the madhouse.'

'But are the children safe with her?' Ian asked.

'She has never tried to harm them.' He poured a dram for himself and settled back into a broken chair. 'Yet.'

Linty looked at the pathetic eyes: 'You canna go on this way, Michael. I'm not speaking for us now – we didna know how it was – but for you.'

'But I am speaking for us,' Ian said. 'She is poisoning your daughters with the tale that John is a bastard. You may let your innocents suffer, but by God, mine shan't. I grant your wife is a problem, and I'm sorry. But I shan't have my son held to ridicule by a woman out of her wits. If John catches on, what then? Bastard is only a word to him now, like "villain" or "oaf." He has no idea what it means, only the insult behind it. But later—'

'I grant Sheena has hurt folk,' Michael said, 'and I'm sorry. But if you think I'll put her away for your sakes, you are asking too much. And besides, she only speaks the truth.'

Ian rose. *What did you say?*

Michael said, tiredly, with a sigh, 'I'll not fight you. To say that John's not Johnny Brown's child would mock all the evidence of our eyes. How could you think folk didna know? The hair, the eyes, the chin?' He lifted his own chin, as if to ready

211

it for Ian's fist. 'Am I to put away my wife for a flaw in yours?'

Linty sprang up and caught Ian's arm. 'He doesna know what he's saying! He's fou, can't you see?'

'He's not! Michael, you've one minute to apologize—'

'For the truth? Why care? Nobody cares. It's an old story better buried. The gossip, the chuckling's been over these many years.'

So wearily he said it, not seeming to care that Ian stood over him with a red glare in his eyes and his face twitching-white. 'You can kill me; it won't alter facts. And I'm past caring.'

Linty hung on to Ian's arm. 'Please,' she said, fearful that his body was coiling away from her, 'let's go. What good is it to hurt Michael? Just to repeat a bit of gossip, dead like he says it is? Oh God, Ian, come away!'

He lunged forward, slapped Michael hard across the face and said, 'We're going. But if I hear of one more ugly word from your children, there'll be trouble.'

On the way home Linty tried to comfort him, knowing how rawly his pride suffered, but he said nothing. Aye, she thought, he could be a saint about everything but this – that the village thought him a cuckold. 'It's years ago,' she said, 'and only just suspicion. You will forget it.'

Still he said nothing. She couldn't reach him, even in bed. He turned from her and she knew he lay awake in the darkness.

Next morning he had a chill but dragged on his clothes to go to work. Over porridge and tea, Linty noticed that his hands were shaking so that he had to use both to hold the mug. 'You rose too soon from the fever,' she said, 'and last night's walk tired you. I'll tell Mrs. Hayes you won't be in today.'

He made no resistance. She left him to Jean, saying if his forehead should sweat to hurry to Dr. MacRae in the village. On the way to the Castle she told Torquil what had happened at Michael's.

'Likely he just doesna feel like facing folk today,' Torquil said. 'A bit of time and he'll pull out of this and see it as nothing. But he *is* proud.'

They separated at the greenhouses. The day's work dragged, there being little to do. The Queen's economies were peculiar – to keep the staff on but, as the footmen still complained, never silk stockings for them, just cotton. Visiting ladies were shocked that bits of newspaper were used in the water closets instead of soft white paper. She supplied beautiful crystal jars for the rose petals the gardeners dried, but never a drop of brandy to keep the fragrance alive.

Joining Torquil for the walk home, Linty said, 'God help Michael if John reports any more trouble at school.'

'Likely there's been none. Don't fret. Ian's a sensible man; he'll forget this in a day or two.'

When they came in, Jean said that Ian was asleep. John was cheerful at the fire, proud of his bruised eye and missing tooth. Nobody had dared come near him today, he said. The Wright girls had even said they were sorry. Good – so Michael had scolded them.

But Ian wouldn't join them for tea. And during the night she wakened to hear him moan.

'What is it?' she asked, moving to feel his forehead. It was hot. The fever was back.

'My chest,' he said. 'Don't sit on my chest, you're too much a weight, darling. Get off.'

'But I'm not—'

'You're too heavy there. I can't breathe.'

She put on her dressing-gown and ran up the stairs to rouse Torquil. 'I think the fever's back, and he's not in his right mind. Hurry!'

While Torquil went out to fetch the doctor she and Jean stirred up the fire and made tea. Suddenly there was a burst of song from the bedroom, and the women ran in to see Ian getting out of bed like a drunken man, wobbling. 'The room's too small for a party,' he said, and pressed his hands up. 'Push up the ceiling, let go my chest, I can't bear the weight.'

'Ian! Get back into bed!'

It took all of their strength to push him back onto the bed, to keep him from throwing off the blankets. Why must they lie on his chest, he asked? What was there, then, a flatiron? Take it away, take it away . . .

He whimpered and lay silent. The doctor came. He said it wasn't typhoid, but pneumonia. They were not to worry, but he'd just stay on through the dawn. A cup of tea – thank you.

Nobody went to work. John stayed home from school. The doctor remained through a crisis at dusk. Linty prayed. At midnight, gasping, Ian died, a spew of blood on the pillow.

Most of Crathie attended the funeral; Linty and Jean tossed the 'flowers' of ivy and green fir into the grave.

Michael and his daughters edged forward at the gate of the graveyard. 'I am sorry,' he said.

Linty tried to smile. 'Sheena?'

'At home. No better.' Softly he said, 'Forgive us?'

'Aye,' she said, as softly. 'Nothing seems to matter now.' She pulled the black cloth over her bonnet and moved past the lingering crowd down the hill, to join her son who had run ahead to cry in private.

John cried too much, too long, always trying to be alone. He was away from school for a week. His grief somehow made her own easier, for she had to think of ways to try to cheer him. Then, on a Sunday of sick, wan light she said, 'I've been lazy too long. John, will you teach me to read and write?'

His interest stirred a little. 'Why?'

'I want to write Johnny Brown. I doubt if he's heard the news, and he was your father's friend.'

John got his stubby pencils, and paper. 'Here's how you begin...'

She had a lesson each evening until finally it all came clear. The hard work helped to heal them both. Then she wrote to Johnny at Osborne. He would surely not know of Ian's death – or he would have written to her.

His reply came a week later, formal and stiff, as if he knew the family would see it. They all had his sympathy. He would likely see them in the spring.

Never had a winter seemed so long, so dreary, though now Linty was able to read the easiest of John's books. In Balmoral library she progressed to some of the romances the Queen approved, but they didn't seem real, all about fine ladies who masqued as milkmaids for fear of fortune hunters, and milkmaids who turned out to be fine ladies so they could marry earls. Always there were happy endings, and that wasn't like life at all.

But for John's sake she tried to be serene. She encouraged him to bring playmates home after school, when Jean had plenty of food for them. He was popular; he was good at sports. On Saturdays Grant took him shooting, and in March he and Torquil fished.

On a May morning Mrs. Hayes told Upper staff that the Queen was expected within the week. There was the usual flurry of polishing. The hundreds of little ornaments that crowded the royal apartments were carefully dusted, and Mrs. Hayes herself saw to the bedroom where Prince Albert's bust and the other scary objects stood above the tartan satin spread.

Linty was allowed a free day to prepare for night duty. She was alone in the cottage at noon when Johnny rode up through the daffodils, and as she came to the door he took her into his arms. Not knowing that Jean was at the Davidsons, not caring who saw them. 'I couldna write as I wanted to,' he said.

'Come in, Johnny.'

Inside, he looked at her anxiously. 'You're all right?'

'Aye,' she said. But not as before. She must have loved Ian more than she'd known, or perhaps she felt guilty. And Johnny now was such a fine gentleman. He wore his kilt as always, and his hair and beard were the same but for some gray. But he had a kind of way of standing there more like a king than that Bertie would ever be. For the first time he made her feel small and shy.

'Will you take a dram?'

'Have I ever refused?' He sat down by the peat fire. 'Linty, does Ian have a proper tombstone?'

'A marker,' she said, bringing the drink.

'You can't reject money now,' he said, 'and I want him honored with his name on granite. And there'll be need of money for you and John. It will be in Ballater bank in your name, as left to Ian by a relative. Wait,' he said as she started to interrupt, 'I ken what I'm doing. It's safe as houses. And you'll never want.'

'Well, then,' she said, 'I can only say thank you. But we don't need much. John's set on farming someday; he's in love with the land.'

'Then he can train at Bush this summer and earn a bit too. Farming's becoming a science now; I can send him to school for it later. Now, what time does Torquil come home?'

'About five.'

'I'll find him in the gardens then?'

'Aye. Why?'

'I want to talk to him about us.'

'What about us?'

'It's too soon to ask you – do you still love me?'

'It's not like it was,' she said, 'Too much has happened. It's love though – I think.'

'May I say that to Torquil?'

'Why must you say anything?'

'Because he's head of your family now. Because I want to come here freely, not sneak about.'

'You mean, you want to sleep here as you used to?'

'When you want me. Meanwhile, just to see you. I'm not forcing anything.'

'You can't,' she said. 'I couldna force myself. But surely you know that. What happens will happen, but I'm making no promises. It will never be the same.'

'I'm asking no promises, Linty. I still can't offer marriage—'

'I know.' In the first real pity she had ever felt for him, she went to him and gently kissed his cheek. We started together in friendship, she thought, and we may end that way; but we will end together. His arms crushed her close but he didn't kiss her on the lips, and she was grateful.

That spring John and Johnny became close. On a free Sunday when the Queen was busy with her relatives, they shot together in the hills, not for game but for practice. John gave Johnny a cairngorm he had found for good luck. Linty was amused that they seemed to have secrets, like two boys.

'It's good,' Torquil said. 'He has a hero again. But you?'

216

'It's just not the same,' she said.

'Not the ghost of Ian?' Jean asked.

'More the ghost of me.'

When he had left Balmoral for Windsor, she scolded herself for her jealousy of the Queen. If she didn't love Johnny, then why her resentment? When she asked among the servants who tended Her Majesty, 'Is she beautiful?' she always got the same replies: fat, dumpy, badly dressed in out-moded black. 'If it weren't for Mr. Brown,' Gordon said, 'she'd look a mess; he's always taking her gowns to the maids to be cleaned or pressed.'

Being on duty at night, Linty had never seen any of the Queen's gowns, which were furbished during the day. But it was said she would wear them out before buying new ones, not out of thrift but boredom. She had been seen in an old black crinoline with egg on the bodice – but wearing the Koh-i-noor diamond at some reception in London. Nonsense! Mrs. Hayes said. Mr. Brown wouldn't have allowed it. Older servants remembered that she had depended on Prince Albert's taste when ordering new clothes.

But there were few appearances in London. She remained in seclusion, but the newspapers said nothing more about shirking, and she did entertain the Shah of Persia in magnificent style. When she returned to Balmoral she must have felt she had earned her holiday, for there were a series of Ghillies' Balls – and again, the only partner she chose was Johnny. 'It isna wise,' Johnny told Linty. 'It offends everyone but the servants, outrages the press. I have told her she is a clever diplomat except on home ground.'

More shocking still, she insisted he take the sacrament with her at Crathie Kirk. It seemed like one scandal had scarcely died before she provided another. Gordon said that at dinner the Queen was forever quoting Johnny. 'Mr. Brown said ... Mr. Brown thinks ...'

English ladies, finally invited to Balmoral after years of being ignored, didn't care what they said when they came with their maids for repairs in the linen room: 'Some lout of a ghillie trod on my hem, mend it.' 'My fan is broken, trod underfoot by those oafs – have you another, in black?'

They chattered like magpies: how could one avoid that odious Mr. Brown; one had to dance with him or offend the Queen.... Fancy her sitting out dances with Dukes, refusing to partner her sons. Oh God, to be out of this brutal cold. How *could* she deny them fires? Lady Ely had warned them, but seeing was believing. 'I had no sooner had my maid light a fire than the Queen herself came in, ordered a footman to smother it and raised the windows wide herself! My dear, I *am* no polar bear; I'll catch my death if I'm another night here.'

Well, Linty thought, these loud-voiced arrogant snobs will return south and bask in the glory of having visited the Queen, so who cares if they must suffer for it? Johnny told her of their despair when they were ordered to accompany Her Majesty on carriage trips up into the mountains. 'Sometimes we even have to *walk* in the *rain*,' he mimicked, 'and that *terrible* Mr. Brown offering his bottle without even *cups*.'

One evening, shortly before another Ghillies' Ball, Gordon came into the linen room. 'Do y'ken where Johnny is?'

'No,' she said, 'He's not in his quarters?'

'He doesna answer.'

'Asleep, maybe? He's been out on the hill, I think.'

'The Queen wants him to help her down and start the dancing. I canna keep her waiting.' He looked scared.

'It's not your fault,' she said. 'Just tell her he's not in his rooms.'

'Does Mrs. Hayes have a passkey?'

'No.' For all the rooms but Her Majesty's and Johnny's and those that had been Prince Albert's.

'Why does it have to be me must tell her he's not there – or fou?'

'But it's not your fault,' she repeated.

'It doesna matter. You wouldna want to deliver a message and have those eyes freeze over – like steel through you. Linty, come with me and see if we can rouse him.'

She was not supposed to leave her post, but she went with him, up and around the corridor. They hammered on the door, waited, then hammered again. Somewhere inside, five bells

218

tinkled – the Queen's. Heavy footsteps came to the door, and it opened.

Johnny was very drunk. 'Lemme alone,' he said, and then, 'Linty! What's wrong?'

She told him. 'Hurry, get dressed; the Queen's waiting.'

'I was sleeping,' he said, and cursed. 'Get Grant, he'll do. Tell her I'm drunk.'

Linty gasped. 'Oh, no! We'll say sick—'

'Then she'd be in with her mourning veil.' He steadied himself against a chair. Beyond it she glimpsed fine mahogany furniture, a couch and loveseat upholstered with the Balmoral tartan, gilt-framed pictures. 'I've told the truth before; Christ, why should I lie now?'

'What about me, having to tell her?' Gordon asked.

'If Ponsonby and Jenner and Clarke can do it, you can. They didna get sacked, or their heads cut.'

'If I get you some strong tea, quick—'

'Och, Linty, dinna be a fool.'

'You're the fool,' she said. 'Come, Gordon, you've no time to waste.'

As they closed the door and hurried back down the corridor she was terrified that the Queen might come out of her suite. But all was silent. Gordon whispered, 'I'm for it, then.' She tried to smile encouragement, then fled to the linen room.

Was Johnny so sure of the Queen that he dared to do this? Or did he want to be sacked? There wasn't a guest downstairs who didn't expect Mr. Brown, Master of Revels, to escort and dance with Her Majesty. It would be as humiliating for her as if Prince Albert had shirked a public appearance for no reason.

The warning bell: the Queen was passing through the corridor. And in what state of mind?

Linty took up a romance and tried to read but the words seemed meaningless. She got up and rearranged a tidy cupboard of pillow cases. If only, if only she had a job of work to pass the hours.

Then, finally, at eleven a lady's maid came in with the usual broken black fan. Was there another? It was terrible how the ghillies whirled, knocking a fan from hands.

Linty brought a lace fan. 'Is it gay, then, the ball?'

'Yes.'

'And the Queen is – dancing?'

'Radiant, like a girl.'

So Johnny had somehow managed to sober up and go downstairs. 'Mr. Brown is a good dancer,' Linty said, in final prod.

'He's not there. I believe he's still up on the hill after game; Her Majesty said a mist had set in.'

So the always-truthful Queen had lied. Or Gordon had. But when Gordon came in at one he said he had merely told the Queen that Mr. Brown was not 'available.' The frown he had feared was an odd little smile. She had said, 'Summon Grant – and keep the fiddles going.'

'You are free at least to entertain Johnny,' Jean said. 'Torquil and I think you should.'

But Linty shook her head. She had finally managed to close her heart to him, or at least protect it with caution. 'If I sleep with him,' she said bluntly, 'it will all start over again – the jealousy and the pain. For I was jealous of the Queen.'

'I think a man can love two women in different ways.'

'That may be. But I won't be begging to get hurt again. I think I'm content.'

With the shabby, cosy wee house; enough money, if not luxuries; plans for John. He worked at Bush farm that summer, proud of earning two shillings a week and prouder of learning how hay should be scythed, and animals cared for. He read the new scientific pamphlets. Aye, he would go to Agriculture School when he was seventeen. But the love of this land was in him; he would return here, and Linty hoped for a happy old age for her, with her grandchildren close.

So the next year, and the next, when Johnny came to Balmoral she asked him to the house only to talk among them all, and it seemed that temptation was past. Johnny didn't press her, and she saw that as an admission that he, too, was past the passion they had shared. But he still confided in her. When Jean and Torquil were upstairs, and John studying in the 'new' room, he would pour out the months' frustrations and – sometimes – what almost seemed like hate of the Queen.

'Baby,' Princess Beatrice, was visiting Balmoral – a lovely blonde of fifteen, she was the last of the daughters. 'It's terrible the way the Queen treats her,' Johnny said. 'It's *wicked*. With all the others grown up and married, she wants to cling to Baby so the child will stay with her and never marry. She's given orders that nobody in the royal household may mention the word "wedding," "marriage," or "babies." She's not allowed to dance with any man but her brothers. Gordon, serving at their private meals, says the poor little Princess dares not discuss anything with her mother beyond the weather, or ponies. God!'

But he was happy about what folk were whispering as Her Majesty's 'love affair' with Prime Minister Disraeli. 'It lets me off the hook to some degree. Of course it's not an affair, but he's given her a kind of romance, and he knows she needs flattery, flattery to the point of mush. I've heard him myself call her his "faery Queen," and she with blushes and eyes like stars. She even asks him to sit in her presence.'

'You are jealous,' Linty teased. How nice to be able to tease, remote from hurt.

'Of *him*?' Johnny asked scornfully. 'He looks like a marionette on stage, wiggy with a big dyed curl on his forehead, gouty, old—'

'You are jealous!' she said, laughing.

'No,' he said seriously. 'I think he means the best for her. She even dresses up a bit, puts on her pearls and diamonds to receive him, has ordered new gowns. There's a battle of flowers – he sending them with love notes, she having his favorite primroses gathered at Osborne. Och, he's got her in his web, all right.'

'Like a spider?'

'A lucky spider, I think. He's waking her up. She says no prime minister ever explained things to her so amusingly, so clearly; she feels, as she said to me, so young again. And clever! He keeps harping on Prince Albert, how only he ever understood her long seclusion as the Great Love of History. If the fellow wasna ambitious for her I'd say he was an oily-mouthed shit. But it seems what I've said in trance is coming true. Somehow he's bringing her luck, and God knows she

221

needs it. I think it was touch and go for a while that she wasna asked to abdicate.'

'And Bertie would have ruled?'

'I doubt the government would have stood for that, but then I'm not one to mess in things beyond my ken. I'm only glad things have taken a turn for the better.'

Better for us, too, Linty thought – this new, safe closeness. She missed him when he left Balmoral, but not with the old cruel sort of longing. I have given up, she thought, and it's as well.

One summer afternoon of the Queen's residence Linty went across the fields to pick blackberries. Turning at a bend in the road, she saw two strangers, a man and woman, just ahead of her. Wondering why they had paused so abruptly, she looked beyond them at an empty pony carriage – the Queen's, with its silver crest.

So that's why these strangers were staring. Then Her Majesty and Johnny, thinking themselves alone, came out from the trees. They stood close together while Johnny pinned a plaid shawl about her. She squealed and said, 'You stuck me with the pin!'

He gave her a rough shake. 'Well, woman, can you no hold your head up?'

'But my chin's bleeding!'

'It's your own fault for not holding steady. Come along now.' And he helped her into the carriage.

As they drove away the man and woman turned and saw Linty. Could it be, they asked, that they had actually seen the Queen and Mr. Brown?

'I dinna ken for sure,' Linty lied. Only of course they knew . . .

The strangers introduced themselves as Mr. and Mrs. Barry-Torr, on holiday. Not journalists, he said, and very much embarrassed by having intruded on Her Majesty's privacy.

Reckless they were, she thought as she went on to gather her berries. Gossip like this was sure to spread, and perhaps damage Her Majesty's new-found popularity.

But the newspapers made a jolly fuss about another incident – The Frogs of Frogmore. England had had a plague of young frogs, it seemed, in the summer of 1875, and thousands descended on Her Majesty's garden. Johnny had set her chair on a tartan rug and she had begun to write when, as he said later, 'All hell broke loose. You can't imagine that many frogs hopping on the rug and trying to climb Her Majesty's skirts. I got a besom and tried to fend them off but had to shout for help; all the gardeners came. Just then the French Ambassador, scared of the frogs but more scared of being late for his appointment with the Queen, came up and made her a low bow, frogs coming up like a sea. And by God! She doesn't turn a hair, she just goes through the interview cool as you please. What a woman!'

The next year the Queen astonished everyone by opening Parliament, although she refused to wear her crown because it gave her a headache. She had been warned that she might expect anti-royalist demonstrations, that her carriage could be overset, that John Brown would be booed or stoned. But Johnny said it all went well, to cheers.

That same year she was declared Empress of India – Her Imperial Majesty. Disraeli, now Lord Beaconsfield, was more than ever in favor, Johnny said, and rightfully.

'Do you ever have the second sight about yourself?' Linty asked him that autumn. 'All you've said has come true for her. What about you?'

'I only know you'll come back to me,' he said, 'but where or how I can't tell you.'

Seemingly, during the next two years, there was no change in Linty's life except that she felt a restlessness, as though she must store the last of her youth against the long autumn, the final winter. Johnny was so generous with money that she could afford the coach into Ballater; she bought a cherry-ribboned bonnet and yards of bombazine for dresses for Jean and herself. With Torquil they spent a holiday in Aberdeen, and she marveled at the sea though it frightened her. Crathie and the cosy house would always be home, and she thought how nearly she had come to leaving it for Johnny and a nomad life without her son.

John was fourteen now, taller than she, finished with school and working full time at Bush Farm. One evening he came home and said, 'There's an awful thing happened up at the Wrights'. Mrs. Wright went out with a rifle – for rabbits, she said. But she turned the gun on herself, into her mouth . . .'

After the funeral, Torquil asked Michael back for a dram. When John had left the room, Michael said, 'Her mind has been darkening these four years. There were times, Linty, I nearly came down to warn you for fear she'd do you harm. It was always Johnny she loved, wanted. She still had some idea you and he – you know?'

'I was always afraid of Sheena,' Linty said.

'You're saying she killed herself for love of Johnny?' Torquil asked.

'In her darkening, yes.'

'He mustna know that,' Jean said. 'What use could it be? He did her no harm; he only couldna love back.'

Michael nodded. 'He's a great man in his way. I wish him well. He's a lot on his shoulders we'll never ken the burden of.'

His children were bedded at the Inver for the night and he said he must go. Like an old man, Linty thought, supported by his oaken staff, weary beyond his years.

Grant, the keeper, died in November. And news came from Windsor that on December 14th – the fatal date – Princess Alice, Grand Duchess of Hesse, had died of diphtheria. But the Queen had never emerged from mourning Prince Albert, and the servants said you couldna go deeper into black than black.

Mourning or not, when the Queen was at Balmoral the Ghillies' Balls continued. The elderly Prince John of Denmark visited, providing Gordon with two stories which, he said, 'If I were gentry I could dine out on. The Prince's English is poor, but he blunders on with it to please Her Majesty. One night at dinner a lady guest was late and the meal had started when she hurried into her chair next to the Prince's. As I served her, I heard her whisper to him that she'd been unable to unlock her bedroom door. Her Majesty sat glaring, so the Prince decided to explain the lady's tardiness. "You see," he said, "it not her fault. She was confined before dinner." '

Later, at a Ghillies' Ball, he told everyone how much he

admired the grace of the Queen's dancing. The following evening at dinner he decided to compliment her by saying that she danced like a spinning top. 'I am agreeable,' he said to her, 'to see that the Queen dances like a pot.'

Had she laughed? Not at first. Then she understood, and was delighted.

Disraeli's visits to Balmoral always put the Queen in good humor, but Johnny was all too aware that Mr. Gladstone had bored her. 'Like a bloody preacher he was, even at table. One night I was standing behind her chair when he went on exhorting – on and on, letting no one get a word in edgewise – and I thought any minute Her Majesty would cut him off and embarrass everyone. So I just rapped him on the shoulder and said, "You've said enough," and he sure as hell stopped.'

In the old days Linty might have thought that Johnny bragged, but not now. Not after seeing them when they thought themselves alone, him scolding her when she complained of the pin-prick. It was like they were a married couple, he so tall, she so tiny, squabbling like any old wifie and her man.

Och, I am well out of it.

In the autumn of 1882 John went to study in Aberdeen. Linty thought he looked just as Johnny had at eighteen, only he was clean shaven and his eyes a brighter blue. A handsome lad, if she did say so herself, and she would miss him until he came home for Christmas.

The court was back, the Queen still depressed about Disraeli's death, for two years could pass and she'd still mourn as if it were yesterday. Prince Albert's rooms remained unchanged, the hot shaving water still brought morning and evening, the razors polished, his dressing clothes laid ready. People didn't talk about it now, and old Mrs. Hayes was not afraid to go in to dust.

But folk did talk about how, at sixty-three, the Queen could dance lighter than a girl, though she had become so plump; her skin was still like the pearls she wore over her black dresses; and her eyes, even in that soft fat of her face, were as sharp and beautiful as ever.

The autumn started beautifully, with its purples and golds, but then it turned to mists. On his last free day after the court moved south, Johnny asked Linty if she'd come on a picnic – never mind the weather, for if they went to the Rain Forest the tall trees would serve as umbrellas, and he would borrow a pony cart.

Why not, then? She prepared food, and it all seemed so familiar, as if she were seventeen again, only wiser and not in love. Loving, aye, ready to share any problem, but prudent.

The pony cart jolted along the Dee, under gray skies. Already Lochnagar wore a small ruffly snowcap; but she was warm in her shawls.

'I brought grouse,' Johnny said.

As if time had turned back. 'I brought sausage and bannocks and apples.'

He turned to smile at her, remembering.

They really had no right in the Rain Forest, it being Farquharson land, but it was a lovely, lonely place. You could look up and up and not see the tops of the trees; it was all a misty dark green hush, where you'd be scared alone, with never a bird singing. Johnny helped her down from the cart, tethered the pony, and they wandered through the towers of firs over heavy mosses. It was sad, Linty thought, the smell of a year's death, leaf mould and little plants breathing their last until springtime.

He spread a rug and they ate, and drank from his bottle. Oddly, they whispered – but perhaps it was like being in church, so still it was. Brownish needles were soft under her hands. She picked up a pine cone, dry and crumbly. Looking up, she could not see the sky, only the movement of white mist.

Later she couldn't remember just why she went into his arms; it wasn't fear – but as if she could not bear the autumn to frost them, to kill them. They lay on the hard ground under the rug in a way she had never imagined, because it seemed like a fight against something and into a kind of heaven.

Och, but there were no words for it, for the peacefulness

226

afterwards. Sitting up, they clung together, then fell back. He kissed her eyes, her lips, her throat, and pulled up her dress again. She turned her body into his.

They scarcely spoke on the way home until he said, 'You must come to London for Christmas. You and John. I'll ask for two days.'

'I'll stay here,' she said, content. 'I want you here, not in a big, strange place.'

'I'll be retiring someday,' he said, 'She's given me my wee house here, though God knows I've no time to be in it – then we will marry.'

Someday, she thought wryly, but without anger. As long as he was needed he would never retire. 'Never mind,' she said as he walked the pony onto the Crathie road, 'Kiss me once more.'

She still felt the bruise of that kiss when she joined her family at tea. The first snow fell, and looking out she said, 'How beautiful!'

John, lying on the hearthrug with a book, said, 'What?'

The darkening violet sky with a half-moon set like a jewel. The way the snow formed a soft white bonnet on the wood-shed. Firelight reflected on the window pane.

'The snow,' she said. But she meant, the world.

On the afternoon of March 28th Mrs. Hayes summoned all of the Balmoral servants into the ballroom. So the Queen was coming early? Another big clean-up, a formal recitation of duties.

'I'm sorry to tell you,' Mrs. Hayes said, a telegram in her hand, 'that Mr. John Brown died yesterday at Windsor.'

Linty, standing next to Gordon, felt his hand tight on her wrist.

'Erysipelas – a fever. That's all it says. But I'd think, out of respect to him we should all observe mourning – as Her Majesty will be doing.'

It was all unreal, Linty thought – the people gathered, the dim ballroom with its stagsheads – something she was dreaming. But Gordon's hand was biting into her wrist. Perhaps he thought she would faint.

'Reverend Campbell has no notification of funeral plans, but for those of you who wish to pray, the Kirk will be open this evening. I am sure we all share grief...'

Linty scarcely listened.

'...struck down in the prime of life ... all of us will miss ... It will be such a blow to the Queen ... she has not been told yet, she being ill with rheumatism ...'

Somehow Linty was out of the ballroom, onto Gordon's horse, home. Torquil, who had spent only a half-day in the gardens, was told the news. He carried her into her room, dismissed Jean, who was hovering with tea, and set Linty up against pillows.

He said nothing, sitting beside her and stroking her neck, her forehead.

'I want to die,' she said. 'Let me.'

Still he said nothing, the gentle fingers stroking. There seemed to be tight bands across her head where the nightmare lay.

'We only had a little way to go,' she said. 'He's not so far.'

From far away she thought she heard Jean and Gordon whispering.

'Is it real?' she asked, turning to Torquil, looking into his eyes.

'It's real, hen. And you're not going to die. There's John. Part of him.'

Part of Johnny, aye. 'But you don't know; you can't know. We were just—'

Falling in love again, and for good and for ever, and never mind the Queen or the winds of the world. We were one person, finally, there on the hard ground, and nothing, no one, could ever break us.

'Hush,' he said, 'you are going to sleep,' and he made her look at him, holding her chin in his hand. Her eyelids flickered and closed. Torquil tiptoed away.

They sent for John in Aberdeen.

A week later he said, 'When I die, I want to die a hero, too.'

That was the way the Queen made it out, and in a way it was true, though Johnny would have laughed at the idea. He had only been at his duty, searching the grounds of Windsor for the Irish revolutionaries rumored to be hiding there. He caught a chill, his face had swelled, and though nursed by Sir William Jenner and Dr. Reid, he had died on March 27th. No one wanted to break the news to the Queen, whose rheumatism was agonizing after a fall down the stairs. It was forty-eight hours before Prince Leopold found the courage to tell her.

Unaware that the news had already spread to Crathie, she sent for Johnny's brothers and broke the news to them herself. When they got back they said that her tears fell steadily. She couldn't stand up. Both her legs were paralyzed for a time. She refused to see anyone or sign anything for four days.

Hugh Brown called on Linty. 'Folk say she's like she was when Prince Albert died.' He looked at her anxiously. 'But you are not to pieces?'

'Inside, I am,' she said. 'But I can't make a spectacle of myself, or show the village how I feel. It wouldna be fair to John.'

Hugh said, 'Johnny gave me orders to see that you'll never want, and there's money in my bank for you. But he dared not make a will. He did ask that when John is through school in Aberdeen he help us manage the farm. He'll be good at accounts, too, Johnny said.'

Linty thanked him. 'You don't think Johnny had some second sight about his death, planning ahead like he did?'

Hugh shook his head. 'Any man over fifty is sensible to plan. Johnny was practical. Lucky he told me he wanted burial here; otherwise the Queen would likely put him in Westminster Abbey or some other fancy foreign tomb.' England was foreign to Crathie folk.

'Why is the funeral delayed?' she asked.

'She wants a special tombstone, and she wants to be strong enough to come here herself.'

So it was not until May 26th that Linty attended the funeral at Crathie Kirk. From the royal pew the Queen's sobbing was audible, but Linty held back her tears — it would never do to cry in public. John had returned to complete his term in Aberdeen, and that was as well ...

During the long service she held tight to Jean's hand. When it was over, she whispered that she couldna bear to see the interment. Let the others follow the handsome coffin out to the kirkyard and lay their wreaths. She would come alone, later, when she was calmer, when she was sure she wouldna cry too much, and not in front of anyone.

For two weeks she resumed work at Balmoral. Rumor had it that the Queen was still in a terrible state of weeping but that she did receive her ministers and attend to her boxes. Johnny would have been proud of her, Linty thought.

But how odd to know, in her silent nights on duty in the linen room – silent because there were no balls, no entertainments – that along the corridor the Queen was mourning just as she did, weeping into her pillow, or pacing, while Linty stood at the window and looked out into the soft spring moonlight that somehow had no glow. Once, hearing heavy footsteps outside the door, she thought, 'Why, it's Johnny come for a gossip,' then realized it was only Gordon coming to share midnight tea.

In early June, John returned from Aberdeen. One look at him and she said, 'Och, you must shave that off!'

'But it's my first beard,' he said, laughing. 'A good plump one, too. Why don't you like it?'

Because you are the image of Johnny at that age.

'Because it's making you look older than you are.'

'I like to look older. I'm keeping it.'

Well, so he had a mind of his own, and she said nothing more.

Next day he wanted to see Johnny's grave. She felt strong enough to say that she would accompany him, and they went to the kirkyard at sunset. No one was there. John removed his cap, and they stood by the granite tombstone and read the inscription

This stone is erected
in affectionate and grateful remembrance
of John Brown,

The devoted and faithful Personal Attendant
And beloved friend of
Queen Victoria,
In whose service he had been for 34 years.
Born at Crathienaird 8th December 1826
Died at Windsor Castle 27th March 1883

'That friend on whose fidelity you count,
That friend, given you by circumstances
over which you have no control,
Was God's own gift.'

Well done good and faithful servant,
Thou hast been faithful over few things,
I will make thee Ruler over many things,
Enter thou into the Joy of thy Lord.

Browning wreaths from lords and ladies and princesses —
even the Empress Eugenie, with little labels. The Queen's own
wreath of lilies, now tarnished, insect-bitten.

'Just to think he was a stableman,' John said. 'Why, it
makes you think you can do anything.'

'Aye.'

She must come here alone so that she could cry, try to
commune. Already she heard footsteps behind them. John
turned suddenly and said, 'My God, I think it's the Queen.'

She walked slowly, supported by two men — probably her
doctors. A thin black veil covered her face, but there were
diamonds on her fat little hands. Linty and John moved hurriedly aside.

The old resentment flamed up — why must she pick this
very hour to come here, when I am entitled to this privacy at
least?

John bowed; Linty curtsied. Over the Queen's shoulder the
sun set in violent pink and gold. Somewhere, far off, sheepbells tinkled, a dog barked.

The roses Linty had brought Johnny were still in her arms.
She couldn't place them now, for the Queen also held roses.
She couldn't leave until the Queen did.

Then Victoria swept back her mourning veil, came forward and placed her roses on the mound. She stood looking down in a sort of daze – or was it prayer?

A blackbird trilled. Over her shoulder the sun was turning from gold to amber to dark violet.

Victoria looked at Linty, expressionless, remote.

And then she saw John and gasped.

It was only the smallest of sounds, but Linty heard it, saw the great blue eyes sharpen and widen. She opened her mouth in a little O and seemed almost about to come forward.

For a long moment she stared at John, then to Linty and back to John again. Then she bowed her head, looked at the ground, veiled her face and moved slowly, erect, past them and down the hill, the doctors following.

'She looked so strange,' John said when they were out of sight. 'Like she'd seen a ghost.'

'Och, she's just upset,' Linty said, and placed her roses next to the Queen's. 'She was that fond of him, y'ken.'

Poor woman, she thought as the sunset deepened toward dusk. I'm sorry it happened. Perhaps she wanted to treasure Johnny as hers. But now she knows, she knows.

Historical Postscript

Historical Postscript

When 'Bertie' became Edward VII he destroyed almost every statue and cairn that Victoria had raised for John Brown. He even took photographs and mementos from his mother's apartments and is said to have burned them. Much of this was jealousy stemming from his boyhood, but it's possible that he also wanted to erase Brown from the nation's memory so that future generations would not be reminded of the old scandal.

When the Queen was preparing *Further Leaves From Our Life in the Highlands*, the Second volume of her journal, she showed the manuscript to Bertie – an odd thing to do considering that much of the book was a paean of praise to Brown. He wrote his mother, 'It is most unwise for the Queen to expose her private life to the public.' The Queen was furious, and pinned a note to his letter: '... strange, considering how much talk and want of reticence there is in this house and how little he keeps anything to himself. It is strange that objection should come from this quarter, where great strictness as to conduct is not generally much cared for.'

Henry Ponsonby, her Private Secretary, learned the following year that she had written *The Life of John Brown* for publication, and also planned to release his personal diary. E. E. P. Tisdall, in *Queen Victoria's Private Life,** says that when Ponsonby read the two mauscripts 'his blood ran cold.' He felt that publication was out of the question. If necessary he was prepared to defy the Queen and burn the manuscripts. He pointed out to her that, in her exposing of her innermost and most sacred feelings, readers would misunderstand.

His ally was the Dean of Windsor, who also tried to dissuade the Queen and wrote her as tactfully as he could. The

* Jarrolds, 1961.

Queen sent him a message saying that this was none of his business. The Dean replied that if she overrode his objections he would resign his post.

A few weeks later the Queen ordered Ponsonby to destroy the Brown manuscripts. Evidently, as Mr. Tisdall suggests, she realized that 'One inevitable result must have followed their appearance; everybody would have used their imagination in conjecturing what items the royal editor had expurgated.'

What does remain to us is extraordinary in its indiscretion. The Queen sent Brown a New Year's card which pictured a coquettish maid:

> I send my serving maiden
> With New Year letter laden
> Its words will prove My faith and love
> To you my heart's best treasure.
>
> Then smile on her and smile on me
> And let your answer loving be
> And give me pleasure.

(Signed)
To my best friend J.B.
from his best friend V.R.I.

Then there is the letter she wrote to Brown's brother Hugh:

I found these words in an old diary or journal of mine: 'I was in great trouble about the Princess Royal who had lost her child in '66 and dear John said to me; "I wish to take care of my dear good mistress till I die. You'll never have an honester servant."

'I took and held his dear kind hand and said I hoped he might long be spared to comfort me, and he answered, "But we all *must* die." '

Afterwards my beloved John would say, 'You haven't a more devoted servant than Brown' – and oh! *how* I felt *that*!

Afterwards so often I told him no one loved him more than I did or had a better friend than me; and he answered, 'Nor you – than me. No one loves you more.'

Mr. Tisdall recounts a fascinating experience in his book. In order to gain useful biographical material he placed an advertisement in a national newspaper asking people with family records or personal memories of Victoria and Brown to write him. One letter was particularly interesting, typed, unsigned, with a telephone number but no address. Enclosed were photostat plates of a letter with a black mourning border. There was the Osborne House address, printed, Queen Victoria's monogram in the middle, and two handwritten words *Burn This* heavily underlined.

The letter reproduced by the photostats had been torn into tiny pieces but reassembled and pasted onto sheets of old brown paper, and the handwriting appeared to be the Queen's, with her frequent underlinings. The sender of this letter said it had been received from a royal footman at Osborne, back in the 70s, who used to carry messages between Victoria and Brown. He had noticed that Brown often tore up the messages after he'd read them, so the scraps pasted on brown paper had been fished out of Brown's wastepaper basket.

The letter was not addressed to anyone nor was it signed. It was an order for a bathing machine for Helena (Princess Helena?) for the afternoon. And then, from matter-of-factness to this astonishing line: 'Oh, forgive me if I offend, but you are so dear to me, so adored, that I cannot bear to live without you.'

We are aware that Victoria and Brown had their rows; this appeared to be an appeal to make up. Mr. Tisdall believes that if the letter were forged, it would have been crude, a shocker to show the boys in the pub. The people to whom he showed it felt it to be genuine. But, strangely, the photostats disappeared from Mr. Tisdall's home in 1946.

Something that has not vanished is a letter Victoria wrote to her daughter: 'My heart's in the Highlands ... and I must fight and struggle against it.'

I have often been asked whether I believe that the Queen

really loved Brown in a romantic way. One strong indication is that a woman in love cannot resist talking about her man. Victoria bored and exasperated her family and associates by constant references to John Brown, verbally and in letters. In *Further Leaves From Our Life in the Highlands* he is mentioned, as one titled lady said to me. 'Ad nauseam.' And it's interesting to speculate how much of the journal may have been edited.

Love affairs are not always consummated sexually. If their relationship was physical, we will never know. That it was love on her part seems obvious. His own devotion was proven by steadfast and loyal service. For both, I believe, it was a long and strange enchantment, spanning her tragic decades, enduring malice, ridicule, slander. If there is survival after death, one likes to think that Johnny Brown was aware of her last glorious years, saw her in all the dazzle of her Diamond Jubilee, sixty years a Queen, eulogized by the press, cheered in her state progress through London. She wrote 'No one ever, I believe, has met with such an ovation as was given to me, passing through those six miles of streets ... the crowds were quite indescribable ... the cheering was quite deafening, and every face seemed to be filled with real joy.'

But Brown might have been proudest of all had he known what she said during the humiliating disaster of the Boer War. She looked over the casualty list of Colenso Hill, and said nothing. Then she ordered her secretary to clear the lines. She wanted to telegraph her troops.

Princess Helena Victoria said, 'Grandmama, it is only customary for the Sovereign to address the troops if they win a victory.'

The old Queen drew herself up to her scant height, rage in her voice. 'Since when have I not been proud of my troops in success or in defeat? Clear the line!'

The Famished Land   40p
Elizabeth Byrd

'A vivid and moving re-creation'
Susan Howatch, author of *Penmarric*

A memorable novel of Ireland in the 1840s when the flower-soft days of Ballyfearna became a hunger-ridden nightmare as blight turned the blossoming potato fields to vile, black decay ...
... and young Moira McFlaherty must cope with family, fever, passions, jealousies, threats of eviction and the roving eye of the man she loves.

'Splendidly readable ... Moira, the red-haired heroine is not too good to be true – she existed then, I'm sure, and still does' *Daily Telegraph*

'Superior ... with wonderful flashes of Irish humour and compassion' *American Publishers Weekly*

Immortal Queen   40p
Elizabeth Byrd

A chill morning in the Great Hall at Fotheringay,
February 8th, 1587

Elegant and still beautiful, an anointed queen prepared to die
as bravely as she had lived.

On the black scaffold, clad in a red camisole embroidered
with gold, Mary realized how she had forged her own destiny
with link after fatal link ... Catherine de Medici ... Elizabeth
... John Knox ... Darnley ... Rizzio ... and, above all,
Bothwell – whose name was the last word her lips uttered as
the headman's axe fell.

'A book which could be read over and over again with fresh
enjoyment each time ... as fine and as stirring an historical
novel as has been written' *British Book News*

'Establishes Elizabeth Byrd as a novelist of high order'
Edinburgh Evening News
'A joy to read' *Daily Express*

These and other PAN Books are obtainable from all
booksellers and newsagents. If you have any difficulty
please send purchase price plus 7p postage to

PO Box 11, Falmouth, Cornwall.

While every effort is made to keep prices low, it is sometimes
necessary to increase prices at short notice. PAN Books reserve
the right to show new retail prices on covers which may differ
from those previously advertised in the text or elsewhere.